Serenading the Shadows

Ellie~
Listen to the music of your
heart.

Jodie Larson

JODIE LARSON

Serenading the Shadows
Copyright © 2016 by Jodie Larson

ISBN-13: 978-1539001577
ISBN-10: 1539001571

Cover Design by Murphy Rae at Indie Solutions by Murphy Rae
www.murphyrae.net

Interior Design by Champagne Formats
www.champagneformats.com

Editor: Tee Tate
www.teetate.com

Serenading the Shadows

Prologue

"WHY? I DON'T UNDERSTAND WHAT THE BIG DEAL IS. Can't you just move it so I can go out and live my life?"

Another crack of lightning illuminates the sky. The responding thunder rumbles in the background as the torrent of rain falls upon the ground. The cold, bitter wind howls against the glass as it presses forward, matching the mood inside the car.

"The big deal? Adrienne, you're sixteen years old. There is no way we're going to let you go to an overnight concert two hours away with that boy," Mom says from the front passenger seat.

That boy? Ugh, why does she have to say it like he's a disease? Just because Brian isn't from our side of town doesn't mean he's not good enough. Sure, he dresses in nothing but baggy jeans and leather jackets, but he listens to me, treats me like a human and not a piano playing robot. In fact, half the time we're able to sneak away together, the piano never comes into the conversation. I don't have to pretend to be someone I'm not with him. I can just be me, whoever that is. Most days I'm not even sure anymore.

"You know how important this weekend is to your career. You need to be there," Dad adds.

I let out a frustrated groan and stomp my foot. "No! I'm sick and tired of playing on your schedule. You're always trying to run my life. When do I get to have a say in what I do, or where I go, and when I play?" I run a hand through my hair, yanking at the roots. "You know what? Maybe I'll give up the piano altogether just so I can be a normal teenager for once in my life!"

Playing the piano has been my world since I first crawled onto the bench at the age of three. My fingers hit the keys and played a simple melody: *Twinkle, Twinkle Little Star.* I had listened and watched my mother play it so many times I knew exactly what to do. That's when my life, my freedom to choose, ended. Piano lessons, performances, traveling concerts, scholarships to private schools to work on my music, voice lessons, and anything else related to better my ability. Not once have I been able to go out on a Friday with friends. Those nights were dedicated to showing everyone that the local piano prodigy is going to make a name for herself.

"Sweetie, you have the rest of your life to do what you want. What we're doing now is helping you succeed for the future. You have a gift, and it shouldn't be wasted," she says. "Trust me, Adrienne, you'll thank us later. Besides, it's only for a few more years." She turns and pats my leg. "I wouldn't be surprised if the orchestra asks you to play with them for the new season."

"Maybe I don't want to play with the orchestra. Maybe

I want to do something for myself." I can feel the heat crawl up my neck the more this conversation doesn't go my way. Time for the kill. "You can't live your life through me. Eventually, you're going to have to deal with the fact that you're a washed up nobody who can't play the piano anymore, Mom."

A twinge of pain hits me as I watch my mom's face fall from the sharpness of my words. It's not like I'm asking for much. One weekend of normalcy is all. That shouldn't be too much to ask for.

"Adrienne, you're not going, and that's final. You *will* go to this performance, and you *will* play the piano. And when they offer you the seat with the orchestra, you *will* accept." The scowl Dad gives me in the rearview mirror almost makes me shrink back in my seat. "We are done talking about this. It's what's best for your future," he says with the utmost finality in his voice.

I lift my face to the ceiling and let out a frustrated yell. "You don't understand! I hate you! I hate you both! I'm nearly an adult. I should be making decisions about *my life!*"

Angry bolts of lightning flash across the sky, creating a distraction from the deafening rain pelting the car. Within seconds, the car shakes and rocks with the roar of thunder and gusts of wind. Darkness surrounds us again as the sky opens up, releasing its fury.

Suddenly, the car jerks and we float across the water on the road. Dad's knuckles turn white before he corrects us. The wipers can barely keep up, making it nearly impossible to see.

Dad turns his head to say something, only he never has the chance to speak.

Mom clutches his shoulder, pulling at his shirt.

Everything moves in slow motion. Scenes flash before my eyes. Blinding white lights pour in from the oncoming vehicle. Our screams echo in my ears as I brace for impact.

And then there's nothing.

No sound.

No lights.

Nothing.

I don't know where I am or how much time has passed. Faint voices sound above me, while machines beep in the background. I can't move. I can only listen to what the voices are saying.

"We need to get her to an OR, stat," a man says.

"How's her pressure?" someone else asks.

"Eighty over forty." The woman's voice grows fainter as the darkness threatens to pull me under again.

"Now, people, move it! We're going to lose her."

I want to move, but nothing works. I want to cry, to scream, to ask what happened, but I have no voice. Something's wrong. Why won't my body respond?

Sounds fade in and out, the voices and machines are a constant now, the only reminders I'm still here.

"She's stable now," a familiar masculine voice says. "She'll need to stay here in ICU for a while, though. How's her family?"

"Died on impact," another voice says. "They never had a chance. She was lucky she was in the back seat."

Darkness.

Quiet.

Alone.

It's what I wanted.

It's what I asked for.
I guess what they say is true.
Be careful what you wish for.

One

I LOOK OUT MY WINDOW AT THE GRAY CLOUDS IN THE SKY. Such a gloomy day, but for me, it's normal.

It beckons me, the piano sitting in the corner of my small apartment. Days like this is when the remorse crashes on me like the force of hitting a brick wall. Some call it survivor's guilt. I call it karma. Things happen for a reason. It's the universe's way of telling me I should have been thankful for what I had instead of pissing it away and being an ungrateful, spoiled child. Even after ten years, the feeling hasn't gone away.

The soft notes of "Moonlight Sonata" float in the air as my fingers glide across the keys. Each note painting the sad picture of a life once forgotten. This piece was to be my promise of a bright future. It was all my parents wanted for me. I guess they knew better than I did.

As I get lost in the music, I close my eyes and transport myself back to a time where scars didn't mar my body and nightmares didn't plague my dreams. I can still see their smiling faces in the crowd as I play various pieces by Mozart, Bach, and Beethoven. I don't play them anymore. Too many memories are attached to each one, chipping away at the broken life I've created for myself.

I'm startled when a gentle hand is pressed to my shoulder.

"Holy shit!" I jump high off the bench and clutch a fist to my chest. It's like my heart is trying to escape the safety of my body as the hairs on the back of my neck stand on end.

My best friend, Quinn, takes a seat next to me and sighs. "I've been calling you nonstop for the past hour. Have you been playing the whole time?"

I turn my head fractionally and begin playing again, quieter, though, so she can hear me.

"Yes."

I knew she would show up today. She's taken on the role of my protector, making sure I don't fall too far down the rabbit hole. She'd seen it enough times after the accident when I came to live with her parents. Quinn understands better than anyone the demons living in my head.

"Adrienne, you know you need to stop this, right?"

The sorrow in her voice hurts, threatening to shake the control I'm barely holding onto. Every time she looks at me like I'm made of glass is just another glimmering reminder of what I once had. I ignore her statement and continue playing, focusing on the keys.

She sighs. "Come on. Let's go. You need to get out of here. You're not spending your one day off moping around your apartment."

"You know I like it here. Besides, what are we going to do?"

"Something that doesn't involve here. Come on, get out of your jammies and put on real clothes. I mean, my God, look at you."

I glance down at myself and shrug. "What's so wrong about me? Besides the obvious. Who am I trying to impress?"

She rolls her eyes and drags me across the room to my dresser. "Nobody, but seriously. Sweatpants and a Hello Kitty shirt?"

I almost laugh. Almost.

"You used to love Hello Kitty."

Clothes fly out of my dresser as she rummages through my stuff. "Yeah, when I was five. You know we're a little older now."

After selecting a pair of shoes from the rack, she stands in front of me with her hands on her hips. What is she waiting for? Gratitude for treating me like a six-year-old who still needs their mommy's help? I raise an eyebrow to her. "You know I'm perfectly capable of dressing myself, right?"

She looks me up and down. "I can see that. Humor me, will you?"

"Fine. We'll do it your way."

Quinn giggles like a schoolgirl and does a little hop. I roll my eyes. "Thank you for seeing things my way. Now hurry up and shower. You look like shit, and I refuse to be seen in public with you like this."

This time, I do laugh as I gather up the clothes and head into the bathroom. After I'm done showering, I wipe the steam off the mirror and stare at myself. The roadmap of scars covering my shoulders and sides always catch my eye. Constant reminders of what happens when you act selfish and think of only yourself. Those are easily covered. It's the one by my ear that disappears into my hairline that's harder to hide. The angry white, jagged line always draws my attention. No hairstyle can hide it, so I cover it as best I can. When I emerge, Quinn's rummaging through my refrigerator, acting as if she lives here.

"Why don't you ever have anything good in here?' she whines as she takes out a can of Diet Coke.

I pull down a glass and fill it with ice for her, placing a cherry on top because I know she likes it that way.

"I have lots of good things in here. It's just not the crap food you like to eat."

"It's not normal to have this much healthy food."

"Says the nurse practitioner."

She laughs and slugs my shoulder. "You're not one of my patients so I'm allowed to tell you to eat junk food every once in a while."

"So, where exactly are you forcing me to go tonight?" I ask, taking a sip of my soda.

"You'll see. Dinner first, then fun."

I groan. "Why must you torture me so?"

She drains her glass and sets it in the dishwasher. "Because I can."

I do the same and turn to face her. "Okay, let's get this shitshow on the road, then."

"Yay!" She claps her hands like an excited child. "And just so you know, I'm highly offended. You know it's not going to be a shitshow. It's going to be fun. Come on, say it with me. Fuuuuuuuuuuuuuuun."

I grab my stuff and turn on the light above the stove. "Fun. There. I said it. Now let's get this over with."

Soon enough, we're piling into Quinn's BMW, a gift

from her parents after she finished grad school. It's hard to believe she's in charge of patients and performing medical procedures considering she used to faint at the sight of blood when we were kids. I told her when she started the whole process she should have been a doctor. She said they were too stuck up and worked ungodly hours. This was the next best thing.

The Kansas City lights flash past us as we drive down the familiar streets. "So how did your date with Pete go?' I ask.

She shrugs and pulls into the parking lot of our favorite little Italian restaurant. "It was fine. We went to a movie, then he took me home."

We exit the car and walk inside Emilio's, finding our usual table. It's dressed as your typical cheesy Italian bistro, complete with the red gingham tablecloths and old-world decorations hanging from the ceiling. Candles adorn each table, as well as a single white daisy.

"What was wrong with him now?"

We take our seats, and she sighs. "I don't know. I just didn't feel that spark. He's nice enough. Maybe a little too nice?"

"Is there such a thing as too nice?" I ask.

Pete is just another name on a long list of dates left behind. She's starting to become more like me, afraid to commit or open herself up to someone. And I don't want that for her. She deserves better than the life I've resigned myself to.

She doesn't respond because Matt approaches our table, wearing his usual white dress shirt, black tie, and blinding grin aimed directly at Quinn.

"My favorite girls. How are you tonight Quinn,

Adrienne?"

Quinn straightens in her seat and fluffs her hair for a second. As if she really needs the help. I've always been envious of her thin figure and flowing blond hair. Heck, she even developed a good two years before me, turning every boy's head in our neighborhood. But it's her blue eyes that draw people in. They're icy blue in the middle with a darker ring around the edges. Way prettier than my dull honey-colored ones. It's obvious she has a crush on him, and, judging by the way his eyes slowly roam over her snug pink shirt, he does too.

"Hey, Matt. I'm doing awesome. Just dragging my pill of a friend out of the house for some fresh air." She leans into her hands, placing them neatly beneath her chin.

"*The pill* is doing just fine tonight," I say.

He laughs and pulls out his notepad. "So, ladies, do you need menus tonight or is it the usual?"

"The usual," we both say in unison.

He scribbles down our order and turns to head back to the kitchen. As soon as he's out of range, Quinn sags into her seat. "Damn, he's looking good tonight in those glasses."

"Yeah, I'll say he is. Why don't you ask him out? Maybe you can find that spark with him?"

She shrugs and takes a sip of her water. "Yeah, wouldn't that be classy? 'Hey, I know I'm just your annoying customer, but would you like to maybe go out on a date with me? Oh, and can I get more parmesan cheese?'"

I laugh. "Well don't say it like that. You'll scare the poor guy off before he has the chance to say yes to the date."

Matt arrives with our salads, and I swear he winks at Quinn, who instantly turns pink.

"I can't. It'll be weird."

"I'm supposed to be the awkward anti-social one. You're the upbeat, way-too-perky-for-her-own-good best friend." I pause. "Wait, this isn't still about Brad, is it?"

The look she gives me could freeze hell in an instant. "No, absolutely not. I'm not giving that assbag another thought."

Okay, apparently her only long-standing relationship, which ended six years ago, is still a cause for contention. I raise my hands defensively. "Okay, okay. It's not about Brad. Then what is it?"

She looks off to the side. "It's just…it doesn't seem right for me to date when you're…you know."

My fork clanks against my plate as it falls from my hand. This is exactly what I was afraid of. "Just because I'm not currently attached to someone doesn't mean you don't have to be either."

She shrugs and finishes her salad before Matt arrives with the rest of our food. "Did I tell you about the flu epidemic going around the office?" she says, changing the subject. I shake my head. "I've had five kids this week who had to be hospitalized due to severe dehydration. Why is it so hard for parents to bring them in at the first sign instead of letting it progress to that point?"

"That's horrible. Those poor kids."

A twinge of pain runs through my heart as I think about those little kids sitting in hospital beds, hooked up to tubes and who knows what else. Hospitals still give me the creeps. I haven't set foot in one since the accident, nor do I plan on ever going back there again. Not that I planned on being there…the first time.

Quinn kicks me under the table, bringing me out of my head. "Am I boring you?"

"No," I say, shoving my plate away. "Just zoning."

Matt brings us the check, and I move to grab it only Quinn snatches it from my hands.

"Come on, I'm pretty sure it's my turn to pay," I say.

She sticks her tongue out at me and digs two twenty dollar bills from her purse. "Nope. You're a struggling musician trying to make your way through the world. I've got this."

"I'm not a struggling musician and you know it. Playing one night a week at an upscale lounge isn't exactly a career."

"No, but you're playing, so it's something."

When Matt asks if she needs change, she waves him off with a smile. He returns her animated grin, but she drags me out of the restaurant before he has a chance to say anything else. And I thought I lived my life in a constant state of avoidance.

"Okay, so where to next?" I ask when we get back into her car.

"You'll see."

We drive a few blocks when I see it come into view. You can't miss it. It's a giant building, taking up half the block. The Warehouse is the hotspot for local talent where everyone comes to get noticed. That was my draw to working here. I never had ambitions to be a bartender. Far from it. Instead, I get to watch others fulfill their dreams of becoming a musician.

There's a good mix of bands and solo acts who come through here. A few have made it big. Others still struggle to get by and are happy to play to whoever wants to listen to them. And we hear it all: jazz, metal, oldies, grunge, and even the occasional classical pieces.

As we walk into the open area, I notice several people hanging around the tables off to the side. The main floor has been left open as a makeshift dance area. Whoever is playing tonight must be pulling in a huge crowd.

We make our way to the bar and take the first two available seats near the end. My boss is working behind the counter and smiles as he turns to face us. Gabe Olson is older than we are, but not by much, early thirties or something. He doesn't act like it, though. Probably because he's worked here for the past ten years. It's hard to take yourself seriously when you're working in a bar. It's free rein to be as much of a smartass as you want.

That was another draw for me. It allows me to pretend to be someone I'm not.

"Trouble one and trouble two. How'd I know that you'd be here tonight?" he asks.

Quinn narrows her eyes at him. "I'm not trouble and you know it. This chick," she says, pointing her thumb in my direction. "Now she's the troublemaker. Can't you do something about her? I mean, really. It's getting kind of hard to take her out in public anymore."

I jab Quinn in the shoulder with my fist.

"Ow!"

I roll my eyes and slug her again for good measure. "Do you always have to be so sassy?"

She shrugs and looks up at the ceiling. I shake my head and turn my attention back to Gabe.

"So how's the band looking for tonight?"

"They're good," he says. "You should have seen them

audition. The lead singer, Kade Evans, is incredible."

"What's the band name again?"

"Lightning Strikes."

Figures. Quinn thinks she's so funny. She knows my phobia of storms and anything related to them. I'm sure she practically peed herself when she thought of this brilliant idea.

I try to focus on something else. "What kind of name is Kade?"

Gabe slides a soda in front of me. "Don't know, don't care. As long as they bring it tonight, that's all I care about."

Quinn decides to rejoin the conversation. "So tell me about this lead singer. Is he hot? Is he tatted? Piercings? Blond? Dark hair? Cut like a motherfucker? Come on, spill it!"

I can't help but stare at her. It's like she's bipolar some-times. One minute she's acting all sweet and innocent in front of a guy she finds cute, and the next she has the mouth of a sailor and the filter to go with it. My brain aches just trying to comprehend her actions sometimes.

Gabe, however, doesn't find her quite as amusing as I do. His eyes show his waning patience with her, pinning her with a stare that's crossed between longing and irritation.

"I guess you'll just have to see for yourself," he says curtly.

It's a shame she isn't on the same wavelength as Gabe. They would make the perfect couple. Both are hard-headed and childish at times. But it's obvious Gabe adores her, even if he acts hard on the outside. It's his tell. Like the boy in el-ementary school who pulls your hair on the playground all the time because he likes you.

The lights dim low and we turn in our seats to face the stage. I never noticed when the crowd came in, but the place is packed now. The crowd is female heavy, of course. Figures. Rock shows tend to draw a large female population. All scantily clad in flashy clothes, high heels, and enough makeup to choke an ox.

The drums start a punishing beat to get the crowd's attention. Quinn leans forward in her chair. Her curly blond hair hangs over her shoulders, and she turns her beaming smile to me. I raise my glass to her and stare back at the stage. Blue lights begin to illuminate the blackness, soon joined by red and green ones, swirling together as they dance across the walls. A guitar strums in the background, then a bass and another guitar. Then the lead singer takes the stage, causing every girl in the audience to scream as if they were dying.

The white spotlight stills on him as he begins singing the first lines of "Country Song" by Seether. I freeze and time slows as I stare at him.

Oh. My. God.

I've never been one to follow the crowd. But I feel myself wanting to strip out of my clothes and run around the stage naked because my body feels like it's on fire.

Looking at him, I get why every girl in the area is here tonight. His sexiness is off the charts. The hole in his black jeans right above his knee gives the smallest glimpse of tanned skin, while his white, sleeveless shirt showcases his muscular shoulders and arms. Black tattoos trail down to his biceps. Add in the perfect mess of black hair, defined cheekbones, and his five o'clock shadow, he's every girl's dream and every mother's nightmare.

The perfect bad boy.

I sit mesmerized as they sing song after song, mixing it between covers and some of their own original stuff. Each time he opens his mouth I can't help but focus my attention there. The little smiles he gives to the crowd, the twitch of his lip when he hits the rougher notes. Everything pooled together makes him like no one I've ever seen before.

"Damn, they're good!" Quinn says when they take their first break. "Gabe wasn't kidding. And that lead singer? Hot as fuck."

I nod in agreement.

Suddenly, my skin prickles from my head to my toes. It's an unfamiliar feeling, one that should put me on edge, but doesn't. I close my eyes as I inhale the sexy scent that's close to me. Sweat mixed with spice fills my nostrils. A lethal combination to any woman's defenses.

Opening my eyes, I turn my head to the side, following the sexy trail to find the source. And there he is, standing right next to me, leaning against the bar. I quickly scan his body from head to toe, getting a better appreciation of his sexiness. And it's so much more than what I can do from a distance.

When I look over again, he turns to me and gives me a sexy grin. "Hey, babe." He gives me a once over, letting his eyes trail slowly up and down my body. "Nice hoodie."

Oh fuck. I completely forgot that Quinn dressed me in my usual attire. Skinny jeans and a hoodie aren't exactly screaming "take me now", unlike the rest of the girls who are practically panting over him with scraps of material covering all the necessary parts. And for some, that's even debatable.

My brain misfires while trying to come up with a witty comeback. *Don't be lame! Make a joke or something!*

"Nice shirt."

Fuuuuuuuuck!

He looks down and a bead of sweat trickles from his hairline down the side of his face, getting lost in the scruff on his jaw. My skin tingles and my heart rate kicks up a notch as a fantasy of tracing his jawline with my tongue plays before my eyes.

Get a grip, I remind myself. He's just a guy. A hot, sweaty, completely fuckable guy, who probably has a bad reputation and the notches on his bedpost to prove it. He could have said, "Hey, I love your eyes" or "Hey, I want to bend you over the bar and fuck your brains out". But he didn't. He said he liked my hoodie. Not exactly the statement you're looking for to give an indication that he's into you.

Our eyes lock and the room quiets around us. The crowd disappears. The lights dim, except for a spotlight in my mind, showcasing us. Everything is lost to me except for Kade. His eyes, a dazzling deep shade of blue, one that I've never seen before, keep me locked onto him like a tractor beam.

In my twenty-six years, I have never been more aware of another human being in my life. There's just something about him, something dark and dangerous that makes me want to throw all caution to the wind. Forget my fucked up past, forget my reasons of self-pity and loathing.

And he's barely said more than two words to me.

Gabe sets a water glass in front of him, effectively breaking our trance. He downs it in two gulps, and I watch his Adam's apple work to move the liquid down his throat.

I never would have thought that a throat could be sexy. But his? Yeah, his definitely was.

Kade wipes his mouth with the back of his hand and the empty glass thuds against the counter. He gives me another onceover and I think he's about to turn without saying another word to me. But to my surprise, he reaches forward and tucks a stray curl of hair behind my ear. He leans in close and his sensual scent invades my senses again.

I flinch slightly as his finger trails down the side of my face. I want to turn and hide my imperfections to this seemingly perfect god, but he holds my stare, making me unwilling to break it. "I really do like your hoodie," he whispers low in my ear.

A million sensations run through me all at once before gathering together between my legs. One simple statement has rendered me into the woman I swore I would never become.

He pushes away from the bar and disappears back into the masses. The crowd parts like the Red Sea as he makes his way back to the stage. And I'm left standing here stupefied.

Quinn is speechless for once; her mouth hanging wide open. She squeals loudly, piercing my ears and dragging me back to the real world as she shakes my shoulders. "Oh my God! Did that just happen?"

I shake my head, refusing to let my hormones rule my head. I have to stay in control, of myself, of the situation, of everything around me. Bad things happen when my control slips and wanes.

I wave Quinn off. "Whatever. He's just a guy," I try to say calmly and casually. But my voice gives me away. My heart is still trying to beat out of my chest, and my cheek still feels the presence of his finger where he caressed it.

How could one encounter do this to me?

The music starts up again with "Riot" by Three Days Grace. Kade scans the crowd, playing the perfect performer as he hits every note. Then he looks in my direction and stays there, eyes searching until they find mine. We stay that way until the very last note. The crowd roars to life again, including Quinn who's practically dancing on the bar.

Kade winks and starts another song, this time playing it up for the girls in the front row. But that wink, that little gesture, I know was for me.

And as I watch him strut across the stage, the lights illuminating his sexual prowess and magnetism, I can't help but wonder what it would be like to be with him. Something that's never crossed my mind before because I'm content in my single life. No one to count on other than me, no one to dictate my life.

So why do I all of a sudden wish for the opposite?

Two

THE SIMPLE MELODY OF "JUST MY IMAGINATION" FLOATS through the air as I work out the final details of my set for Copperfield's tomorrow night. It's been in my head most of the day, humming along absently as I tidied my small apartment. Once a song gets stuck in my head, the only way to get it out is to just play it. And ever since I've touched the ivory keys, it doesn't take long for me to figure out the notes to any song I hear.

It's why I was called *The Prodigy.* My teachers spent hours working on the classics with me, but when I got home, it was the pop culture songs that intrigued me, despite my parents' disapproval. It became a game with my friends at first. They'd yell out a song and I'd play it almost perfectly the first time, as long as I knew the melody. Soon I'd challenge myself by listening to the radio and then playing the song right after, just to see if I could do it.

After making the last few notes in my notebook, I stand and walk toward the giant floor-to-ceiling windows, just a few steps away from my piano and sit on the floor. Pulling my knees to my chest, I hug the notebook close. Pinks and purples paint the clouds as the sun sinks further into the horizon.

My parents always loved this time of the day. They would spend every night they could on the front porch swing, cuddled together just to watch the sunset while I stayed inside, forced to practice my music until my fingers cramped. Not that I cared. Watching the sunset was never a luxury I had. There were too many other important things going on that prevented me from admiring one of life's simplest pleasures.

I rest my chin on my knees and sigh. Knowing what I do now, I would have stopped and taken the time to breathe, to enjoy my parents company rather than resent it. Or take a mental break to alleviate the stress put on me. As I look out at the sky now, I can see why my parents wanted to do this as often as they could. It's beautiful. A simple reminder to stop and appreciate the little things in life.

My cell phone rings and breaks the moment. Pulling myself off the floor, I make my way into the living room where the dancing phone is skittering close to the edge.

"Joe's Chicken Shack," I say.

Quinn laughs on the other side. "Yes, I'd like to know if you choke your chickens?"

I smile and sit on the couch, tossing my feet onto the table in front of me. "Of course, but the special sauce is extra."

"Gross!" she exclaims, laughing uncontrollably. "Okay, so what are you doing right now?"

I check the time. "Well, since I have to be to work in about an hour I was going to jump through the shower quick and then go. Why?"

"No reason," she says over the noise of the wind in the background. "I'm going to stop by and help you pick out something to wear tonight."

The notebook lands with a thud on the table as I lean forward. "Quinn, really. I'm a big girl. I can dress myself. I know you think of me as your own personal Barbie doll and everything, but it's Wednesday night. Nothing's going on. Just some unheard of band playing tonight. And from what Gabe said they're really more of the garage type anyway."

"Move it! Have you heard of a goddamned blinker?" I pull the phone away from my ear in an attempt to save my eardrums. "Sorry, some dipshit just cut me off."

"Okay, Queen Road Rage, I'm hanging up now. Just let yourself in, as if I really need to tell you that."

She laughs until I hear the sound of her horn. "Asshole! Okay, I'll be there in a few."

We disconnect and I set the phone on the table. Why on earth does she want to come down here to dress me up tonight? I mean, if Gabe said it's a garage band then it's going to be a bunch of punk rock wannabe's. My standard hoodie or black shirt would be more than sufficient. But I know it's pointless to dwell on it. Quinn's going to do what Quinn's going to do. It'll be less painless for me to just go with it.

By the time I exit my bathroom, Quinn is rummaging through my drawers, pulling out several items and tossing them onto my bed. "About time," she says, still pushing things around. "Okay, so here's what I'm thinking. I love these destroyed jeans paired with this off-the-shoulder white shirt and the hot pink bra underneath. Or, we can do the green wrinkled cami with your black skinny jeans and a whole mess of bangles on your wrist."

I walk closer to her and she finally looks up from her destruction of my dresser. "Okay, so why am I getting the special treatment tonight?" I ask.

She flings a thong at me and winks. "Because you need to look hot tonight."

I narrow my eyes at her as I slide the scrap of material over my legs while clinging to the towel still wrapped around me. "Okay, now tell me why."

She shrugs and points to the outfits laid out on the bed. "Just pick one please?"

Both really are not my ideal thing to wear at work. They show off more skin than I like to in front of crowds. The more of my body is covered, the better.

"Where's the bra for the cami outfit?" I ask.

A mischievous smile appears and she wiggles her brows. "No bra with that one. You are going to be bouncing solo there."

Ugh.

"Well, that makes my choice easy then." I pick up the hot pink bra and fasten it over my towel. After straightening myself out, I toss the towel over Quinn's head, making her squeal.

"Hey! Your naked body has been on that. I don't want your shit touching my shit."

I fluff my hair after putting on the pre-selected clothes. "Whatever you say." I do a slow spin. "Am I appropriate now?"

Her resounding cat call is answer enough.

"Damn. I'd fuck you if I swung that way."

Always the comedian. I push on her forehead as I walk to the bathroom again, which only makes her laugh. When

I reemerge, Quinn is sitting on the edge of my now cleaned off bed.

"What?" I ask.

She's giving me that look that I know means trouble. She's hiding something from me, I can just feel it. And she's a horseshit liar.

"Nothing. I was just thinking that you're going to have so much fun tonight."

"What are you talking about? I'm working tonight. There's going to be a whole bunch of drunken idiots walking around and generally annoying me with their lame pick-up lines. Not exactly what I call a fun time."

Her mischievous smile comes out again and this time I'm certain she's hiding something. What exactly is she up to? With a sigh, I grab my suede brown boots and zip them up. "Ready, nut job?"

"Ready," she says with a bounce and a clap. "Let's get this epic night going."

"Fuck, what is up with you tonight? Did you slip yourself some pills that weren't yours before you left work?"

She shakes her head. "Can't a girl just be excited to accompany her best friend to work?"

"No. Not without an ulterior motive," I say, grabbing my keys and purse from the counter. "And you, Ms. Jacobson, have an ulterior motive."

She clutches her hands above her heart and gasps loudly. "I'm hurt. Offended, even, that you would think that I, your bestest best friend in the whole wide world, would have an ulterior motive."

"Because, bestest, best friend, I know you. There's something up your sleeve. I just haven't figured out what it could be yet."

She slings her arm around my shoulders and winks. "Then I guess you'll just have to wait and see."

The bar is already packed by the time Quinn and I walk through the back employee entrance. Gabe is running around like a mad man, filling drink orders and looking flustered. Quinn nods and heads to her usual spot while I sign in at the other till and hit the floor running, filling drinks as they're being yelled to me from the crowd.

Usually Wednesday nights are not this busy. The band playing tonight must be really good. Or at least have a cult following around town. I haven't seen a crowd like this since Sunday, when the Lightning Strikes, and their sexy-as-sin lead singer, were here.

Kade. How could one short meeting with some guy who's probably not good for me affect me this much? I mean, yeah, he's gorgeous with that smoking hot body, tattoos, and fuck-me eyes. I've never wanted to be one of those screaming girls in the crowd before, but that night I wish I had been.

Not that our interaction was bad. It just could have been better. I'm not even sure we said more than ten words to each other. And yet, here I am, drawing fantasies from a two-minute interaction. *Get a grip on yourself, Adrienne.*

Beer flows over the top of the mug, spilling onto my hands and bringing me out of my thoughts. If I keep this up, I'll be wearing most of these drinks instead of serving them.

After the crowd thins out around the bar, Gabe turns to

me, wiping his brow with an exhale.

"Hey, thanks for that. I'm not sure how it got so out of control so fast. They just came out of nowhere."

I stack some clean glasses on the bar and flash him a smile. "No worries. It's my job, remember? Just a good thing that I showed up early tonight."

He laughs and helps me wipe down the mess we made. "Yeah, I know, but Melanie wouldn't be able to handle that much chaos."

I place some mugs in the blast chiller and shut the door with a thud. "That's why she's the daytime bartender and not me."

But he doesn't hear my statement because his gaze has already drifted over to Quinn, who's casually chatting with some guy sitting next to her. She lets out one of her fake laughs while placing a hand on his arm. I notice the guy's demeanor change, his eyes becoming more predatory than friendly as he moves them across her body.

Gabe stops cleaning and stares at her. The poor man has it bad. I walk up behind him and gently brush my hand across his back.

"Don't worry, she'll come around," I say just loud enough for him to hear me.

He grunts something unintelligible and resumes his task. I shake my head and begin stocking the coolers, taking out some six packs and bottles from the back liquor room. Quinn smiles at me when I glance up again, letting her eyes go wide as if telling me that she's into this guy. Luckily, Gabe has retired back to the office for the moment, so he's out of the line of fire, so to speak.

The speakers crackle and come to life as the sounds

of a tuning guitar fill the area. The crowd shifts and floods the stage area, leaving the bar pretty bereft. Which is fine. It gives me a few extra minutes to stock everything that Melanie didn't bother getting to earlier today.

Gabe reemerges and stares at Quinn again, who has started getting friendlier with her bar neighbor.

"Gabe, can you check on the sound system?" I ask. "There's an awful lot of feedback coming through the speakers. I have a feeling they've been playing with the settings."

He drags his eyes away from Quinn and nods to me. "I noticed that too. Can you hold down the fort until I figure it out?"

I shove him away from the bar with a laugh. "Go! I've got this."

And he couldn't have left at a more opportune time, as I see Quinn drag the guy's roaming hand back above the bar with a fake scold. She glances over at me, letting me know she's okay for now. Over the years we've set up a silent communication to get each other out of situations. Not that Quinn has ever needed it. She can handle herself.

Several hours, and a splitting headache pass by and the crowd has doubled in size again. I can barely hear what the lead singer is saying. Either he's talking about gym socks or making some kind of sexual reference that I just can't understand. His screeching is kind of hard to follow. A few of the songs I've recognized by the melody, but it's mostly originals they've written themselves. Probably with a crayon and a napkin. While in an LSD haze.

Something crashes on the other side of the room. Bodies start piling together while voices get louder and more aggressive.

"Fuck, now what?" Gabe says as he sprints over to see the damage. The mosh pit has grown and Gabe is swallowed up by it as he tries to pull bodies away from each other, leaving me to fend for myself with the angry, thirsty crowd.

I wipe the sweat off my brow, wishing I had gone with the cami instead of this shirt. Braless or not, it would have been a hell of a lot cooler. With all these bodies, it's about a million degrees in here. Plus I'm running around like a crazy woman. That doesn't help.

"I said get your fucking hands off me!" Quinn's voice rises above everyone else's, dragging my attention to her. Her now intoxicated friend has both his hands shoved up her shirt as she's smacking him in the face while trying to get away.

"Hey, buddy, back the fuck off!" I scream at him.

He turns and his bloodshot eyes focus on me. "Who the fuck are you and what are you gonna do about it?" he sneers. "She and I are just having a little fun."

White, hot rage courses through my veins as my hands ball into fists, hearing my knuckles pop with the intensity. "Look, asshole, get your fucking hands off of her or I'll make you do it."

He moves his hands away from Quinn's body, but grabs her face instead, forcing his lips upon hers. Quinn desperately claws at him, trying to push him away. I round the bar, which gets his attention. The pain that shoots across my knuckles is completely worth it, when I see the red mark form on his cheek a minute later.

"Get the fuck out." My heart feels like it's going to fly out of my chest. All I can see is red. I can't even remember a time I've been this enraged before.

He brings his fingers up to his lip. When he pulls them back to inspect them, they're tinged red from the small cut that has formed in the corner of his mouth. Quinn falls to the floor as he shoves her away, choosing to grab my shirt and forcefully drag me to him.

Panic starts to set in as I try to wiggle away. *Why the fuck isn't anyone doing something to help? Can they not see this guy getting physical with two women?*

"Look bitch," he says, bringing his face close to mine. "I'm not in the habit of hitting chicks, but since you threw the first punch, I may have to return the favor."

I try to push against his chest. It's no use, like pushing against a brick wall. His hand rears back and I close my eyes, bracing for the blow. Only it doesn't come. When I open my eyes, my would-be assailant is sprawled across the floor with a hand over his face and curled up in the fetal position. The crowd swarms in, making us the spectacle instead of the band still playing on the stage.

I pull Quinn over to me, inspecting every inch of her to make sure she's okay.

"Who punched him?" I ask.

Quinn points to the guy next to me, her lips slowly turning up in the corners. Why the fuck would she smile about any part of this situation? When I turn to thank my savior, my breath leaves me in one swift whoosh.

Kade.

He looks pissed, like he's still ready to fight. Nostrils flaring, hair mussed up like he's been running his hands through it all night, wearing a well-worn Royals t-shirt that hugs his chest just right and a pair of faded jeans. Hardly the same man I met the other night, who was more like a sex god than the everyday Joe who's standing next to me. Both personas have me reacting in the same way: shortness of breath, heart racing, palms sweaty, ache between my legs. It's enough to make me forget the last five minutes and what would've happened if he hadn't shown up.

"Are you all right?" he asks. That gravelly voice, it's so deep and sensual. My mind completely blanks. He did ask me a question, right?

Quinn jumps to my rescue by holding her hand out for a high five, which he returns. "Yeah, we're cool, thanks to you," she says.

He shoves his hands into his pockets, causing his shoulders to scrunch up to his ears. "I tried to get over here sooner, but the crowd around the bar was too thick." He turns to me and jerks his head to the guy on the floor.

Our two bouncers finally decide to show up and pick the douche bag off the floor. He's barely conscious as they drag him to the entrance, unceremoniously throwing him on his ass.

Turning, I face Kade again and smile. "Thanks for the help."

He flashes me a wide smile, showing off his perfectly straight teeth and a hint of a dimple in his right cheek. His five o'clock stubble is back, causing my fingers to itch to touch it.

What the fuck is wrong with me?

"Anytime, babe."

He holds his hand out to me and I take it, placing my much smaller hand in his. The air crackles and electrifies as we touch, sending a shiver down my spine and my stomach to flip. I suck in a quick breath of air and watch as his eyes dilate when they meet mine. All we've done is shake hands and I want to jump him right here, right now. But I need to slow down. I need to remember who I am, the broken girl who isn't good enough for anyone. Destined to be alone because that's what she asked for all those years ago.

I slowly remove my hand from his, noting the coldness setting in. Goosebumps erupt across my skin as his heated gaze looks me over from head to toe. I drag my bottom lip through my teeth and quickly run my tongue over it. He shifts closer to me, but stops when Quinn's voice breaks through our moment.

"So I don't think we've been formally introduced. I'm Quinn," she says, giving him a wink. "And this is Adrienne."

He briefly pulls his eyes away from mine to acknowledge Quinn's statement. "Kade," he simply says before returning to me.

I need to get away from him before I completely make an ass of myself. Back behind the safety of the bar, I start putting away empty bottles and wiping up the mess on the counter.

Gabe comes storming behind the bar, eyes lit with fury and a matching red face. If he could spit fire, I'm sure he would.

"What in the hell happened back here?" He looks between Quinn and me before noticing that I'm favoring my right hand. He gently moves it over, examining the discoloration forming across my knuckles.

"Nothing. It's handled," I say. I try to pull my hand away from his and wince when I flex my fingers.

He strokes the top of my hand gently with his thumbs. "You shouldn't have done that. I mean, you need your hands to play. Why didn't you let Keith and Joe handle it?"

"Because there wasn't any time. It all happened so fast. Plus the crowd was crazy packed. There's no way they would have gotten here in time."

While Gabe continues checking me out, I glance over at Quinn and Kade, who are now sitting at the bar. Quinn looks ashen, but Kade is murderous. What is his issue? Gabe is my boss. Everyone knows that. The V between his brows deepens. He's positively fuming right now. But why?

Gabe turns his attention back to Quinn, who sheepishly casts her eyes away. "Okay, now tell me why my bartender had to punch someone?"

"The girls got into a bit of a situation, but they took care of it," Kade says when no one responds.

"A situation?"

"Adrienne hit the guy for me, but then Kade hit him when he was about to punch her," Quinn says, her voice dropping low.

"What the fuck?" Gabe yells.

Two guys show up and I hand them a fresh round of beers, steering them away from the argument at the end of the bar. I've never seen Gabe so pissed before. I mean, I get it. He went to go break up a fight on the main floor and comes back to his wounded bartender and an unconscious man lying on the floor.

"You should put some ice on that otherwise you're never going to play tomorrow night," Quinn says when I rejoin them.

I flex my hand again and wince, staring at the purple color now slowly crossing my skin. Grabbing a clean towel, I put some ice in it but struggle to keep it closed when I put it on my hand.

Kade grabs the towel and gingerly places it on my swollen hand. "Here, let me help."

Resting my hand in his, he lightly presses down until I can feel the cold permeate through the towel. I suck in a harsh breath and close my eyes.

"Wow that hurts."

He pulls the makeshift ice pack off and examines my hand. "It's not broken. You probably just bruised it a little. I'm guessing you don't hit many people, otherwise you would have done it so you didn't hurt yourself."

He places the ice back on my hand, the cold making the throbbing slow down to a dull ache. Our eyes meet as his thumb slowly strokes along my wrist, my hand still cradled in his. It's been a long time since I've allowed anyone to take care of me, and I'm not sure if I like it. What I do know is he can keep touching me for as long as he wants.

Nerves get the best of me, though. "Thanks, I got this now." I pull my hand from his and hold it close to my body, slowly backing away.

"Take some Ibuprofen. It'll help with the swelling."

Quinn digs through her purse and produces a bottle with a smile.

"Got some right here for you, Rocky."

Popping three pills into my mouth, I wash them down with a big gulp of water, which proved to be a more difficult task than I thought. Kade's eyes follow me as I move behind the bar, attempting to do my job while still nursing my hand.

Part of me wants to start up a conversation with him, but the words are never there when he's close. It's like I've forgotten how to speak or maybe English isn't my first language. Instead, I stare and avoid him like a shy teenager.

I walk back to where he and Quinn are talking and bump my hand on the way, making me cry out in pain.

"Go home," Gabe says, resting a hand on my shoulder. "I'll split the tips and save them for you when you get back Friday night. I've got this."

"Are you sure? I mean, it's been a madhouse in here." Only it's not anymore. I glance around quickly. Wait, the band's gone? And where the hell is the crowd? Probably finding another bar to destroy. Only a few stragglers remain at the other end of the bar, whispering to each other as they glance in our direction.

My shoulders sag. "Yeah, I suppose. Hopefully I didn't do too much damage. Can't believe I was stupid enough to punch him. God, I'm such an idiot."

Quinn perks up a little. "You should have seen her, Gabe. She was all 'Hey, fuck off, asshole' and he was all 'Shut up, bitch' and then she went all cage fighter on his ass. It was so fucking sweet."

"That's not how it went and you know it." I roll my eyes, earning me her middle finger. "You're such a drama queen. No wonder why I hated playing telephone with you when we were younger."

Kade hasn't said much since I walked away from him. Just kept his hands folded in front of that mouth made for sin. His eyes follow my every move, creeping me out slightly but somehow making me calm. Almost like I'm protected. Again, something I'm not used to.

It makes me nervous, but not in a bad way. I don't think he'd ever do anything to hurt me or make me feel uncomfortable. Granted, I don't know that for certain, but the simple fact he came to my aid tonight says volumes for his character. That fierce protectiveness is a huge turn on, drawing feelings to the surface that I've avoided for way too long. Emotions are messy and it's easier to just leave them out of the equation.

Kade is a temptation, dangling in front of me like forbidden fruit. Every part of me wants to pick him from the tree for a taste, even though I know I shouldn't.

One bite never hurt anyone before, right?

"Whatever," Quinn says, pulling me out of my head again. "I speak the truth."

"Uh huh." I turn back to Gabe. "Last chance. Are you sure?"

He laughs and hugs me lightly. "I'm sure. Go home, rest up, and I'll see you Friday. No more fights, got it?"

I mock salute him. "No problem there. That was my first and last fight. Hurts too damn bad and I'm a wimp."

Quinn jumps off her stool and tosses an arm over my shoulder. "Let's go, Bruiser. I've got a bottle of tequila with your name on it."

"Ugh," I say, pulling away from her. "I'm just going to grab my stuff out of the back room."

Quinn follows me and leans against the doorjamb as I gather my things together.

"You know he's totally into you."

"What?" I say, shutting the locker door.

She steps to the side and nods her head toward Kade when we're back near the main floor. "You should go for it."

"No."

"What? Why the hell not? He's hot and single, you're hot and single. Together you'd be on fire."

I shake my head and find myself unable to look away from him. "Distraction," is all I say.

Her face falls and she puts both hands on my shoulders. "It's not your fault. Your parents would want this for you. They'd like you to find someone to spend your life with. How are you ever going to find that if you never go out?"

I shake her off. "That's not true. You've seen me go out with plenty of guys."

"You are a serial first dater. When I say go out, I mean *go out*, like on more than one date. Overnight, even. Multiple times."

"Maybe I'm meant to be alone." I sigh.

Giggles and high-pitched squeals come from two girls who've flocked to Kade, not taking notice of his inattentiveness. They paw and rub up against him in a desperate ploy. He doesn't once acknowledge them. How do I know that? Because his eyes haven't left mine since he saw me come out of the back room.

"Listen to me." She grabs me by the shoulders once more. "You're a good person. What happened isn't your fault. Please don't live in the past. Live for today. Live for tomorrow. Just live."

I try to tune her out, but only partially succeed. She's not entirely right. Everything that's happened to me so far has been my fault. I begged to be left alone, wished to make my own decisions about my life. Wish granted. Now I have to live with the consequences. Plain and simple.

"Sure."

With a final wave to Gabe, we turn toward the front entrance. The loud screech of a chair draws my attention back to the bar. Kade stands, leaving the two babbling blonds mid-sentence and stunned. In a few short strides he makes his way over to us; my heart beats just a touch faster.

Quinn greets him with a smile. I don't.

"Were you going to leave without saying goodbye?" Ugh, his voice. Every time I hear it, my knees weaken and I'm *not* that kind of girl.

"Goodbye. There. Happy?"

Quirking his lips up, he lets out a quiet chuckle. Butterflies swarm in my stomach, looking for a way out. Every time he smiles at me like that.

"You're kind of sassy. I like that."

Something comes to life when he calls me sassy. I can't explain it. Maybe it's the way he pronounces the word, caressing each letter as if he was making love to them. No, that's not right. I can't see him making love to anything.

Fucking. That's what I see. He's fucking those letters until they cry out, begging for release.

Another rush of heat gathers between my legs, creating another ache.

"Kade, can you walk us to our cars? You know, in case that guy is lingering around?" Quinn asks.

A look passes between them. Quinn still hasn't figured out that I know when she's up to something. Or she just doesn't care. And really, when did they get to be so buddy-buddy? I mean, she just met him tonight. Or did she? Wait, did she set this whole thing up?

That's impossible. I mean, she wouldn't do that.

Like fuck she wouldn't. This is exactly the sort of thing she'd do.

"It's not necessary. We'll be fine. Besides," I jerk my head toward the girls who are throwing dirty looks at Quinn and me. "It seems as if your fan club would like you to stay a bit longer."

Kade closes the gap between us, backing me up until I'm flush against the wall. He tucks a stray hair behind my ear, letting his hand linger just as he did on Sunday. "I was going to do it anyway."

My scalp tingles as his fingers run through my hair. Clearing my throat, I readjust my stance.

"Fine, have it your way. Do what you want."

Pushing off the wall, I quickly walk to the door with Quinn and Kade slinking behind. Whispers, coy glances… they've been doing it all night. It's no different when I glance over my shoulder in the parking lot.

This can't be good. *What is she up to?*

The lights flash on my car and I open the door. "Well, thanks for making sure we didn't get attacked in the parking lot, or attacked by some masked ne'er-do-well."

Before I can sit down, Kade reaches out, grabs the door, and leans against my car, like he's still in protection mode.

"I would never let anything happen to you."

I try to swallow past the lump in my throat. How can this man be so frustrating and fascinating at the same time? I don't need distractions in my life, yet I find myself wanting to be near him. Maybe it's his fierce protectiveness or the way he doesn't give a fuck about what others think. I only wish I had that kind of confidence. I can fake it with the best of them, but when it comes down to it, I'm chicken shit.

Our eyes meet again and I quickly look away. "Um, thanks again, Kade, for saving me tonight."

"Anytime, babe."

That's the second time he's called me babe. Each time it

makes my stomach flip and heart beat faster.

Quinn finally reappears and gives us a small wave.

"Okay, I'm out. See you tomorrow for our weekly makeover session. Later."

She gives Kade a wink before driving away, leaving us alone. Pressing my lips together, I shift on my feet and kick at the rocks. The awkward silence grows the longer I stare at the ground, while I can feel Kade's eyes begging me to look at him.

"So where are you playing tomorrow night?" he finally asks.

"Um, nowhere?"

His sexy laugh fills the air and I fight to keep my lips from turning up.

"Then why is Quinn coming over tomorrow to fix you up?" His eyes darken. "You have a date instead?"

This time I do laugh. "No, I don't date."

He moves closer. "You sure about that?"

"About dating? Yeah, positive." I swallow hard. "I don't have time to deal with my own needs, let alone someone else's."

I focus on his fingers gripping the door. Musician's hands. Long, slender fingers, calloused on the ends from playing the guitar. Working man's hands. Skilled. And distracting.

"You never answered my question," he says, leaning in close.

God, he smells good. Almost as good as he did on Sunday, only without the mix of sweat. Which is a shame really. There's something about it that makes his skin smell stronger, more primal. It makes you think of sex, which is probably the last thing I should be thinking of when I'm this close to him.

Please don't let him see how turned on I am through my shirt, because it's been a long, long time since I've felt this way.

Backing away, I bite my lip and lower myself into the car. "I guess you'll just have to figure it out."

Poking his head into the car, he asks, "Is that a challenge?"

"Take it however you want." I shrug. "Night, Kade."

The shit-eating grin on his face makes me smile as I stare at him in the rear view mirror. Did I just issue a challenge as I left him standing there with his hands in his pockets?

Well, shit.

Three

"ARE YOU LEAVING ANY HAIR ON MY HEAD?" QUINN jerks my head to the side for the millionth time. My neck aches as she teases my hair into a giant frizzy mess. I'm failing to see what the outcome of this is going to be, other than I'll have to shave my head when this is all said and done.

"Shut up and let me work. God, you're whinier than some of the two-year-old patients I see."

With a heavy sigh, I shut my mouth and let her work her magic on my hair. Quinn's going all out tonight. She even surprised me with a new dress, which I told her was stupid. She waved me off as only she can and said I deserved it after saving her last night.

And it's absolutely gorgeous. A royal blue A-line style with a boat neckline, capped sleeves, and comes to about mid-thigh. I drew the line at shoes. After pulling out my nude peep-toe heels with the ankle strap, we both agreed they would be perfect.

Which brings me to the current torture I'm enduring. Quinn calls it a makeover. I think we've agreed to disagree on the subject. I brush the mess away from my eyes to look at the mirror.

What the fuck has she done? Is this some sort of payback for being a hermit? Did I give her a shitty birthday present when we were kids and she's waited this long to exact her revenge?

"I look like I stuck my finger in a socket. What exactly are your plans, other than making a complete mess of my hair?"

"Patience," she says. "You'll see. You're going to look gorgeous when I'm done."

There is no way I can see the bigger picture with this mess. How does she expect me to go out like this?

"And why the special treatment tonight? Who am I going to impress? Everyone who goes to Copperfield's is either married or from the upper-class society, which I'm not a part of anymore." My throat tightens at the last thought, reminding me of what I once was.

Quinn shakes her head as she gathers up half of my hair, pushing it so there's a slight bump at the crown before securing it with a myriad of bobby pins. Each shove brings a new meaning to the phrase "pain is beauty".

"Will you just hold still? Seriously!" Quinn clutches the comb between her teeth, squinting as she concentrates while curling the ends of my hair. Using the flat iron, she elegantly sweeps my bangs to the side and secures them with a blue jeweled pin. Her eyes narrow slightly as she places a few more curls at the back of my head. One more jerk, and few forcefully placed pins, she puts her hands in the air in triumph.

"Ta-da! Damn, you're sexy. Here." She hands me a mirror and I take it, nervous to see the end result. Wow. I'm stunned, speechless, and, well, amazed. This can't be my reflection staring back at me. This girl is polished, refined, and put together. Definitely red carpet worthy.

"Quinn, it's amazing. I can't even begin to thank you. I love the curls in the back. And the diamond accents you put in are so classy. I feel like I should be walking down the aisle." She raises her eyebrow and I laugh. "Okay, maybe not quite. How about prom?"

She presses her cheek to mine when I turn around to examine the front one more time. "I would have said marriage, but that would involve you dating. Then again, the same can be said for prom. You need a *date* in either of those scenarios."

I roll my eyes and stand from the chair. "Whatever. So are you doing my makeup too, or am I being left to my own vices for that?"

A pained look spreads across her face and I can't help but giggle. "Oh my God, absolutely not. I haven't gone through all this trouble for you to do your own makeup. If that's the case, you might as well go roll in the mud right now." She shrugs. "No offense."

"I'm used to your lack of filter."

"Besides, I have it all worked out in my head. I need you drop dead, no holds barred, stunningly beautiful tonight."

I quickly strip out of my button-down painting shirt and work the dress up my body. The silk material glides over my skin, hugging me in all the right places. "My God, Quinn, you really shouldn't have. I mean, I'm glad you did because this outfit is exceptional, but it had to have been crazy expensive."

She waves me off and points to the chair again. "I told you, I owed you for last night. Now no more talking until I'm done."

After a half hour of more torture, I'm finally stepping into my shoes and admiring her handiwork in the full length mirror by my bed.

"God, I wish I didn't love cock as much as I do. Otherwise I'd be all over your ass."

Seriously? Her filter must be non-existent tonight. Only Quinn could get away with saying something like that. Dropping my jaw, I turn and stare. "Oh my fucking God. I can't believe you just said that."

She laughs and grabs her purse off the bed. "Well, I did. So let's go. Are you riding with me?"

I nod before grabbing my own clutch and turning on the stove light. "Might as well. I wouldn't want to mess myself up before I get there." We laugh and head out the door.

Copperfield's is packed again, just like it is every Thursday. It's kind of amazing I've managed to pull in such a large gathering of people. Obviously everyone must agree since I have my own night here and from what the employees tell me, it's their busiest work night of the week.

As soon as we walk through the front doors, Shane Eiserman, the manager, greets me with open arms. "Adrienne, you look absolutely stunning." He kisses the back of my hand, and I blush slightly. He's attractive enough, but a little too old for my tastes. With his salt and pepper hair and the amount of wrinkles around his eyes, I'd put him around his early forties. But I could be wrong.

I run a hand discretely down the front of my dress in an attempt to smooth out any wrinkles that may have formed on the car ride over after glancing at his perfectly pressed attire.

Shane laughs at my gesture and links my arm through his. "Don't worry, my dear. You look divine. Shall we?" We start walking into the lounge, turning heads as we go.

I hand Quinn my clutch. "If you need a drink, just give them my card. I'm buying."

She waves off my statement and heads over to the bar area. "Your money's no good here," Quinn says over her shoulder. Her pink lace dress sways as she walks down the few stairs, picking a seat close to the stage.

Shane leads me to the piano and gently rubs his hand up and down my arm. Unease settles in, though I try to brush it away. He's never been this attentive before and it's creeping me out. When he leans in close, alarm bells ring in my head.

"Maybe tonight after the show you and I could get together for a few drinks back at my place?"

I turn toward the piano, placing my hand on top for balance. "Um, I don't know. I mean, Quinn drove me tonight so I'll need to leave when she does." A feeble excuse, but I hope it works.

"I can drive you anywhere you want after the show, or you could stay at my place." He closes the gap between us. Is he serious? If this is how my night is going to go, I should leave. Now. Who cares if the tips are good and the paycheck is enough to keep me coming back.

A glass shatters, followed by the bartender cursing loudly, drawing his attention. I breathe a sigh of relief. Shane turns back to me and slides his hand down my arm. "Think about it."

A chill runs down my spine as he walks away. What the fuck just happened? I was feeling on top of the world before I got here, and now I just want to crawl into a hole and never be found again. Shane's never done this before. Why he's being so aggressive tonight?

With a calming breath, I take my seat on the bench, finally at peace. All I need is to start my set, and then everything will be fine. When it's just me and the piano, life makes sense. After a brief struggle with the microphone stand, I address the crowd. Instinct takes over as my fingers dance across the keys, filling the room with the first few notes of "If You Don't Know Me By Now" by Harold Melvin and The Blue Notes. Glancing around, several people smile and stop their conversations. This is why I love coming here. The atmosphere is so different than the bar. Yeah, the clientele is higher class, but the ease and relaxed environment recharges me, prepares me for the craziness the weekend will bring.

And it doesn't smell like a million sweaty bodies that haven't showered in days.

The oldies are a huge hit. People sing along to the melodies, prompting me to finally pick a song I'll sing to. I try to sprinkle a few of them into the lineup, depending on the crowd. It's not that I don't have a good voice. Just the opposite, though I still get shy and self-conscious about it.

Quinn's face stands out in the crowd, sending me encouraging smiles and random thumbs up. Tears prick my eyes. I don't know what I did in a previous life to have her here now, but I thank God every day. The woman is my rock, the person who grounds my feet when all I want to do is fly.

Halfway through "When Will I Be Loved", I glance at

Quinn, who's chatting with someone new, wearing a three-piece suit complete with a blue dress shirt and ivory tie. He looks like every other guy in here, only...

Wait. That profile, the just-fucked hair begging for me to run my fingers through it. The clean-shaven look is new. I long for the scruffy five o'clock shadow I'm used to seeing.

My body recognizes him before I do, and everything south of my navel ignites with awareness.

If you saw him on the street dressed like that, you'd never know it was Kade Evans. The tattoos are covered and it surprises me how disappointed I am. I can feel his stare and my heart beats a smidge faster. That shit-eating grin he wore when I left him in the parking lot last night is plastered across his face.

Cocky son of a bitch.

I play a few more songs before taking my first break. With a small bow, I tentatively make my way to them. Kade stands to greet me and flashes his damned come-fuck-me smile. Judging by my body's response, it wants to accept the challenge.

"Adrienne." Holy hell. How does the sound of his voice make my brain turn to mush? I blink repeatedly, which only makes him laugh. "So I found you. What's my prize?" He lifts my bruised hand up to his lips, placing a gentle kiss upon my knuckles.

My face burns as I focus on his lips caressing my skin, feeling my body temperature rise. His lips linger before looking up and making eye contact with me. I'm not quite sure if this counts as an appropriate public display, though I could care less. Actually, he could throw me on top of the bar and fuck me until kingdom come and I wouldn't give two shits about who was around.

"Prize?" I say, once my higher brain function returns. "Who said anything about a prize? I only said you'll have to find out. There was no challenge issued."

His thumb moves across my hand, and my stomach flips and flutters at the feel of his skin stroking mine. When he leans closer, my breath hitches. I warned myself to avoid his magnetism, but with each passing second my resolve weakens. The way he looks at me...it's like the world completely shuts down and we're the last two people left standing. If we needed to repopulate for the survival of the human race, that's a sacrifice I'm willing to make.

Quinn clears her throat. Oh yeah, forgot she was here. "That first set was so good, but please tell me you have something more modern to play?"

Rolling my eyes, I sigh. Such a music snob. If Ryan Seacrest hasn't featured it on his AT40 chart, it's crap according to her.

Kade tries to hide his laugh by disguising it as a coughing fit. Smooth. "No, nothing modern. This whole night is dedicated to the Fifties and Sixties. You're just going to have to suffer."

"You're no fun." Quinn groans loudly. "Kade, seriously, how can you be attracted to someone who is obviously a bore?"

Seriously? I quickly snatch my hand from his, only now realizing he never let go. Quinn shrugs off my glare.

"All right, let's get something straight here. One, no one is attracted to anyone. Two, where in the hell do you come off saying shit like that, Quinn?"

I don't mean to sound like a raging bitch, but she

stepped over the line this time. Sure, Quinn can be brash – and doesn't always use her filter – but it's not normally directed at me. What's worse, she doesn't even look remotely apologetic for her remark, as if she's trying to get a rise out of me.

Mission accomplished.

Kade shoves his hands into his pockets and shrugs. "What can I say? I like them feisty and sassy."

Quinn throws another sardonic smile at me and laughs. "And you've got one. Good luck, buddy. She's all yours."

"Okay, I'm right here." I turn to Kade and jab a finger into his chest. "And don't mistake this for another challenge."

The look in his eyes says otherwise. It's like he's stripping me down, peeling back all my layers to get a better look at me. He wants me. But could I be with someone like him? Do I even know how to be happy anymore? I've resigned myself to a life of solitude. A man like Kade would shake my foundation, letting pieces crumble to the ground. Would it really be so bad if he was the one to pick them up?

Kade moves closer, bringing his sinful lips next to my ear. "I told you, I like you sassy."

He pulls back and I struggle to find a breath. We're practically strangers. Two brief run-ins, not counting tonight, and a handful of conversations together isn't enough time. Or is it? I'm not exactly the best judge of these things. One look, one drunken mistake, and then the walk of shame in the middle of the night. That's what I'm used to. Not this. Not this constant feeling of something more.

I lick my suddenly dry lips. My pulse quickens as I watch his eyes dilate slightly and his nostrils flare, just like that first night. Taking him in slowly, getting my first good look from head to toe, desire starts running through my bloodstream. I want to run my hands up his coat and slide it off his shoulders, just so I can get a look of him in his vest.

Kade twists his lips to the side and, as if he could read my thoughts, starts to unbutton his coat, letting it slowly slide off his arms and shoulders. He tosses it carelessly over his chair and leans against the bar to grab his beer.

Holy Mary, Mother of God.

This man, this rock god or whatever he is, is hands down the hottest thing alive. The way the vest accentuates his narrow waist and muscular torso has me speechless. I think Quinn is as well because she's literally stopped doing everything altogether and is blatantly staring at him, leaving her glass suspended in the air just inches from her lips.

"I –"

Kade smirks and places his beer back down. "You were saying?"

Ass. He knows exactly what he's doing and how to make me into a puddle of stupidity. I need an escape. Shane spots me and taps his watch, indicating my break is up. *Oh, thank God.*

"No time for your head games. There's a piano calling my name."

I turn toward the stage, but stop when Kade's fingers wrap around my arm. He leans in close, pressing his hard chest against my back. The heat emanating off him has me panting and needy.

Yeah. That's the reason why.

The air seems too thin because it's hard to catch my breath. Once again his lips come close enough to my ear so only I can hear him.

"I love watching you up there," he says, nodding to the stage. "Do me a favor?"

"What?" I pant, trying my best not to sound desperate. There's so much adrenaline running through my body, it's making me light-headed. I need to put some distance between us before I completely embarrass myself in front of society's finest.

Brushing his lips against my cheek, Kade wraps an arm around my waist, catching me before my knees buckle. Suddenly, an image of Kade holding me like this every night pops into my head. Something so natural and easy, giving me a sense of security and safety. His fingers press into my stomach and I stop breathing altogether.

"Play the next song just for me."

Turning my head fractionally, I look at him out of the corner of my eye. A song for Kade? This could be dangerous.

On the way back to the piano, I ram my side into a table while trying to get through the mass of people. The pain briefly distracts me from picking out a song. Something for him? I skim my finger down the list. What could I play that would scare Kade away? Maybe I could play...no, that won't work. Or maybe...not that one either. Scrunching up my nose, I blow out a quick breath. Forget it. I'm sticking with the plan.

"Fuck," I say quietly enough so the mic doesn't pick it up.

Hesitating, I hover my fingers above the keys. If I play this, I know he'll read into it. How could he not? I mean, Heath Ledger sang this to Julia Stiles in *10 Things I Hate About You* and managed to win her over. If he hears this, there's a good chance he'll react the same way. If only he knew how appropriate it truly is though. Because as much as I fight it, as much as I deny it to myself, I am attracted to him. It's getting harder and harder to look away every time he's near.

Risking a glance in his direction, Kade smiles, letting his dimple come out to play. Fuck me sideways, he would go and do something like that. He knows I'm a sucker for that damn thing. Heat climbs up my face and I release a slow breath.

You have to sing this one.

Closing my eyes, I start singing "Can't Take My Eyes Off You". Instantly the crowd stops murmuring, some even sway in their seat. I've put my own little twist on the song, slowing it down even more, making it more sensual than the original. Quinn leans up and whispers something in Kade's ear. What is she doing? It's not fair. She gets to be close to him while I'm stuck up here, quasi-pouring my heart out. Not that I'd be bold enough to whisper anything in his ear. But I would like to know what my Judas best friend is saying.

Our gazes lock and everything fades into the background. Almost like a spotlight is shining down on Kade so we're the only two people in the room, the lyrics flow effortlessly from my lips. He's too good to be true. And I can't help but follow his every movement, drawn to him like a magnet.

That's when I notice the change in Kade's eyes, an intensity I've never witnessed before. Those blues that first drew me to him watch over me so intently, I can't help but daydream what it would be like if we were together.

We're in my apartment, me sitting at the piano and Kade leaning against it, brushing the hair away from my face. I can feel each stroke of his fingertips against my cheek before lowering himself to the bench. His arm touches mine and I scoot closer to him, convinced we're not close enough. Our thighs press together and he leans over slightly to whisper in my ear...

Forcing my eyes open, I play the last few notes. The roar of applause is humbling, especially since I don't consider myself a singer. But there are only two opinions I value most right now, and they're sitting beside each other. Quinn lets out her usual whistle of approval, with a few cat calls thrown in there. My gaze drifts to Kade, giving me a satisfied smile. He likes it. Heat runs through my veins and it's taking everything I have not to run into his arms with the look he's giving me.

Baby steps. He likes how you sing. Let's not jump ahead of ourselves here.

A few songs later, I finish my set and gracefully rise to take a bow. After thanking the crowd, I remind them I'll be here next Thursday, which is their cue to start bombarding me with questions as I step off the stage. Most want to give their congratulations, a few slide their business cards into my hands, asking me to do private parties or wonder if I want to branch out to other establishments.

On the outside I'm cordial, polite, everything my parents taught me when I was younger. Inside, I'm a mess. The attention makes me uneasy and I start to shrink back into myself. All I want is to find the security I seek when I'm near Kade.

Before I reach Quinn and Kade, Shane's arm snakes around my waist and places a firm kiss on my head. Chills run down my spine and I get a sudden sick feeling in my stomach. I try to push away, but he pulls me closer into his side.

"Great job, Adrienne. You had a record night. We've never had this many people in the lounge before."

Shifting uncomfortably in my heels, I glance back at Kade. He's fuming, flexing his fists at his side. The vein on the side of his neck starts to poke out. I think...I think he's jealous. Definitely showing the same signs as last night when he laid the guy out at the bar. If Shane doesn't let go, he may be forced to in a minute. Even though Shane is acting completely out of character, I don't want to see anyone get hurt. Grabbing his hand, I pry it off my hip and quickly step to the side. "Thanks, Shane."

"Look, I'd really like to drive you home tonight. Tell Quinn she can take the night off. I'll look after you, cupcake. I'll take real good care of you."

He trails a finger down my arm. Alarm bells scream in my head, making my skin crawl where he's touched it. Why is he doing this? Why now? Why tonight? Bile burns my throat while I try to choke it down. I need an escape, an exit strategy.

"Shane, I..." is all I can get out before Kade steps between us. He wraps his arms around my waist, pulling me into his chest. I instantly relax into his body, molding into him as if I belong there.

Then his lips crash down on mine, moving quickly at first, but then slow to a sensual dance. I can taste his warm breath and I lightly gasp when his tongue reaches out to gain access to my mouth. He takes advantage and sparks ignite when the tips of our tongues brush against each other for the first time. I place my hand on his chest as he moves me around so I'm fully against him; his hands running up and down my back in the process.

I lose myself in this kiss, in Kade because deep down, I want this. Gripping the nape of my neck with his hand, he plays with the curls around my shoulders. I run my hands up his chest until finally, *finally*, I get the first feel of his hair running through my fingers. So soft, so silky, and…*good God*. Why does he have to groan like that when I tug?

Shane clears his throat next to Kade, forcing us to break away. I drag my tongue slowly over my swollen lips, his taste still lingering on them. Sweet and addicting. A low growl emerges from his throat as he watches my every move. He flexes his fingers at the small of my back; the hand in my hair pulling gently until I'm looking up at him. Kade kisses my nose and smiles.

"Sorry, man." Kade shrugs unapologetically. "Couldn't wait any longer. My girl killed it tonight, like I knew she would."

I moan softly at his words while keeping my gaze locked with his. Either he's a really good actor, or…

I'm not sure what to think anymore when it comes to Kade.

Wrapping my arms around Kade's waist, I place my head on his chest, giving Shane a weak smile. The rhythmic beating of his heart fills my ears, pounding slightly faster than normal, which I assume is from our incredibly inappropriate PDA session.

"Shane, this is Kade Evans," I say, holding my hand out between them. "Kade, this is Shane Eiserman, the general manager here at Copperfield's."

I pull back slightly, expecting Kade to release me and extend his hand to Shane, but he doesn't. Instead, he tightens his grip on my waist, keeping me locked to his side.

"Funny. Adrienne's never mentioned a boyfriend. Why haven't I seen you here before?" Shane asks, tucking his hand away with a scowl. He puffs out his chest slightly, and I want to laugh. *Oh, Shane. You don't want to go toe to toe with Kade. Just back away and everyone should still be able to walk out of here on their own accord.*

"Unfortunately, prior commitments have kept me away, but I made it a point to be here tonight." Kade places a kiss on my temple and I smile genuinely at him. He looks down and winks. "You did well, babe."

When I look back at Shane, his shoulders are slumped forward as he huffs a breath. "Yes, well, I need to get back on the floor. Pleasure to meet you."

Kade releases one arm from me, shaking his hand with that same shit-eating grin I've seen on numerous occasions already. The awkward exchange only lasts a moment until Shane turns and walks away. I try again to pull away from Kade. This time, he lets me go.

"What the hell was that?" I ask, trying to hide by breathy tone, but fail miserably.

Kade points in the direction Shane left. "That guy is a creep. You looked like you were about to throw up or pass out when he touched you. Forgive me for coming to your rescue. Again."

He's really pissed. That deep V has set in between his brows and the vein I saw earlier is still throbbing on the side of his neck.

"What is your issue? It's not like I asked you to come over and save me. Or stick your tongue down my throat and make me–" I press my lips together and close my eyes. Shit.

I didn't mean to say that. Maybe I stopped myself in time. Maybe he won't read into what I'm trying to say.

Too late. The smirk is back. Dammit.

"Make you what?"

Kade pulls me closer until each and every hard muscle of his body is pressed against mine. He's too close again and I can't think. Well, that's not true. I'm imagining what he would look like without this suit on. Based on what's pressing against me now, I'm betting it's six-foot-two inches of pure sex.

My face instantly heats up as Kade traces a finger down my cheek. He leans in, his scent invading me again, turning me into a wanton harlot of desire and need when I'm trying to stay mad at him.

"What do I make you do?" he quietly asks. Hot breath tickles my ear, weakening my defenses again. I need to stop this. I need to get some distance between us because I can't think with him this close to me. After that amazing kiss we shared, the only thing that comes to mind is what he would be like in bed.

"I...you...I..."

Apparently English isn't my native language. I can't even form a coherent sentence, let alone a thought. He laughs and dips his head lower. My eyes widen. I think he's going to kiss me again. Leaning forward, I pucker my lips and start to close my eyes. That is, until Quinn appears. I quickly put some distance between us. It's about damn time she showed up, even though she's a few minutes too late. Although I seriously doubt she would have jumped in sooner. Pretty sure she has a master plan working for us.

"Great job tonight, Rin. Your best set yet."

She looks between the two of us and her lips twist to the side. Kade's breathing heavy and hasn't taken his eyes from mine. With each rise and fall of my chest, my lungs inflate more, regulating my breath into a normal rhythm. Still, I can't look away from Kade.

"So are you ready to go?" I need to get out of here, away from Kade. Truth be told, I needed to leave about five minutes ago, before he mesmerized me with that amazing first kiss. Just the thought of his tongue as it swept inside my mouth, tasting and savoring me, has my rebellious body wound up again. The lust building inside me is screaming to take him home and let him do that again, and in places other than my mouth. It's almost too much for my brain to compute.

The sardonic smile is back and I already know what she's going to say before it even leaves her traitorous mouth. "Sorry, but I have an emergency I need to deal with. One of my patient's needs me." She turns to Kade. "Can you take her home?"

His face splits into a heart-warming grin and I actually feel myself mirroring it.

"I'd be more than happy to take her home." He turns to me. "What do you say? Wanna go for a ride?" He wiggles his eyebrows and heat spreads across my body before finally gathering between my legs.

Quinn taps her foot, waiting for my answer. I want to call her out on her meddling ways, but I just can't. There's something about this that feels right. And I know I should fight this, know I should keep him far away from me so I don't poison him with my toxic soul. But for the first time in a long time, I have a chance at happiness; something I thought could only ever be a dream.

"Fine." I give Quinn an accusing glare and she averts her eyes to the ceiling.

"Good," she says, finally looking back at me. "I'll call you tomorrow during my lunch break. Night, you two." She gives us both a quick wave and practically runs out the door. Could she tell I wanted to jam my heel into her eye for putting me on the spot? However, as my body tingles with Kade's close proximity, how mad can I be?

"Look, I'm pretty tired," I say. "I can call a cab. You don't have to drive me home if you don't want to."

Hurt mars his beautiful features before transforming into a heart-warming smile. Kade grabs my hand and wordlessly starts leading me out the exit and toward his car. A set of lights blink in the dark, illuminating a path for us. He squeezes my hand quickly before releasing it.

"This is yours?" I give a low whistle. "Nice car."

The sleek, black Nissan 370Z Coupe is not exactly what I was expecting Kade to drive. Actually, I saw him more as a Harley kind of man, a lone rider, burning up the highway on his two-wheeled death machine. But this sports car could also fit the bill; fast and dangerous, mirroring the path that we're heading down. The kick plates illuminate when he opens the door and I run my hand over the soft, supple leather once I'm nestled safely inside.

"Are you sure you want to take me home?" I'm almost afraid of the answer, but he puts those fears to rest quickly when his hand comes up to gently cradle my cheek, his palm warm against my face. Instinctively, I lean into his soft touch and hold back the sigh that wants to come out.

Kade's eyes shine under the glow of the electronics, but

I think it's more than that. I can feel it in his touch, the way he watches me, how his eyes are constantly seeking something from me. And as much as I refuse to acknowledge it, there is something more between us.

"I'm taking you home. After tonight, I need to make sure you get there safe."

What does he expect to happen? Sure, Shane was creepier than usual, but he would never hurt me. At least, I didn't think so before tonight.

Kade drags his hand from my face, leaving the area cold and bereft. The city lights pass by the window as he navigates his way to my apartment from the directions I'm giving. Out of the corner of my eye, I keep a silent watch on him in a debate of my will and strength, figuring out if this is something that's worth pursuing. Opening up my soul to another human being, letting myself get hurt, counting on someone other than myself, when that was the opposite of what I had wished for.

With Kade, there are so many uncertainties, and the only thing I know for sure is every time we're together, I want it to last longer. I may be crazy, but the voice inside me says to trust him.

And I do.

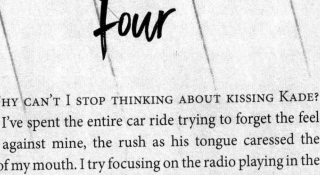

Four

WHY CAN'T I STOP THINKING ABOUT KISSING KADE? I've spent the entire car ride trying to forget the feel of lips against mine, the rush as his tongue caressed the inside of my mouth. I try focusing on the radio playing in the background. It doesn't help. Music has always been my go-to distraction, but when I have Kade to look at, everything fades away.

Each stolen glance makes my heart pound. Those pouty lips, those cheekbones, and the dimple in his right cheek have me entertaining thoughts I shouldn't. When my face heats, I return my stare to the window hoping he didn't notice. Tonight I saw Kade, the real man behind the rock god persona. He's kind and caring, so why in the hell do I continue acting like a bitch? All I do is push him away. Maybe I should try to be human. After all, he has saved me twice so far this week.

The car jerks forward when he parks outside my building. Kade slams the door and before I can open mine, he's there helping me out. Huh, I didn't think guys did that sort of thing anymore. I figured chivalry only played out in movies or books. Because let's face it, fantasy and reality are hardly ever the same.

Placing a hand on my lower back, he ushers me to the stairs. The contact is minor, yet he's caressing my whole body from that one tiny spot. It's firm yet soft, strong but not overly powerful. It's a rush, a high greater than any illicit drug or alcohol can give. And like a junkie, I don't want it to end.

We stop at the outer door. The butterflies in my stomach have now turned. Maybe this wasn't such a great idea. *It's a little late to have second thoughts.* Should I invite him up? Should I ditch him on the street? Oh God, I think I'm going to throw up.

I turn on the top step to face him, trying to figure out what to do. He focuses on my lip, watching as I repeatedly run it through my teeth. Reaching up, he tugs it free, letting his finger slide down my chin.

I swallow hard before meeting his eyes. "Look, Kade, I just want to say thank you for tonight. You know, saving me from Shane. It…I just." I look away. "He's never acted this way before."

He closes the gap between us, moving up a step until we're eye to eye. The moonlight dances in his eyes, making them sparkle as if they were magic. "I didn't like the way he was looking at you," he says, reaching up to rub his thumb across my shoulder. "I saw your face when he approached, and I knew instantly I wasn't going to like the guy."

"But why did you kiss me like that?" I whisper. "I mean, all you had to do was come up and pull me away. You could

63

have even used the guise of being my friend and us going out later." I turn my head, wanting to hide the flush crawling up my face. The memory of our kiss plays on a loop in my head.

His hand travels down my arm to lace his fingers with mine. Bringing my knuckles to his lips, he kisses away the events of last night. Everything except for him.

Pressing a palm into his chest, I revel in its firmness. Finally, I meet his eyes again.

"I kissed you because I wanted to. And judging by the way you reacted, you wanted it too. The way you melted into me...*fuck*, Adrienne." He runs a hand through his hair. "I know I'm not in this alone."

My heel catches on the step and I wobble, but Kade's arm snakes around my waist, saving me once more. Heat pours off his body as we anchor ourselves to each other.

"Why do you keep fighting me?" His brows draw together. "Why are you always trying to run away?"

This is it – my chance to tell him to fuck off – to deny that I'm not interested in him. But pain lances through my chest instead. I can't. His blue eyes plead for me to hold on when all I'm trying to do is let go. I have to. Then, hurt shimmers in his gaze and the pressure in my chest increases. In just one look, Kade shatters every wall I've created to keep people out.

I hang my head, but he places two fingers beneath my chin, tilting my face back up. Kade's eyes search mine, darting back and forth, trying to find the answers I'm unwilling to give.

"What are you afraid of? Your eyes are so sad all of the time. Why is your first instinct to always run?"

I swallow thickly as the last ten years crash through me: anger, pain, loss, depression, solitude, penance. But I can't tell him that. He wouldn't understand. No one would. I know how fucked up my head is; it wouldn't be fair to drag someone else into it.

I kick a small pebble and sigh. "Look, I really don't want to have this conversation right now, especially outside on the front steps of my building."

He graces me with a sheepish smile and the corners of my mouth turn up slightly. He's so beautiful when his face lights up like this.

"Yeah, I suppose this isn't an ideal place to have such a deep conversation."

"You know, when I first saw you I never would have imagined having a deep conversation with you," I laugh. "I thought you were more superficial."

He cocks his head to the side with a smirk. "So if you weren't imagining a *deep* conversation with me, were you thinking of something else we'd be deep into?"

My jaw drops and I playfully slap his chest. "Oh my God! Seriously?"

He throws his head back and laughs. I stop and watch his Adam's apple bob up and down while the sexiest sound I've ever heard escapes his lips. His voice is so smooth, yet has a rough edge to it. I can't help but want to listen to him speak about nothing and anything all at the same time.

An awkward silence falls upon us and I shift from foot to foot. Should I invite him up? Would he even want to be here with me?

Fuck it.

"Do you want to come up for a drink or a bite to eat? I

mean, it's the least I could do since you drove me home and all."

He gives me that dimpled smile and nods. "Yeah, a quick something would be good. Plus, I'd really like to get out of this fucking suit."

Discretely, I look him up and down again. *Yeah, I'd like to get him out of that suit, too.*

I turn to unlock the door and freeze when his chest presses against my back. The keys in my hand shake and almost fall to the ground as Kade places a hand on my hip. The area instantly warms, traveling all the way through my body. He surprises me by keeping his hand there until we walk into the elevator.

As we ride up to the top floor, I sneak another peek at him. Man he cleans up good. His suit hugs him in all the right places, accentuating his assets. The silver belt buckle catches the light when he stretches his arms above his head, drawing my eyes like a magnet. Is it hot in here or is it just me?

He clears his throat and smirks when I drag my eyes back up to his. "Babe, my eyes are up here."

Oh my God. My whole body is on fire. He laughs even harder. Fuck if I didn't get caught checking him out. If this elevator suddenly decides to plummet, I'd be okay with that.

"Isn't that the woman's line? I mean, for some reason, men are always talking to these." I wave my hands in front of my chest. I laugh when Kade bobs his head up and down but keeps his eyes firmly locked on my breasts.

"Okay, point made. You can look up now," I say as the doors open to my floor.

When we enter my apartment, he follows behind me,

turning in small circles. "Nice place you got here. It's kind of small though, don't you think?"

He takes a seat at one of the bar stools and I move away from him. Maybe it's the cologne he's wearing, but there's something about him being next to me, in my apartment, which has ideas floating in my head. Ideas I don't need to be thinking, but so many deliciously dirty thoughts circulate anyway.

"No, I don't think so," I say, handing him a glass of water. "I don't need a lot of space."

"Yeah, I suppose. It's very open, that's for sure."

I nod. "On the plus side, it's easy to keep clean. You know, in case people show up. My laundry is always done and everything is tidy. Simplicity at its finest."

The loft design was one of the features that drew me to this place. The open concept, very few walls, and high industrial ceilings are perfect when practicing my music. The sound fills the space so it feels like I'm back at the concert halls performing. And the neighbors appreciate the fact I spent a lot of money soundproofing the space so they can't hear me play at all hours of the day and night. You can't call it traditional, like my parent's house. With no bedroom walls and the bathroom being the only enclosed space, it's anything but traditional. Just another way of proving I could make my own decisions as an adult.

He smiles, standing gracefully from his chair, and wanders around my apartment. Rather than follow him around like a paranoid freak, I'm rooted in my spot, watching him explore.

Kade runs his hand over the back of my couch and leans down to thumb through the magazines Quinn left on the table. An amused grunt escapes him and I assume there's a National Enquirer or some other trashy gossip magazine in there.

"You like to read?" he asks, reading the spines on my favorite books. He pulls a few out from the shelf, thumbing through the pages before returning them. Curiosity gets the best of me and I close the distance between us.

"Yeah, on my downtime. Which I have a lot of, so I guess it's more than a hobby for me."

He picks up another book and holds it up to show me, trying to suppress his amusement with a sideways grin. "So is this more for educational purposes or a How-To book for you?" This time, a snort escapes him.

I quickly snatch my prized, signed, hardcover away from him and gently place it back in its spot. "For your information, that book is a beautiful love story."

He rolls his eyes. "Yeah, okay. I know many love stories that start out with a guy wanting a girl solely for his kinky pleasure."

Now it's my turn to roll my eyes. "That's why it's called fiction. That doesn't actually happen in real life. Just like nobody has sex as often as these couples do in books. I mean, seriously. Most of them are going at it like four times a day, with the guy having multiple orgasms each session. It's just not realistic."

Kade straightens and looks down at me with a heated stare. He cocks an eyebrow and runs his finger down my cheek, sending a trail of fire and lust coursing through my body. "Are you sure about that?"

I swallow hard. "Yes."

Cupping my cheek, Kade brings his face within inches

mine. "Maybe you haven't been with the right man."

I wet my suddenly dry lips. My palms begin to sweat and I can feel the tremble run through my body as his finger brushes against my earlobe.

"Why? Do you know someone out there who is up for the challenge?"

The heat from his lips calms the tremors, making me seek out his body. Soft and slow, our lips mold together, not rushing or pushing the other to open. It's one of the sexiest and most sensual kisses I've ever received.

We pull back and the lust burning in his eyes blinds my own. His chest moves up and down quickly beneath my hands. The pulse between my legs increases as Kade's arousal strains against my stomach.

"You have the most beautiful eyes I've ever seen. Such a unique shade of honey and gold."

My lip disappears between my teeth again while I twist my fingers together. "Um, thanks."

Something catches his eye and he quickly walks over to the corner of the room, to the black, shiny instrument taking pride and precedence in my place.

Kade runs a hand over the smooth, polished wood before letting them drop to the keys. He assesses the piano carefully, his face lighting up as he plays a simple, yet beautiful melody. In mid-piece, he pauses and looks to me with childlike wonder.

"You have a Steinway?"

"Yes." I walk over and lean against the piano. Lowering himself onto the bench, he cracks his knuckles, this time playing something more challenging. It's still incredibly beautiful. He fills the space with colorful notes and I watch as he loses himself to the music. Kade stops briefly to remove his coat, handing it to me before unbuttoning his vest and loosening his tie.

I place the coat on the back of the couch, but not before discretely sniffing it like a creepy stalker.

When he plays the final note, my resonating applause sounds around us. He stands and gives me an over-exaggerated bow, along with my favorite smile.

"Thank you. Thank you."

He slides over on the bench and extends a hand to me. I readjust my dress as I sit next to him. "That was beautiful. I didn't know you played. I just assumed you were solely a guitar guy."

Before I know it, I find myself mindlessly playing a classical piece. When I realize my mistake, I quickly change to something more modern. Kade frowns.

"Why'd you change pieces? I love Bach."

The music stops as my hands settle in my lap. Out of the corner of my eye, I can see him studying me.

"It's a long story," I sigh and rub my eyes with the heel of my hands. "I don't play classical music for anyone anymore."

"Why not?"

I hesitate before placing my hands back on the keys. "Something happened... that made me stop playing." I start to play again, ignoring everything I just said. Kade tilts his head and listens as my hands glide across the keys, playing a sad, wilting tale.

"What happened?"

I shake my head. Tears threaten to fall, building up to the crescendo, pouring every ounce of pain I have into it. He continues to silently sit next to me, soothing me with his presence alone. Normally I'd only find a calm like that through music. This is different, but good.

The final note echoes through the room and my hands stay immobile on the keys. After a few seconds, I bring my hands into my lap and risk a glance at Kade. There's awe in his eyes, not pity, as I was expecting to see. He opens his mouth, but then quickly closes it. I look away. He must think I'm crazy. Or some pathetic waif who has too much emotional baggage to even put the effort into.

I start to stand, but he grabs my elbow, gently bringing me back down next to him.

"That was breathtaking. I've never heard anyone play Mendelssohn like that before. So passionate and soul inspiring. I'm just...wow."

I bite the inside of my cheek to keep from crying. Hard. "You know the piece? Hardly anyone knows the pieces outside of the popular composers."

He nods and trails a finger down my face. "Some of the first pieces I played were classical ones. Of course I was taught how to play Beethoven, Mozart, Bach, and the likes, but my favorites are Tchaikovsky, Grieg, or Handel."

"I love all of them." I turn toward him. "But my favorite, my go-to is Chopin. There's just something about his music that sings to me. It pulls me out of whatever funk I'm in." I shrug. "Maybe it sounds crazy. It's hard to explain sometimes."

His eyes soften. "You're so passionate about your music. I don't understand why you don't play these pieces anymore. I mean, you have a gift. It's a shame no one ever gets to hear it."

I stand from the bench. This time he lets me go. Guilt

starts to set in as I walk to the windows and stare out into the night sky, wrapping my arms around my waist. I can see Kade's reflection in the window, watching me carefully. He doesn't move to join me, which I appreciate. Instead, he lets me have my space while I gather my wits together.

"I just can't. It's too complicated. And it's my punishment." I turn to face him, hardening my features so he won't see my pain. "Trust me. It's best if you stay away. I'm toxic and will only bring you down."

Kade stands and slowly walks toward me. I back up with every step he takes until the cool window presses into my back. He's close enough to feel his body heat, but he never touches me. Just looks me over, focusing on my face.

Tentatively, he raises his hand and finds the scar by my ear, tracing the raised white tissue with the tip of his finger. Pain crosses his face and I turn my head away, letting his hand fall away.

"What happened?"

A lone tear slips down my cheek, but I brush it away before he sees. My lower lip trembles as I tighten my arms around my waist.

"I'm broken," I whisper, barely audible.

Kade shakes his head and places two fingers under my chin, gently lifting it up to meet his eyes.

"No, you're not."

"Yes, I am," I squeak. "It's best if you just leave and forget me. I don't want to hurt you."

Pain pierces my heart again, sending an ache coursing through my body. But then it stops. The ache eases as Kade's warm lips find mine, and I slowly open up to him.

I respond in kind, meeting his pace as I kiss him back.

A real kiss. One that speaks more than words ever could to him. He rests his forehead against mine.

"You won't hurt me. And it's impossible to forget you. Have you ever felt something so powerful you can't look away, but you don't know where it came from or if you can trust it?" I open my eyes and stare into his. "That's what I feel when I see you. It's the strangest damn thing. Something changed the moment I saw you, and I knew then you were special. I want to learn everything about you, but you've got to meet me halfway." His hand brushes across my lower back. "Don't shut me out before I can even get in."

Kade pulls me into his chest when another tear falls down my cheek. We stand silent for a moment, him softly consoling me without knowing the problem.

Pulling back, I wipe my eyes with the back of my hand. A small, nervous giggle escapes as I attempt to lighten the mood. "Don't say I didn't warn you."

His chest rumbles with laughter. "I'll take my chances."

I must look like a mess. There can't be a scrap of make-up left on my face after all the tears I've cried. I look at the black on my fingers. If this doesn't scare him off, I'm not sure what will. "I'm sorry about that, you know, breaking down and crying."

He shrugs. "It's not a big deal. My best friends have sisters. Trust me, there was enough estrogen growing up to choke a donkey. Tears, PMS, mood swings...I'm used to it all, babe."

"Oh you poor thing," I say with a smile. "Always surrounded by women. Must be a curse."

He taps the end of my nose and chuckles. "Yeah, well there's only one woman I'm interested in being surrounded by, and she's standing right here looking as beautiful as ever."

I roll my eyes and walk to the couch. "I think you need glasses."

Kade follows and sits on the opposite end of the couch. Tucking my feet beneath me, I lean my head against the cushions.

"So not only have you surprised me with your piano knowledge and talent, but also with your suit." I wave my hand up and down between us. "I never would have pegged you for the polished kind of guy."

He laughs and shakes his head. "Believe me, it's not something I do often. You know, doesn't mesh well with my rock god image."

"Hey now, that's my nickname for you. You can't use it."

"Why not?"

I smile. "Because it's mine."

He rolls his eyes. "What? Do you own the copyright on it?"

I laugh. "Maybe."

This time he laughs too. "Whatever, babe."

"So if you don't wear suits for fear of your image being tarnished, why'd you do it tonight?" I trace the sleeve of his shirt, intrigued by the cufflinks he used. Silver with musical notes stamped on top. Not surprising, considering he's a musician.

That sexy smirk appears again, putting his dimple center stage. He leans close as if he's divulging a secret. "You'd be amazed at what I'd do to see you."

I scoff. "You'd risk your image to see me?"

"Absolutely," he says with a wink. "Besides, if it backfired, I could have claimed to be completely out of my mind or wanted to know how the yuppie side lived." His face gets serious for a moment. "Alien abduction and insanity are both viable options, too."

I shove at his knee but Kade grabs my hand, rubbing his thumb across my knuckles. His touch causes a tingle to run up my arm in the process. I stare at our joined hands and my chest aches. I can't do this – pull him into my world – but denying my feelings are getting harder by the second.

I don't want to crash and burn, but when I'm around Kade, all I can think about is the fall. He said he needed to know me based off a feeling when we first met. It's crazy and insane. Only he's right. It's there, between us, and the more we talk, the more it grows, making it harder to ignore.

Meet him halfway? If I follow this road, I'm afraid of what I'll find. Opening up to someone else is something I haven't done in a really long time. I'm not really sure who I am anymore. But the more Kade gets to me, the closer he is to discovering my past.

Five

Tha-thump. Tha-thump. Tha-thump.

What is that noise? It's not my usual alarm. Every time I move my head, the noise gets louder. *What?* And why is my neck all cramped up? I flex my fingers. This is not my bed, unless I suddenly started sleeping on something other than my pillow top. Confused, I stretch out my arms and collide with a solid figure.

"Ow! What the fuck, babe?" The husky voice, thick from sleep, does more than startle me.

"Ah!" Sitting up, I clutch my chest and teeter on the edge of the couch before moving safely to the corner. This is it, my first heart attack. Okay, now I'm awake. The pounding in my head matches the one in my chest. The fog slowly starts to lift. Let's recap the night: went to Copperfield's, tried to avoid creepy Shane, came home and played the piano with Kade…

Kade!

He's still here. With me. In the morning. *Oh God.*

Kade scratches at the day-old stubble along his jaw and my mouth dries. In the morning light, with his shirt slightly open, showing off his tanned skin and defined pecs, I'm swooning all over again. He's the absolute sexiest pillow I have ever slept on. The funny thing is I don't even remember falling asleep with him here last night.

It's not fair that he looks so amazing and I look like... what do I look like? I cringe. One can only imagine. I do my best to fluff the rat's nest on my head when it hits me. *He stayed here last night and we slept together on my tiny couch.*

Quinn would have a field day if she saw us.

Kade stretches his arms above his head, letting out a grunt in the process. Damn, if he doesn't make the sound sexy. His shirt rises higher and I get the barest glimpse of his six-pack abs and the sexy V thing that makes every woman a complete idiot. When does he find time to work out? I can barely find the time and I'm not in a band. But now I have an image of him at the gym stuck in my head. Sweat slicking his shirtless body as he lifts weights, making each muscle flex and ripple. Kade running on the treadmill, or pounding on a heavy bag...

Hmm. Suddenly, working out doesn't seem so bad.

He rubs his eyes with his fists and blinks a few times before flashing his million-dollar smile. If it wasn't hot in here before, it is now.

"Morning, sunshine." Oh. Good. Lord. His voice is still raspy with sleep, doing absolutely nothing to stop the flush from crawling up my face.

I clear my throat, hoping to sound somewhat normal. "Morning," I squeak out.

Fail.

He laughs and holds out his hand to me. I stare at it for a moment. What does he want? Does he want to shake my hand, like friends?

Maybe I'm not as awake as I think I am.

He cocks his head to the side and smirks. "Are you going to come here or not? After all, we did sleep together last night. Think we're past the 'Hey I might like you' thing by now."

Smart ass. Cautiously, I extend my hand, linking my fingers with his. The pull toward him is still there, guiding me into his body. In no time, I'm snuggled into the crook of his neck as he places a gentle kiss on my head.

"I'm always awkward so I'll never get over it." I pause when Kade's fingers run through my hair. "I don't even remember falling asleep last night. What were we doing?"

Kade continues stroking my hair, which is still half-up and lined with the million bobby pins Quinn had put in there yesterday.

"Well, after I made you come at least ten times, you begged me for more, but my poor cock needed a break from your wild sexual appetite."

My head snaps back. Is he…is he serious? My wild sexual – ugh! God, how can he be so frustrating and so adorable? The prick doesn't even attempt to hide his amusement as peals of laughter escape him.

"Oh, that *so* did not happen."

He starts removing some of the pins sticking out of my hair. "How do you know? I could have rocked your world a million times over."

With a roll of my eyes, I let out an exasperated breath. "I wasn't drunk, you goon. Mind-blowing sex isn't something you forget, especially–"

Kade doesn't need to know that I haven't really had sex in a year. Well, at least good sex. The few one night stands were something less than spectacular and most definitely forgettable.

Sex with Kade? There's no way a girl would forget that. He oozes sex with little to no effort. I can't help letting my gaze travel up his body once more, taking in his bed hair before falling onto his deep blue eyes. Probably my favorite thing to look at. I could get lost in them for days.

Tossing the last pin on the counter, Kade weaves his fingers through my hair, massaging the pain away. I can't help the moan that escapes because this. Is. Heaven. It's so good; I sway in my seat and close my eyes. He draws tiny circles with his fingertips before gently pulling at the roots. Another moan escapes and I peek through an eye to look at him. He's sitting there, all sexy and edible, with his gaze firmly locked on me. Kade gives my roots another tug, causing a pleasurable moan to part my lips.

"Oh, God. I never knew that hair pulling felt so good." I snap my eyes open and quickly slap a hand across my mouth. *What the hell is wrong with me?* Dammit! I've seriously got to watch myself. Even in the short time we've been together, I'm getting relaxed. Too relaxed, and it's scaring the shit out of me. The rational part of me isn't talking like she normally would, telling me to hide myself away to avoid getting close. But with Kade...

Kade cradles my face. Lust and desire swirl in his eyes. He licks his lips. I can't look away from him. I just...can't.

This is bad. This isn't me. Attachment isn't my thing. But every time I look at him, it's all I see; the attraction between us. This is new territory and I don't know how to navigate it. Not to say he is thinking the same as me, but the way his eyes follow me, it's unnerving. He looks at me as if he can't help himself.

Just relax.

Before I can talk myself out of it, I straddle his lap. A moan crawls up my throat, begging to escape, but I suppress it with a gulp. His thumbs draw tiny patterns on my cheek, lighting me up inside with each and every touch.

"Babe, you have no idea how good hair pulling can feel." He leans forward and rests his head against mine. "You'll beg me never to stop."

Ugh, him and that stupid nickname. I push against his chest. "Okay, what's up with the babe thing?"

He smirks. "What about it?"

I roll my eyes. "Maybe I don't like it. Did you ever think of that?"

"Maybe I don't care."

"It's a little possessive, considering we've known each other less than a week."

He leans forward again, lust filling his eyes. "Time has nothing to do with it. Maybe that's exactly what I want to do." He weaves his fingers into my hair. I gasp, breathing faster. Why does the idea of him possessing me turn me on?

I swallow thickly at his insinuation. My senses are failing me; I can't speak, can't think, can't hear anything outside of our collective heartbeats. My focus lies solely on the man in front of me, undressing him with my eyes and imagining all the dirty things he could do to my body. I touch his cheek, feeling the stubble beneath my fingers. It's rough and prickly, but feels oh-so-good.

He leans forward at the same time I do, and our lips meet in a soft and slow, teasing and tasting kiss that drives me crazy. I trace the well-defined lines under his shirt before running my hands up his body and linking them behind his neck. Kade jerks me to him, angling my head as his tongue sweeps over my bottom lip. My body responds before my brain can overthink and I open my mouth, granting him access. His chest vibrates against mine with approval as our tongues reacquaint themselves. Even for early in the morning, he still tastes so good, just as he did last night.

Only this kiss is even better.

There's a stirring underneath my ass and he flexes his hips. How have I gone this long without this kiss? Hours were wasted when we should've been kissing. His lips…I never want anything else but his lips in the morning. They trail over my cheek and down my neck while I move my fingers to his hair, gently pulling on the black strands as he did to me moments ago. An ache builds between my legs as he kisses the hollow space behind my ear.

"Kade," I pant out.

I need to stop. If I don't, one of us will get hurt. With every sweep of his tongue, my resolve weakens. Each touch, each second his hands stay on my body, makes me crave more. More of Kade, more of this attraction; I'm finding harder to fight.

Kade gently cups my aching breast and I lose it. His fingers tease the nipple, making it harden and peak through my bra. His other hand mirrors his actions and my head rolls back, leaving it vulnerable to his mouth. I pull on his hair again and he bucks his hips up to mine. When I shift on his lap, I can't help grinding down on his erection. He hisses through his teeth, and I almost give in to the passion building inside.

"Fuck, Adrienne." Our gazes lock as he cups my cheek, pushing away some straggling hairs from my face. "You're so beautiful." I dig my nails into his shoulders and he grabs my hips, rocking into me until he hits the sweet spot between my legs. I almost buckle over with need.

Kade takes his sweet time unzipping my dress. He's enjoying this torture, this little tease. If he takes any longer, I'm going to rip the damn thing off myself. The wanton harlot in me is loose, wanting everything this man can give me, and just a little bit more. I haven't felt this alive in years.

Kade trails his fingers down my naked back while exploring every inch of my mouth with his tongue. Maybe if I let go, cave to my lustful needs, I can forget how screwed up I am. Live in the fantasy that he wants me as much as I want him and everything will be fine.

No, fantasy is not reality. Not now.

I press my hands against his chest, instantly regretting my decision when confusion colors his eyes.

"What's wrong?" he asks breathlessly.

How do I explain this without sounding like a crazy person? I was so close to getting what I desired. The stupid voice in my head stops me every time something good is about to happen. Even though the attraction between us is so strong, there's still a small part of me trying to hold out.

"I just...I...I don't think it's a good idea. I mean, you know, we haven't even been on a date. I'm not exactly going to just give it up without at least dinner and a movie first."

Kade searches my eyes, looking for emotions I hope he won't find. They must betray me because the slow, sexy smile I adore graces his face again as he pulls me close. I rest my cheek on his chest, feeling his heart beat while my fingers absently play with the buttons on his shirt.

"You're right," Kade says, softly kissing my head. "We should do dinner and a movie first." He leans back to search my face and I turn away. This is embarrassing. Only I could go from grinding on his lap to shutting him down without a valid reason. What the fuck is wrong with me? He turns my head back to face him and my lower lip disappears between my teeth. *Quick, make an excuse.*

"I don't want you to think I'm easy."

It's not entirely a lie. I don't want him to think I'm someone who sleeps around with every hot guy I meet. He's the exception. Not that we've slept together...yet. He's just someone who makes me feel more than anyone else ever has. Point proven as those long, slender fingers drag down my throat until stopping above my heart. Each strong beat presses against his hand.

He brushes a stray tendril away from my eyes. "Never once crossed my mind. The easy part, that is. Not the sex part. That crosses my mind every time I think of you."

Then he goes and says something like that. We should be ripping our clothes off and fucking on this couch right now instead of having this conversation. All I can focus on is sex with Kade; above me, below me, fucking me into oblivion.

"Friends," I say quickly, tucking some hair behind my ears. "We should be friends first. We know nothing about each other. I mean, you could learn that I'm a neurotic head case and go running to the hills. Or I take up the whole bed when I sleep and you can't handle that."

He blinks several times, his face impassive, which is a stark change from the happy one he had moments ago. "That statement makes abso-fucking-lutely no sense." His eyes narrow. "That's a waste of time and you know it." He leans in close. "We could be in the bedroom." He nips my earlobe. "With me inside you."

My nipples harden again. Damn him. Yeah, I want that, more than anything. But I shouldn't. Can't. Won't.

I shrug and climb off his lap. His hand slides from my body as I put some distance between us. Sitting on the opposite side of the couch doesn't diminish my longing for him. In fact, it gives me a better view of his body and everything I'm missing.

"Maybe this'll be a good thing," I say. "You know, us starting out as friends."

Suddenly, Kade pulls me back onto his lap. I yelp in surprise as he laughs. "I don't know about this whole friend thing," he says, using air quotes. "Do friends kiss and make out? Because if you think I can go without kissing your sweet lips again, you're fucking insane."

Heat spreads across my body. "Friends don't kiss like we do." He starts to open his mouth, but I place a finger over his sexy lips before he can protest. "But for you I'm willing to make an exception."

Kade's megawatt smile brightens the room as he picks me up. I hold his face while wrapping my legs around his waist, nipping and tugging on his bottom lip. Could I really have said no to never kissing those again?

"We'll see how long this friend thing lasts. I bet you break first."

Kade carries me to the piano, then plops me on the

bench. Why did he bring me here? I'm about to ask, but he starts working my shoulders over with his hands, massaging out kinks I didn't know were there. With every knot that loosens, my body relaxes and melts into his.

I know he's right. If I didn't lie to myself, I could see me falling for him. It's in his eyes, in his touch. He wants more than friendship, but can I give him that? What if I completely fuck this up?

I turn, halting the fast-building connection between us. If I allow him to continue this much longer, I'm afraid I'll cave – give in to his offer of being more than friends. With a smile that covers my inner turmoil, I say, "Why'd you bring me to the piano?"

He smirks and gives my shoulders one last squeeze. Warmth covers my lips again and I can feel him smile against them. "I want you to play while I make us breakfast."

The smile from seconds ago drops to a frown. With the exception of last night, it'd been way too long since I've played classical music in front of anyone. My pulse kicks up, making my palms sweat. The inside of my mouth is cotton; my tongue sticking to the roof with each attempt at swallowing. Kade has the power to undo me completely, break down the walls I've carefully constructed to protect myself. And it scares me to no end.

I force the smile back on my face. "What do you want to hear?"

"Ladies choice," he says, zipping the back of my dress up before walking over to the kitchen.

Thank God he didn't ask for another classical piece. And this open-ended request allows me to show him what I can do. Perhaps I could even sing a few of them.

Maybe not.

I hover above the keys before finally locking down which song to play. So, Kade wants a relationship? I smirk. Let's see if he can read between the lines with this one.

As the melody fills the space, coloring the air with hope, I sneak a glance over my shoulder to see if he recognizes the song. I'm not quite sure what his favorite genre of music is, especially since he's in a rock band, but I'm hoping he knows it. Something tells me we're going to do our best communicating through music. It's what we musicians know. Speaking without saying words, letting the music be our voices when nothing else will break through.

Kade raises his head from the frying pan and smirks. "Teddy Geiger?"

I nod and he smiles while continuing his breakfast mission. I hum the words, singing them loud and clear in my head, too afraid to say them aloud. All I need is a bit of confidence in me and our potential relationship.

Songs come effortlessly now, creating a fun game of name that tune. Sitting with him, playing music, laughing, all of it feels easy. Right. Until my head gets in the way and I bury how great he is with doubt and potential pain of when he'll leave me.

Even though we don't know much about the other, the music ties us together. It's the only thing that's ever made me feel normal, at home. Sharing this with Kade, it takes away the guilt always lying underneath. Makes me feel less alone. But as wonderful as this moment is, I know we have to take it slow. Friendship is an important step. If we miss it, we'll fall into a hole we may never get out of. And I don't want that. I want us to work. I want the chance for an us to exist.

I jump when Kade wraps his arms around me during a song. He doesn't ask me to stop. Instead, he straddles me from behind, placing both his hands on either side of mine. We play in harmony and once again I'm amazed at his talent with the piano. I watch his hands as they glide across the keys, paying close attention to his long, skilled fingers. *What else would those fingers be good at?* I shake my head, dismissing the thought immediately. Friends don't do that. Do they?

The last note hangs over us and Kade runs his hands over mine. He pulls me close and my head falls back against his shoulder. This feels like heaven, sharing my most favorite space with someone else. I turn my head so I'm facing his neck. Before I know it, I'm nuzzling into the space, my lips making contact with his skin. I've been mesmerized by his throat since the first night and wanted my lips there for just as long. Now, finally, I have it and it's exactly what I thought it would be. Everything about this man sets me into a tizzy. He's nothing but hard muscle and masculinity.

I trace the pulsing vein on the side of his throat with my tongue, unable to stop the action. My body has taken command and I'm nothing but a slave to its whim. I want him more than I'm willing to admit. His hands travel up the length of my arms, caressing my skin, kneading it into relaxation. I didn't even realize how tense I was until just now.

Kade clears his throat when I nip lightly at his jaw. I almost fall off the bench when he stands abruptly. He catches me, setting me upright in front of him. Pushing the hair away from my face, Kade plants a soft, chaste kiss on my lips. "Don't start anything you're not willing to finish, *friend*."

I sheepishly gaze up at him and avert my eyes so he

can't see my embarrassment. "You're right. Friends don't do things like that. I'm sorry."

"I'm not sorry, but I want to make sure we abide by the boundaries you've laid out, even if they're stupid." He shakes his head and grabs my hand, leading me to the kitchen. "Come on, *friend*, you need to eat."

He says the word like it's a sour taste in his mouth. Which it kind of is. Saying we're just friends doesn't sound right. *This is the right step. We need to go slow and know each other. Then you can scare him away.*

We talk nonstop while we eat, both taking turns to ask questions. Most of the questions I answer. Some of them I blatantly ignore or skim over completely. He raises his brow to those, but shrugs them off. I know eventually I'm going to have to give Kade the answers, but right now they need to stay hidden.

We clean up the kitchen and a small bubble of laughter erupts from me.

"What are you giggling about?"

I wave a hand around the kitchen. "Us."

His brows draw together. "What about us?"

Can he not see this?

Confusion crosses his face, like he's stuck on a New York Times crossword puzzle and the answer is not appearing. "What?"

I try my best not to roll my eyes but just can't help myself. "Our clothes."

Oh how I love the sexy way his lips curl up at the corners when he's amused, finally seeing what I'm getting at. "Oh, that. Well, who doesn't clean up a kitchen wearing a now wrinkled suit and cocktail dress?"

A plan forms in my head. Not sure if I should go through with it, but my mood is so light and airy now with him in my place. *Should I or shouldn't I?*

I should.

I stalk slowly toward the sink. He eyes me carefully, following the sway of my hips, causing his tongue to dart out and run across his bottom lip. My steps falter, but I'm more determined now to go through with it. "You know what's worse than cleaning up in a wrinkled suit?"

Kade shakes his head, then cocks it slightly to the side. "No, what?"

I reach behind me, grab the sprayer and quickly move to the side while simultaneously turning on the water. "Cleaning with a wet, wrinkled suit."

Water shoots out and completely soaks his shirt. His surprised gasp has me laughing as his hands attempt to block the stream of water hitting him. Kade moves forward, reflecting the water back at me. We wrestle over the nozzle, but I end up losing and wind up drenched.

It's been years since I've done anything like this. Spontaneous and childlike. The last person to make me feel this way was Quinn, and usually that involved copious amounts of alcohol, just to make my brain shut off. With Kade, I get that same high, without the hangover after effect.

I get my bearings and reach behind me to shut the water off. The nozzle clunks loudly into the sink before Kade pulls me into him, warming me with his body heat. My arms wrap around his waist as he rests his cheek on top of my head.

"That was fun," I murmur into his chest.

I feel his head nodding in agreement. "I haven't done

that in a long time."

"Me either."

Kade holds me out in front of him to inspect the damage. Heated eyes travel slowly up and down my body. His gaze alone heats my blood, sending little shocks through my system as he looks at me with something akin to wonder and awe. He strokes his finger down my cheek, then honks my nose like I'm a two-year-old.

"Okay, friend, now that you've got me completely soaking wet, I should probably go home and get out of these clothes."

Disappointment travels through me at the thought of him not being here anymore. I chew on my bottom lip, but he reaches out and tugs at the abused skin. His eyes betray him, telling me he really doesn't want to go. Not that I want him to go either, but I don't know how to ask him to stay.

"I should probably get some things done today as well."

Kade slides his hand into mine and we walk to the couch to retrieve his vest, coat, and tie. He slings them over his arm and rests a hip against the couch. Silence falls over us once more. I twist my fingers nervously in front of me. *Just ask him to stay. Say you know how to dry him up. Then he'll never leave and you can keep feeling happy.*

"What are your plans for the day?"

"Well," I start, twisting my lips to the side. "I need to get my laundry done before heading to work tonight. Nothing big. What about you?"

"Band practice tonight, which usually leads to a raucous out on the town later."

I raise an eyebrow to him. "A raucous? I didn't think people still used that word," I tease.

He grins and links our hands together. "Debauchery? Is that better?"

I shake my head and laugh. "Only if you're eighty, which you definitely are not."

We walk to the door, the air in the apartment cooling off. It's like someone had left the freezer door open, chilling everything down to arctic, taking with it all the humor and ease of the morning.

Kade opens the door but stalls in the entryway. He pulls me close to him and leaves a scorching kiss upon my lips. My hands thread into his hair as my head tilts to the side to better accommodate him. It's hot and sexy, deep and teasing. My heart flips in my chest as my body tingles to life. He is, hands down, the best kisser I've ever met.

We can be friends and still kiss like this, right? This is taking it slow in some universe.

When his lips finally leave mine, I feel like a puddle, completely melted from the inside out. He gives me a wink before grabbing the door knob.

"I'll see you around."

"If you're not causing too much of a raucous around town, maybe you guys could stop and see me for one," I suggest, still trying to catch my breath and my wits.

He smiles, flashing me that dimple again. "I'll see what I can do. Later, Adrienne," he says before shutting the door behind him.

I stagger on unsteady feet back to my bedroom, throwing myself face first into the plush comforter like a frustrated teenager. A loud groan escapes me and I wish like hell I could shut my brain off for two seconds.

What the fuck did I just agree to? Friends with Kade?

There's no way I can just be friends with him, not when I want to tear his clothes off every second he's around me. My lips still taste of his and I bury my face further into the bed.

Maybe I should have suggested friends with benefits instead.

Six

*B*UZZ. *B*UZZ. *B*UZZ. *B*UZZ.

What the fuck? My phone dances across my night-stand, waking me from a dream. The annoying racket stops, but it's too late and I'm now awake. Groaning, I pull my head up from under my pillow to check the clock.

Eleven o'clock.

Who the hell is texting me this early in the morning? Everyone knows I sleep in until noon after I close down the bar.

But my curiosity is piqued because there are only two people who text me and they ought to know better, unless they want to endure my wrath.

I pull the phone off the table and focus my bleary eyes on the screen. I don't recognize the number.

Unknown: You sleeping the day away?

I frown at the message. Maybe it's a wrong number?

Me: Who is this?

Unknown: Really?

What the fuck is this person's problem? No one has this number except Gabe and Quinn. Unless it's…

It couldn't be.

Unknown: Do you want to reconsider this whole friendship thing and continue what we started yesterday morning?

Kade.

Me: Sorry, Kade. Still just friends.

Kade: Bummer. Don't worry. I'll wear you down. ;)

I smile and settle back under the warm covers, determined to see what exactly Kade wants.

Me: So what are you doing up this early?

Now, I realize it's not early to everyone else. Just me. However, if he's going to pursue…whatever this is, then he better start learning my little quirks. Like, no one wakes me before noon. A grumpy Adrienne is hell to deal with.

Kade: It's hardly early.

Me: Says you. I've only been home for eight hours.

Kade: Exactly. You should be rested and ready to go.

Seriously? Who the hell does he think he is? He's in a band, playing late nights at bars and clubs. He should know better. Plus, it takes me forever to fall asleep. So technically I've slept only five or six hours.

Me: Let's get one thing straight here, buddy. I do not get out of bed before noon unless I have to, especially when I close.

Kade: Wimp.

Me: Seriously?

Kade: Damn straight.

Me: Whatever. Just keep that in mind the next time you feel the need to wake me out of a dream.

Kade: What kind of dream was it? Was I in it? Tell me it was hot.

I roll my eyes, but somehow a smile finds its way on my face. That's such a guy thing. As soon as a girl says she had a dream, they instantly bring it straight into the gutter. It's like they can't think of anything other than sex. I'm surprised they all don't walk around with raging hard-ons all the time.

Time for a little payback.

Me: Well, there was this guy. Sexy smile, hot as fuck. Drove me crazy with the things he could do with his mouth.

Kade: Yeah?

Me: I was begging for more.

Kade: And?

Me: Had me gripping the sheets, he was so good. And then...

Kade: Don't hold out on me!

Me: Then some jerk texted me and woke me up.

Kade: What an asshole.

Me: Yep. So now I've got that hanging around.

Kade: Should I fix that?

Me: Nope. I'm just going to lie in bed for a little while longer and pretend that no one interrupted me.

Kade: Want some company?

Now there's an interesting question. I guess that depends on how he wants to keep me company because I have the sneaking suspicion his version of keeping company will differ from mine.

Me: I don't think you could behave in a friendly manner.

Kade: Oh I'll be friendly.

Me: I think we have different opinions on this whole friendship thing.

Kade: Ever heard of friends with benefits?

Me: Nooooo. Never heard of that. What kind of benefits we talking about? Medical? Life Insurance? Sick leave?

Kade: Funny.

Me: Don't think it's a good idea.

Liar. If that's what he's offering, I'd be all over it.

Kade: Why not? It'd be fun. Besides, I already told you I'm not giving up the kissing. Your lips are too sweet to resist.

I pause before typing my response. He likes kissing me. Now there's something I never thought someone would tell me. And against my better judgment, I'd have to agree. I like kissing him as well. The way his lips feel pressed against mine, how they mold together perfectly. And his tongue, good God, I can only imagine what he could do to the rest of my body. His kiss ignites something deep inside and a part of me is scared to explore it. The other part of me wants to let go and move away from my past, move away from the fears that always lie dormant beneath the surface.

As I type my response, the screen changes to show an incoming call. I hit the green button and press the phone to my ear.

"Did I scare you off?" Kade asks in that deep, sexy voice of his.

"No, not at all. I was just typing my response."

"So you really don't get up before noon? That's a waste of the whole day. What if I want to take you out for breakfast?"

I laugh. "On the rare occasion you want to take me out

in the morning, I guess I'll have to wake up earlier. Or you'll have to learn which days I'm not closing down the bar. That way you'll know when I'll be sleeping in so you don't wake me unnecessarily."

Kade laughs and the sound echoes through my ears. I love his laugh. It's so carefree and easy, as if he really doesn't have any problems in the world. "Okay, fair enough. So now that you've been forced awake, what are your plans for the day?"

"Nothing really," I say on a stretch. "I'm closing again tonight so I don't have to be there until seven."

"Good. I'm coming over and we're doing something."

"What?" I bolt upright in bed. He can't be serious. "Are you kidding?"

"Don't believe me? You should know better than that. I won the challenge, remember."

"Okay, first off, I did not issue a challenge to you," I say, propping myself up against my headboard. "If your brain twisted my words to appear as a challenge, that's on you. Secondly, I'd hardly call it finding out when Quinn told you where I would be."

That piece of information I finally squeezed out of her last night when she came to see me. Conniving little wench admitted to telling him where I was playing while I was busy running around the bar helping others. Somehow she had gotten his number off a flier they left for Gabe and she put this whole thing into motion, starting with Wednesday night when he just happened to show up to save me.

He laughs again. "Semantics. Either way I found you. And let's be honest, you were glad I showed up."

He's right. I was glad he found me. The memory of him

standing there in that suit with the rest of high society is definitely not something I'll forget anytime soon. And the way he saved me from Shane damn near knocked me off my feet. The power in that kiss was explosive, setting my blood on fire and igniting a need within me that I've ignored for way too many years.

"Okay, yes. I was glad to see you there and thankful for your intervention with Shane. I don't know what had gotten into him. He's never acted that way before."

I hear a faint grumble at the mention of Shane's name. Is he seriously jealous? What is this proprietary feeling he has against me? Again, we're just friends. We're not dating, we're not a couple. We're just…I don't know what we are. As much as I want to say we're just friends, the words leave a bitter taste in my mouth. They're not the right words to describe us. But, for now, they'll have to do until we can get to know each other better.

"He's lucky I didn't knock him on his ass when he grabbed you."

"Okay, Mr. Caveman. Besides, I think you more than scared him off with that kiss you gave me."

Kade gets quiet for a minute. "I can still feel that kiss, Adrienne." His tone is low and seductive. A chill runs through my body as the memory pushes to the front of my mind. "I can still feel how your body responded, how you pressed against me, trying to get closer and cop a feel."

Goosebumps run up and down my skin.

"Kade, I–"

"Adrienne, please. I need to see you today."

I chew on my lower lip. Do I want to see him today? Who am I kidding? Of course I want to see him. "Okay," I whisper.

If you could hear a smile over the phone, I swear I just heard his. "Excellent. Now open the door for me."

My head jerks back slightly. "What?"

"Adrienne, I'm starting to get pity looks from people walking by. Or they think I'm homeless. Hurry up and let me in." He hangs up without another word.

He can't be. Not possible. When I look out the window, after launching out of bed and damn near killing myself, I see Kade's sleek sports car parked outside. And there, sitting on the concrete steps, is Kade, in all his bad boy glory, complete with leather jacket and black jeans. But in the few times I've been with him, I know that's all it is. An act, a show, a second personality. Kade is anything but bad. He's sweet and kind, gentle and caring. Perhaps it's only with me since I don't have anything to base it off of, but I can sense he's sincere around me. Like he wants to be with me. And if him showing up at my apartment is any indication of how serious he is in wanting to know me, then I should maybe invest the same interest in him. Push away the dark shadows that are always lurking around so I can find out what it's like on the other side.

I hit the buzzer to open the front door and wait the few minutes for him to ride the elevator up. I rush to the bathroom, brushing my teeth and rinsing with mouthwash because I don't want to kill him with my morning breath. Although he didn't seem to mind yesterday during our impromptu sleepover as we were making out on the couch. Again, goosebumps run over my skin as I think about yesterday morning and the need building between the two of us.

"It's open," I yell when Kade knocks on the door. The faint sound of it opening and closing makes me scrub my face a little faster. Water splashes all over the floor and counter in my haste to be presentable. And frankly, I don't care. I'll clean it up later.

"Adrienne?" Kade calls out from the front room.

I slip on a clean shirt from the back of the door and turn in circles. "Where the hell are they?" Dirty clothes fly from my hands as I practically fall into the hamper looking for my jeans.

Kade laughs from the doorway, and I feel the flush crawl across my face.

"Did you get eaten by your laundry?" he asks, amusement lacing his voice.

"Shut up." I yank the hem of my shirt over my ass, but it's futile.

"Nice panties." He whistles.

"Feel free to leave at any time, buddy." I huff a breath while standing up and placing my hands on my hips. "Damn," I mutter under my breath.

"Need help, babe?" He moves closer.

I attempt to smooth the rat's nest my hair has become through my failed effort to find my jeans. Kade keeps coming toward me, slowly, predatorily. His indigo eyes gleam in the light and a lazy smile crosses his face.

My breath hitches at the first contact of his hand against my hip, pulling me into him. He smells good. Just pure man and spice, a heady concoction made especially for him. The white shirt under his leather jacket helps with the bad boy image, making him look dangerous. And to me he is. Not like he'd hurt me. No, Kade is dangerous to my heart.

I brace my hands against his biceps, trying to keep a comfortable distance between us, even though my body is screaming for more contact.

"No, I'm good," I reply to his question, sounding a little breathy and girly. Kade smiles and lowers his head to rest his cheek against mine.

"I like this look. Did you wear this just for me?"

His hand runs along the hem of my shirt, grazing the top of my ass. That one simple touch sparks something to life. I want to see his face, look into his eyes to see what he's feeling. Those indigo irises speak more words to me than his beautiful lips. I'm drawn to them every time he's around.

Kade laughs when I try to wiggle away, pulling me flush against his body instead. "No. Remember I just got out of bed because *somebody* doesn't have a concept of time?"

His breath tickles my ear as he lets out a quiet laugh. "I believe you're the one who doesn't have a concept of time. The rest of the free world wakes up around seven or eight to start their day." He squeezes my ass, making me jump. Only because I'm surprised by how much I like it. Kade laughs then releases me, and I lean against the vanity for stability. He reaches up and trails a finger along my hairline, the tip brushing against the jagged white scar near my ear. I flinch away, not wanting him to focus on my imperfections, at least the ones he can see.

"I suppose I better finish getting dressed," I say quietly.

He roams my body as his tongue darts out to lick his lower lip. "Or you could stay like that and I'll help you get *un*dressed."

I smack his arm and laugh. "Nice try, buddy. Remember, we're doing the friend thing. No nakedness."

"You know that's not true," he says, following me to the bedroom. "I see Brecken naked all the time and we're friends."

I laugh as I pick up the pair of jeans I was looking for. "And who's Brecken?"

"My band mate."

"Ah, so you're telling me you'd like to fuck Brecken?"

Kade's face is expressionless, staring at me like I had told him the world was flat. He shoves his hands in his pockets while scrunching his shoulders together. I can't tell if he's annoyed or angry. All I know is the air in the room dropped a few degrees and a chill runs up my spine.

"Is that all you think I want from you? To fuck you?" he asks quietly.

I sit on the edge of my bed and twist my fingers in my lap. "No. Yes. I don't know. I guess I don't see your attraction to me. You have girls hanging on you everywhere you go. Beautiful girls. Skinny girls. Girls who aren't fucked up in the head or damaged due to some past trauma." I trace the scar by my ear and sigh.

Kade joins me on the bed, taking one of my hands in his and gently running his thumbs across the back of it. "Adrienne, you're not damaged or fucked up in the head. Yeah, you've had something terrible happen and it changed how you've gone about your life. Everyone has scars," he says, moving a finger to trace over the line by my ear. "Yours make up who you are. Those other girls, they're nothing. There's nothing real about them. Hell, even their body is made of plastic for fuck's sake. You're real. You're funny, kind, caring, and the most amazing piano player I have ever heard in my life. You have a talent that's begging to be shown to the world and I want to be there when it happens."

His shoulder brushes against mine and I let my body sag against it. "This is way too deep of a conversation for us."

Kade's quiet laugh lifts my mood. Leaning my head against his shoulder, we sit in silence; not wanting to break whatever spell is being cast over us.

"Just so I'm clear, though," he whispers against my hair. "I want more from you than just your smoking hot body. I want inside that amazing brain of yours, to see what makes you tick and listen to all your secrets and dreams. More importantly," he pauses, pulling his phone from his jacket pocket, "I want to make music with you because that's who you really are, whether you want it to be true or not."

He scrolls quickly through his playlist, finding the Mendelssohn piece from the other night. Out of all his works, he found the one I was brave enough to play for him.

"You remembered."

He doesn't reply right away. Just nods while he runs his thumb across the back of my hand. "I remember everything about you."

"Well, seeing as I just met you less than a week ago, I'd sure as shit hope so."

His light, carefree laugh lights up his eyes, bringing a smile to my face, especially when his dimple makes an appearance. I pick my head up and start to stand. "So, what's the plan?"

Kade glances at his watch. "We have approximately seven hours until you need to be at work, right?"

"Yep."

He claps his hands. "Let's have some fun."

"Anywhere in particular?" I eye my outfit, hoping I'm dressed appropriately. Then again, it's Saturday, so anything goes.

"Do you trust me?"

Now there's a loaded question. Do I trust him? I look into his eyes to find my answer. It's been so long since I've allowed myself to trust anyone outside of Quinn, and maybe Gabe. Am I even capable of letting someone else in?

He's the perfect person to try and find out with.

His right hand brushes the stray hairs away from my cheek and tucks them behind my ear.

"Just say yes." Kade's warm breath next to my ear sends a thousand tiny bumps over my flesh.

"Yes." I pant, loudly. Fucking embarrassing.

"Good answer." He takes at my hand, leading me toward the door.

No matter how many times I tell myself I keep my distance, I always end up in his hands. Every time he touches me, it's like I can't control myself. "Wait, I need my purse," I say, dragging him slightly behind me.

"No, you don't. I've got it covered."

I raise a brow. "Can I at least grab my keys to lock my apartment?"

He huffs a frustrated breath. "Fine."

Kade's eyes follow me as I grab my keys off the counter. In no time I'm standing next to him again. The distance, though short, creates a frigid ache within that immediately warms when I'm close to Kade. It's as if he's my sun that washes away every dark and dreary day. God, I don't want that to end.

"Ready," I say.

"Good. Let's go." He brushes a feather light kiss on my lips before leading us out the apartment.

Seven

"WHERE EXACTLY ARE WE GOING?" I PICK AT MY nails as he shuts the car door behind me. The confines of the car get even smaller as he climbs in next to me, drawing my attention like a magnet.

"It's a surprise. Are you hungry?"

I shrug. "Sure, I could eat something."

"Good."

He drives with a shit-eating grin plastered on his face. I roll my eyes and sit back as the world flies by my window.

Only the scenery inside the car is better than anything out there. I can't keep my eyes off his profile as he drives. He's just too pretty not to look at. The way his skin is perfectly tanned, or the way his brows draw over his eyes in concentration. Even his jaw, still covered in stubble from not shaving this morning, is sexy. All in all, the complete package. And yet, he's here with me. Kade has his choice of women, and he's chosen me. He must be crazy.

I'll give him this, he's persistent. Who calls and texts

someone after a week to invite them out to…whatever it is we're doing. Wait, he texted me this morning. But I didn't -

"How did you get my phone number anyway?" I ask.

Kade turns to me when he pauses at a stop sign. "Quinn," he simply says.

Of course. "When did you see her?"

"I didn't. I called her for it."

What? "You have her phone number?" When the fuck did they exchange information? Heat flames my face. How does Quinn know more about him than I do?

Kade shrugs. "Why? You jealous?"

I narrow my eyes as his lips quirk into a sly smile. Asshat. "Hardly. It sounds like something my conniving best friend would do."

"Would it piss you off to know I've had it since Sunday?"

I grit my teeth through my smile. "Not at all. Again, it sounds like something Quinn would do." I'm going to chew her ass out the next time I see her.

"How exactly did you get it Sunday?"

He smirks, and I swear I see a hint of trouble in his gaze. "According to Quinn, she said you were tearing my clothes off with your eyes. She also said you wanted to jump me in front of everyone at the club."

Dammit! "That's not-"

"Which is exactly what I thought when I came up to you," he finishes. I gulp. "She found me backstage later and gave me her number, said I needed to call her." Before I can object, he continues. "I told her I wasn't interested, but she said it wasn't for her. It was for you."

I stare in disbelief. I can't decide if I want to choke my best friend or hug her, possibly both. Payback will be in order. Oh yes. But seriously, how can I be mad? I wouldn't be here with Kade if Quinn hadn't been, well, Quinn.

"So I happily accepted. Like I said before, I had to get to know you."

"Are you shitting me? We *barely* talked. And I was not undressing you with my eyes." I cross my arms and glare out the side window, refusing to acknowledge his smug expression. Quinn is definitely going to die. "I wasn't one of your little groupies."

"And that's why."

"Because I wasn't falling all over you?"

He shakes his head. "Because you didn't look like someone who's been passed around a hundred times and could suck the chrome off a trailer hitch."

My mouth drops open. "Wow that makes me feel special. Or inadequate. Not sure which way to go on that one."

"You are special. You didn't write your number on a napkin and shove it down my pants or do any other crazy shit some women do to get my attention." He sweeps a piece of hair away from my face. "Instead, you ignored me while subtly checking me out." He winks. "Don't think I didn't notice."

Heat rushes across my face. "That's not...I mean...you were..."

God! He did it again, turned me into a babbling idiot.

He reaches across the console to grab my hand, and then kisses each knuckle. "I scanned the crowd and found you. You, Adrianne. In a packed room, I couldn't stop thinking about the girl hidden under that damn hoodie. I had to know you. Had to learn your story. Why do you think I chose the spot next to you at the bar?"

Kade parks the car on the side of the road next to a large, wooded park. I keep my gaze on the fingers still clutched in his hand.

"Because it was available?"

"Adrienne, I had water backstage so I didn't need to go to the bar. I only walked over because I wanted to be near you."

I bite my lower lip to suppress a smile from breaking out. "Really?"

He nods, a sexy grin gracing his lips. "Like I said, I really liked your hoodie."

In the small, quiet car, we sit and stare at one another. His calloused thumb strokes the back of my hand, sending chills through my body.

The image of him on stage filters through my mind and my body hums with need. Sexy. Powerful. And yet, he picked me. Out of everyone at the bar that night, he saw me.

"Say something," he says, bringing his hand to my cheek. I still can't believe how his touch can create a stir inside me. It's like I'm high on life, high on him. Only I don't know how to separate logic from infatuation. How do I tell which is best for my brain, or my heart?

"Kade, you're not making our agreement easy. Just friends, remember?" We're teetering close to the edge of the friend zone. One swift nudge will send us over and that scares the shit out of me – whether I admit it or not.

Kade's hand falls from my face. Instantly I regret saying it. I want to grab his hand, put it back where it was, and say to hell with our agreement. I want heat and fire; I want everything he can give me because for the first time in a long time, I feel alive.

"Right. Friends." The forced smile makes my heart sink as he shuts off the car and exits without another word.

Smooth move, Adrienne. Way to fuck this whole thing up. I follow him, waiting on the sidewalk while he grabs a few things out of the trunk.

"What's all that?"

"A blanket and cooler," he says with a smirk.

I roll my eyes. "Thank you, Captain Obvious. What are they for?"

He shuts the trunk and walks toward me. "They have many purposes, really. It all depends on what you're doing."

"And what exactly are *we* doing with them?"

Fresh cut grass hits my nose first as Kade guides us through the park. I tilt my head up to the sun as it peeks through the trees, warming my face. And for once it has nothing to do with Kade. "Why can't you just let the surprise happen? Do you always have to ask questions? Let me guess," he starts as he spreads the blanket on the ground. "You're one of those chicks who talk during the movie, aren't you?"

I huff through my nose and sit on the blanket. A light breeze kicks up, blowing strands of hair into my face. There are children playing on some equipment nearby, their laughter carries with the wind. Barking dogs being led by their owners, playing fetch or jumping over each other catch my attention. It's a fairly quiet neighborhood, not one I'm familiar with. Then again, I didn't get out much as a child, so a lot of the city I've lived in my entire life is still new to me. Recreational things like parks weren't exactly part of the rehearsal schedule my parents had set for me.

Kade empties the cooler, taking out three different

kinds of cheese, a loaf of French bread, and several different selections of deli meats, plus condiments. A small tub
of potato salad, paper plates, and plastic silverware come
out next. Where is this all coming from? Did he grab Mary
Poppins' carpet bag on accident?

"When did you do all this?" I can't believe he put this
much thought into lunch today.

He laughs and takes out two chilled bottles of water.
"This morning before I came to see you."

I balk at his nonchalance. "How did you know I'd come
out of my apartment though? Kind of a risk to pack all this
food, let alone buy it, and pray I would go out with you."

Kade settles in next to me, carefully slicing off a piece
of bread and pointing to my choices in a silent question. I
oblige and show him what I'd like.

"I knew you couldn't resist me."

He scoops potato salad onto my plate before handing
it and a plastic fork to me. I raise an eyebrow. "A sure thing,
huh?"

He shrugs and makes his sandwich, fixing his plate like
mine. I watch as he takes a bite when he settles back into a
lounging position, keeping his eyes on me as I nibble away
at my own sandwich.

"Definitely a sure thing."

"So cocky," I giggle.

"That's a sure thing, too," he replies with a smirk.

I cough and sputter loudly, trying to dislodge the food
from my esophagus. He laughs and starts slapping my back,
handing me water once I take a gasping breath. I gulp it
down quickly, still feeling the lump in my throat. By the
time I look back at him, I'm panting and breathless. I can't

help but stare. The small laugh lines that appear around his eyes and mouth have me gasping for air for a whole different reason while his eyes twinkle in the sunlight.

"Not. Funny."

"It kind of was. Just a little. I mean, I'm not wrong."

"About being cocky? No, you're pretty much right on the money there. Anything else that involves your cock, in any way, is a gross misunderstanding."

I brush a strand of hair out of my mouth and start back in on my sandwich, making sure to take as small of a bite as possible. I need to get all thoughts of Kade and his cock out of my head. It doesn't help when I trail my eyes down his body, zoning in on *that* body part. I wonder what exactly it's like. I bet he's skilled, like no one else I've been with. He'd know what to do, how to give it to me without begging for it. Unless he likes that.

Damn him for putting these thoughts into my head.

Kade snaps his fingers in front of my eyes, startling me. "Babe, eyes up here."

Is it possible to *not* embarrass myself in front of him? Heat covers my cheeks again. I roll my eyes, playing it off like I wasn't checking out his package. "I wasn't staring at that."

The corners of his full lips turn up as he leans forward slightly. "You were totally checking me out."

"Whatever." I close my eyes and count to ten as he chuckles and takes another bite of his sandwich.

When I open my eyes, he's still watching me, chewing slowly as his gaze roams my body. I take the same advantage, admiring the flex of his arms and the tattoos peeking out under the sleeves of his white shirt.

"So what else don't I know about you?" he asks.

I shrug and stab at my potato salad. "Not much. I mean, you know more than most people do. I play the piano, but not classical anymore. I work in a bar most nights of the week and I have no life. That's me in a nutshell."

Kade's lips twist to the side. "But I don't really *know* you. I mean, what's your favorite movie, your favorite color, favorite brand of toilet paper?"

I laugh, but only after I swallow the food in my mouth. One choking fit is more than enough for one date. "My favorite brand of toilet paper? Really?"

"That's important information," he says with a smile. "I mean, if I have to bring my own toilet paper over because yours is like sandpaper, or worse yet, it pills up and leaves little flakes, then we have an issue."

I clench my stomach and laugh. Hard. His own laughter barely registers over mine. We draw stares from several people nearby, but we don't care. I wipe away a tear and straighten myself again.

"You are so strange. Honestly, toilet paper? That's going to make or break our relationship?"

He shrugs, tossing our lunch items back in the cooler. "Like I said, important information. I don't care so much about which way you hang the roll. To each their own. But if I'm going to have a chaffed ass because of your toilet paper selection, then we're going to have an issue."

I shove his shoulder. "You are so weird," I somehow manage to get out. It feels good to laugh. It's something I haven't exactly been doing much of the last few years. Only when Quinn and I hang out together and usually involves a movie or board game.

Kade shoves me and I fall onto my back. Suddenly I'm assaulted with his fingers flying all over my body, finding each and every ticklish spot.

"Stop! Stop! I'm going to pee myself if you don't knock it off!"

He hovers over me, no longer tickling me in torture. Instead, his body presses down on mine with the barest of pressure. All laughter dies on my lips. His intense blue eyes mesmerize me the same way they did the first night I saw them. I grip his biceps because I don't know where else that'd be safe. What I really want is to grip his thick, black hair and drag his mouth to mine.

Kade's face changes to a serious one, shifting his weight onto his forearms. I hold my breath as his fingers run through the hair by my face, causing my eyelids to flutter. With this close proximity his cologne is stronger, and I resist the urge to run my nose along his neck.

"You're so beautiful, you know that?" he says quietly above me.

I shake my head, not believing him. How could he think I'm beautiful? I'm so…imperfect.

His fingertip brushes by the scar next to my ear. I try to turn my head away, but he pulls me back to face him.

"You are beautiful everywhere." He traces the scar again, making me less self-conscious about it each time he notices it. Somehow he's pulling me out of my shell with little to no effort. It amazes and scares me all the same time.

"Kade," I whisper. I don't know what else I could possibly say to him. My emotions are so jumbled together right now; I don't know what to think about them.

Kade lowers his head, brushing his warm lips against

mine. Tingles run across my body and I jerk him to me, needing to be as close as our bodies will allow.

From the back of his throat, Kade groans; a deep, primal sound. Instantly I react, moaning in kind as he settles on top of me. Thank God one of us had enough foresight to keep kissing on the table. Once is not enough, it will never be enough.

A child cries in the distance and I realize we're not alone, but in a public area.

"How do you do it?" I ask, breaking away before things start getting too far.

"Do what?" He rolls off me to prop his head up on one hand as he uses his other to stroke my arm. I mimic his pose and play with the blanket between us.

"Make me forget where I am and what I'm doing. You make me feel...normal. I've never felt that before."

"Never?" His fingers move to my neck, drawing tiny circles before running up to cup my cheek.

I shake my head. "I've played the piano since I was three. Having a childhood wasn't allowed, which meant no hanging out with friends or sleepovers or parties. I've never been to a school dance or football game, nothing *normal* teenage girls do to have fun. If I wasn't studying to pass my classes, I was taking lessons to improve my piano skills, which took up most of my time." I pick at the blanket, keeping my eyes down. "Quinn was the only friend I was allowed to have, and that was because our parents were close. She's been trying for years to help me be," I shrug, "less awkward. Guess I lack the appropriate skills for intimacy."

Kade's hand covers mine. When I bring my eyes to his, I'm surprised to not find any pity, like I was expecting. What

I find instead has my heart fluttering with hope. Something akin to understanding, I think.

"You're not awkward. Inexperienced? Sure. You basically just told me you didn't date or go out often which explains why you're so jumpy around me. But it doesn't explain why you keep pushing me away." He inches closer until our faces are a breath apart. "I've got news for you, Adrienne, I'm not going anywhere. Push and shove as hard as you want, but I'll come back for more." He runs a finger down the side of my face. "There's something between us, whether you want to admit it or not." I freeze and he drops his hand, sighing. "I'll make you see just how perfect we are together."

I'm lost in his indigo eyes, and swallow hard to keep my rational thoughts intact. "It's not that I'm not attracted to you. But I'm not sure how to handle whatever this is between us. I shut people out to protect myself. It's the only thing I know how to do well." How do I keep him at arm's length when all I want is to pull him close?

"This attraction between us, I know you feel it. It's in the way you kiss me back, something I plan to do over and over again. So get that through your pretty little head right now. And as for what this is between us," Kade cups my face, running his thumb across my bottom lip. "It can be the start of something great. We can go slow, just don't shut me out. Tell me when things get crazy for you, and I'll back off." He winked. "I'll try anyway."

"Easier said than done," I whisper.

"Hey." He lifts my chin, making me see him. "Has it been difficult being with me the past couple days?"

"No." I smile, looking away. "But I was in control of the situations, for the most part. Besides, you changed my mind about being a bad boy somewhere along the way."

"I'm not a bad boy, but I won't say I'm good either. There's a fine line between the two. Holding you in my arms, even when you drooled all over my shoulder, was the best night of my existence, Adrienne."

He should write Hallmark movies. Damn he's good, but I scoff anyhow. Always keeping my feelings tucked away, sheltered from possible pain. "I do not drool in my sleep."

"Sorry to break it to you babe, but yeah, you do. Don't worry, I won't reveal your habits, but I gotta say, the drool was sexy as hell."

"Drooling out of my mouth like a toddler is sexy," I say sarcastically.

Kade traces his finger from the corner of my mouth down the column of my throat, blazing a trail of fire in its wake. "Anything to do with your mouth is sexy."

I resist the urge to cross my legs in an effort to quell the ache. It shouldn't be legal to have a dirty mouth like his. With each word spoken, my nipples tighten and the fluttering in my stomach becomes almost unbearable. I wonder what it would be like to be with him – more than the way we're together now. Another shiver races up my spine. If I don't get ahold of myself soon I'm going to make a scene in front of a bunch of strangers. And their kids. "You are such a guy."

Kade cups the front of his pants, adjusting himself. "Yep, definitely a guy."

"Oh my God, seriously?" I shove him away. He stands, brushing himself off before taking my hand, and yanks. I fall into his body, relishing in the heat emanating off him.

"How do you feel about swings?"

I raise an eyebrow. "I don't know, they're swings. You go

up and down, pumping your legs, flying high in the air—" His intense blue stare cuts me to the quick. Something about his expression has the words completely fall out of my head. "What?"

"You just completely turned me on. Do you even realize what you said? How fucking hot that was? Now all I can think about is having sex. With you," he growls low in my ear.

What in the hell? All I said was going up and down, pumping. *Oh, God.* "That's not what I...you can't...I mean..."

There's no way I'm talking myself out of this one. What is it about guys and making everything sexual? Now all I'm thinking about is having wild, sweaty sex with Kade, too. Doesn't help when I feel his cock twitch against my hip. I want to roll my hips into him, see how much I affect him, when he pushes away from me and looks up at the sky, taking several deep breaths with his eyes closed. I clamp down on my lower lip, watching his chest expand with each calming breath. He says he's not a bad boy, but I beg to differ. A number of dirty activities we could be doing right now flood my thoughts.

Kade, now calm and under control, asks, "So, you up to the swings?"

I nod and smile. "Sure. I'd love to swing."

Hand in hand, we amble to the playground area, garnering several confused looks from surrounding parents. I'm sure we look rather goofy, two grown adults swinging next to each other, surrounded by kids and none of them being ours.

"White," I say, lightly swinging my legs underneath me, just hard enough to keep my momentum to match Kade's.

"Huh?" He turns his head to face me.

"My favorite color. It's white. You said before that you wanted to know more about me."

"White isn't a color," he counters.

"It's totally a color."

He shakes his head, leaning back slightly to get more air underneath him. "No, it's not. You can't combine it with anything to make it. It's devoid of color."

"You can't mix anything to make red, yellow, or blue either and those are colors. Besides, you can add white to other colors to create new ones. So it is a color. I win."

"Is that how it is? You say something and automatically it's true?"

I nod. "It's a game I like to play called *I Win*."

"And just how do you play this game?" Kade slows until he's barely swinging. I match him again, unable to keep my eyes off his arms as they flex to keep himself steady.

"Well, whenever we're in a debate, I say is how it's going to be and I win."

"Are you telling me this for future reference? Are we going to have many debates over the years where I'll need to take my foot out of my mouth or just learn to shut up because it's not worth the fight?"

I swallow hard. "I guess I wasn't thinking that far ahead. I mean, unless I do something completely stupid and ruin our friendship; yeah I guess you could call this future advice."

"And what makes you think you're going to do something stupid to ruin our friendship?" He stops and stares at me.

My gaze falls to the dirt. "I know how I am, Kade. I know what it's like to be me and the destruction that comes with it. It's not a matter of if. It's a matter of when."

Kade grabs the chains, dragging me to him. His eyes capture mine, sparking with muted fury. "You are the most negative person I know. Why do you always think there's going to be something wrong? Stop giving up before we even start." He rakes his fingers through his hair. "I want this friendship between us. Every fucking day I want you more because I know it'll lead to something great. You know, the best relationships start as friends. And we, Adrienne, will be great friends and even amazing lovers one day."

"Friendship is all I have to give right now," I whisper, letting his words echo through my head. He's right. The friends thing is going well and considering how hot the kissing is, us as lovers will be even better. We just need the time to get there…

He shyly smiles. "I'll take you any way I can get you." Our lips meet in a feathery kiss before he drops the chains and we separate, resuming our swinging.

We need to get back into safe territory. "Okay, Mr. Smarty Pants, what's your favorite color?"

He smirks and licks his lips. "White."

"Now you're just mocking me."

"No, really. My favorite color is white. It pretty much goes with anything."

"That's what they say about black, which is the color I had you pegged for. It's more dark and dangerous."

"Again, don't be misled by my alternate persona. Yes, the Kade Evans on stage likes the black, but it's the white spotlight that shines on him which sets him on fire. White brightens anything. Makes you see things in the dark that you normally wouldn't see."

It's like he's inside my head. It's the reason I like the color. It brightens the shadows.

"How is it you know exactly what to say at just the right time?" I mutter, more to myself than to him.

He tilts his head to the side. "What can I say, it's a gift."

We continue our game of twenty questions, learning more about each other than I ever thought possible. Kade gets the wild idea to play with some of the kids, causing the moms to straighten up while checking their makeup in their compacts. More than one of the cougars pushes their breasts up, trying to get as much cleavage showing as possible. When the red lipstick comes out, I lose it. Laughter bubbles up my throat, causing me to cough and sputter with each fluff of their hair. It doesn't stop me from fixing my own appearance, using the tinted lip balm I grabbed off the counter before we left my apartment.

Kade pushes a little girl on the swing and her giggles sail in the air. Her brother runs behind Kade and tugs at his pants, wanting his turn. I laugh as Kade pushes them both at the same time, the three of them throwing their heads back with excited giggles and screams as they climb higher and higher.

They move to the slide and the smile on his face grows each time he challenges them to a race down. When he put the little girl on his lap, pretty sure my ovaries exploded. He's so good with kids.

Those thoughts need to leave right now.

After almost getting launched off the seesaw, we decide to call it a day and walk back to the car, hand in hand; me with the blanket and him carrying the cooler. When the trunk closes, he loops his arms around my waist, pulling me close.

"When can I see you again?"

"I don't know. When do you want to?"

"Now." Kade squeezes me tight.

"I'm right here." I place my hands on his chest and can feel the rapid beats under the one over his heart. "Unless you've suddenly gone blind?"

He smirks and his eyes dance with mischief. "Hmm. If I say yes, would you let me use your body as if it was written in Braille?"

I shove his shoulder, causing his smile to widen even more. "Again, you are such a guy. Of course you would say something like that."

"You make it too easy. It's hard to resist when you set it up so perfectly."

"Pig," I joke.

"Does that mean we get to roll around in the mud?" He waggles his eyebrows. Everything I say only feeds his gutter brain.

"No!"

He tsks. "Shame. I'd love to get you dirty."

"Does everything have to be a sexual innuendo with you?"

Kade's head dips down and my breath falters. The closer his lips get, the more images of us hot and sweaty filter through my mind.

"Not everything is innuendo. You have no idea how much I love the idea of getting you naked and making you pant and beg for more." Kade shuts off my thoughts with a searing kiss, and all I can focus on is how soft his touch is. Then, all too soon, Kade breaks away leaving my body cold and aching for his warmth even more.

"Tomorrow," he says against my lips.

For sex? Is he seriously scheduling sex with me? "Huh?"

"We're going out tomorrow. Better be ready when I call this time," he warns. Oh, not sex. Just another date. Well, sort of date. Hang out session? Fuck, why am I making this more complicated than it needs to be?

"You better remember that the world had better be ending if you call me before noon. I'm closing tonight so I'll be home late." I slide into the passenger seat and smile when his lips brush against mine again.

"Do you work tomorrow night?"

"No, I have Sundays off."

"Good. Cause I've got plans for us then." He closes my door and rounds the car.

I bring my knee partly up to my chest while the other leg on the floor. "What kind of plans?"

Kade winks and smoothly pulls us onto the street to bring me home. "You'll see. Patience is a virtue."

"Well it's not a virtue I possess. I don't do well with surprises."

He laughs and places his hand on my knee, causing my stomach to do a little flip at the tender gesture. "Trust me, it'll be fun."

Trust him? Easier said than done. Deep down I do trust him. Outside of Quinn, I trust him more than anyone, which is what scares the shit out of me. But God it feels so right. I want to go with it, follow his lead, and get out of my head to enjoy what life has to offer with him. The question isn't what I want, but if I can allow myself to just be free? God I hope I don't fuck up.

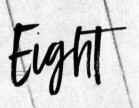

Eight

B Y SUNDAY MORNING, I'VE PACED THE FLOORS OF MY apartment a million times. I couldn't sleep when all I could think of was Kade and the phone call he'd be making. What if I overslept and missed it? Worse yet, what if he doesn't call at all?

After an entire pot of coffee this morning, I keep occupied by doing some laundry, then cleaning the bathroom, even going as far as organizing my kitchen cupboards. At this rate, my entire apartment will be spick and span when my phone rings. I won't have to do chores for the rest of the week.

So now I wait. And wait. *And wait.* I spin the phone on the counter, creating a blur of color as I let my eyes go out of focus. Each little noise has me practically jumping off my chair. My stomach flips. This anticipation thing is for the birds. Why does anyone like delayed gratification? When I look up at the clock again, I hold my breath, hopeful the minutes have ticked away. Only they haven't. The clock shows two minutes later than the last time I stared at it.

"Fuuuuuuuuuuck," *Get a grip, Adrienne. Kade's into you. He won't stand you up.* My pulse kicks up even more. Is it possible to have a heart attack from waiting? On. A. Fucking. Phone. Call!

Forget this. I need a nap. I flop face first onto my bed. I'll just close my eyes for a few minutes. That'll help me relax.

Thwack, Thwack. Thwack.

"What the?"

I gasp, springing upright in bed while clutching the sheets tightly in my hands. My heart hammers, trying to escape my chest with each and every beat. What the fuck is that noise? I follow the thumping in a disoriented haze, leading me through the living room. When I open the door, I swipe at my eyes, and then again just to make sure I'm seeing things right. Kade, dressed in a gray t-shirt and loose-fitting jeans, leans against the doorframe.

Please don't let this be a dream.

And he's smirking. Damn. Is my face giving me away again? "Problems with your phone?" Kade asks, his voice low and gravelly.

I blink several times, still trying to wake up. "Huh?"

He pushes off the frame and enters the apartment, shutting the door behind him. I back up a few steps, giving him room, even though my body is screaming to run straight into him.

"Your phone. I've been calling and every time it goes to voicemail. Wanna explain?"

"I, uh…" How did I miss the damn phone call? Shit! I should have known better than to take a nap.

Kade shakes his head and laughs. "It's fine, babe. Just

giving you some shit."

I can't keep my eyes off of his, getting lost in those blue orbs as they dance with amusement. Asshole's enjoying my discomfort. Enough of this. "Well, I got tired of waiting around and fell asleep."

He raises an eyebrow. "Ah. So you wanted to dream about me?" Kade waves a hand toward my bedroom. "We can put those dreams to reality."

"I think *you're* dreaming." I laugh and try to move away.

Kade wraps his arms around my waist, nuzzling in my hair. Shit. I forgot to see what I looked like before I answered the door. At least I'm still wearing my skinny jeans and black cami instead of my usual ratty, falling apart sleeping shirt and no pants.

I wrap my arms around his neck and close my eyes and inhale. The cologne makes me forget everything except him, not caring one bit about my appearance.

"So you woke up early? What happened to never getting out of bed before noon on the nights you close?"

I pull away and swat his arm. "Do you have to catch everything?"

He chuckles and nods.

"Fine. I was excited for your call and couldn't sleep. So I got up early but needed a nap to calm the nerves. Happy?"

"Extremely."

He's so full of himself, so cocky, so self-assured. I mean, the arrogance of showing up at my apartment, just because I didn't answer my phone. What if I wasn't home? Was he going to sit in the hallway and wait for me?

Wait. Just. A. Second. "How'd you get through the security door? I didn't buzz you in."

Pink flushes his cheeks. "I had to wait for someone to leave, which took forever. Either you don't have a lot of people in your building or they don't go anywhere on Sundays."

"Seriously? Did you rush over when I didn't answer on the first ring?"

"First ring?" Kade moves closer. "Babe, I've been trying to call you for an hour."

What? No way. I make a bee-line to my phone. There are numerous missed calls and text messages, all from Kade.

Pick up your phone.

Not funny.

Okay, now I'm getting angry.

If you don't answer, I'm coming up.

Shit. I must have flicked the mute button when I was spinning it on the counter earlier. Normally I'm good about not engaging it because Quinn freaks out when I don't answer my phone. With a stealthy finger, I unclick the button. Kade moves next to me and peers over my shoulder, seeing that stupid microphone icon appear on the screen.

Busted.

"So. I didn't call?"

I jab my elbow into his side. "Shut up. I left it on my counter."

"And on silent."

"And on silent," I repeat, feeling my face begin to heat.

Kade leans against the counter next to me, his fingers drumming a cadence of irritation. "Were you trying to avoid me? I figured after yesterday you'd want to see me again."

My mind drifts back to our picnic date, the sweet kiss, the fun we had while he proved not to be a "bad boy". "I wasn't avoiding you, promise. I must have accidentally clicked the button before my power nap."

"What time did you start? Because judging by the wrinkles on your face," he says, tracing one of the deeper creases on my cheek, "I'd say you've been asleep for at least an hour. Maybe two."

I glance at the clock and wince. Shit. He's right. Two hours. Can't believe I crashed so hard, but I'm just not used to running off so little sleep. "Uh, guess so."

He runs a hand through his hair while glancing over at my rumpled bed. "At least you'll be well-rested for what I've got planned today. You'll need lots of energy to keep up with me."

I gulp. "Should I be nervous?"

He smiles and kisses the corner of my mouth. "Not unless you plan on wearing this tank top the whole time."

I look down and see my hardening nipples poking through the tank. Kind of wishing I had thrown on a bra. "I'll be right back," I say, pulling back and shaking my head.

Kade's laughter echoes through my apartment as I grab the button-down plaid shirt I was wearing earlier. I fluff my hair and grab a stick of gum from on top of my dresser, but stumble on my way back.

Tripping over nothing is a specialty of mine, only this time it's not the case. No, as Kade moves to me, like I'm prey to his predator, I can't function. He's quite possibly driving me insane with the amount of sexiness he's throwing at me. And he's not even doing anything. That's the kicker. Just the flash of his smile turns me into a stumbling mess. Then he gives me the dimple and I'm a goner. I suppress the moan that wants to escape because it's incredibly hot and arousing. In each step he takes, he exhibits confidence, and what I wouldn't give to absorb just a smidgeon of it. He runs a hand through my hair, and this simple gesture has me willing to do anything he wants.

"Did you have any trouble last night at the bar?"

I shake my head and slip my shoes on. "Why? Are you my guardian now?"

"I worry about you." He leans against the couch and crosses his arms. "A beautiful girl working late at night, then goes home alone? Sorry, but it sounds like the perfect scene for a kidnapping. Or worse."

I turn around quickly and poke him in the chest. "You know I can take care of myself. I've been doing it for years, way before you came along. Already have one person hovering over me, not interested in another."

I'm sure his intentions are good, but I'm not a child. I don't constantly make Quinn check in, although maybe I should. She seems more rebellious than me. Friends don't micromanage.

Besides, if he was my boyfriend, chances are I wouldn't be going home alone every night.

With just a glance he coaxes me into his arms, pressing against the soft cotton shirt covering his rock hard chest. I feel the beat of his heart against my palm and tug at his shirt, forcing him closer to me. He smiles and I capture his lips first, savoring the taste as my tongue darts out to lick the seam. There's nothing like getting that first full taste before he takes over and controls me, tilting my head to the side for the best position. It's primal and heady, quickly becoming my new favorite pastime.

Air escapes my lungs when my back hits the door, the knob digging into my back. But I don't care. I need more, running my hands up his chest until they're twisting and pulling at his hair.

I don't know how he's done it, but he's made me into this vixen who wants to make out more than she wants to talk. Fuck being friends. This is what I want. I want him.

"Mmm, I love when you're sassy," he says, pressing a few quick pecks against my lips. Oh how I love it when he calls me that. "So, you ready for our date?"

"I thought we weren't dating."

He shakes his head with a chuckle. "Whatever lets you sleep at night. You ready?"

I quickly stride over to the counter to grab my phone and stuff it into my purse before standing at his side.

"Ready." Kade grabs my hand and, after locking my apartment, guides us to the stairs.

"Why are we going this way?" He's moving so fast it's hard to stay in step as he tows me behind him.

"Because I have hundreds of ideas floating through my head and none of them are appropriate for public viewing." He winks. "Unless you want to give your neighbors something to talk about."

Damn. Fire races up my neck and face. If I wasn't turned on before, the thrumming between my legs tells me I am now. Would elevator sex be the absolute worst thing in the world?

No sex. Still trying this friend thing.

Right.

Kade doesn't say much as he drives. He gave no indication or clues as to what we're doing. I told him yesterday I hate surprises. The uneasiness of not being in control doesn't work well for me. With his hand on my knee, I forget about my hesitancy. How can such a small gesture make me so stupidly happy? I cover his hand with my own and look over at him. Kade squeezes my hand before lacing our fingers together.

We pull into the driveway of a small rambler about ten minutes from my place. Several cars line the street and the sound of drums and a bass guitar hit me when I exit the car.

"Where are we?"

Kade rounds the car and grabs my hand, pulling me gently toward the garage door. "My place."

The neighborhood is nice and quiet, probably filled with working families and happy children playing in the streets. So very different from the neighborhood I grew up in. I would have preferred something like this, something normal, more suburban, less snobby. With the exception of Quinn's family, of course. Quinn was my saving grace in our neighborhood, keeping what little of my childhood I had alive while my parents tried to keep it locked away. What I would have given to have had something like this instead.

Loud music greets us as we enter the side door. Each person is playing an instrument, laughing while joking with each other about who sucks more or if being tone deaf was a learned sense. The door shuts loudly behind us, and the three of them turn their heads simultaneously. Perfect. Exactly what I don't want.

"Guys, this is Adrienne," Kade says, pulling me farther into the garage. I give a small wave and smile. I remember them from their gig a week ago, but that's about it. Just faces on the stage.

The bass player comes up to me first, engulfing me in a bear hug.

"Hey, Adrienne. Nice to finally put a face to the name. I'm Brecken."

I laugh and hug him back while Kade grumbles something about being too friendly.

"Nice to meet you," I say.

Paxton, the drummer, and Myles, the other guitarist, both shake my hand with their introductions.

"You're right. She's smoking hot," Paxton says, taking his place behind the drums. Kade throws him a scowl before leading me to a stool in the corner.

"You can sit here if you want. It's probably the best seat in the house."

I laugh. "You mean the garage?"

He rolls his eyes. "You know what I mean."

I hook my feet into the rungs of the stool, taking in everything around me. All the garage stuff is pushed to one side and the rest is filled with music stands, microphones, and cords that practically make the floor seem black. I'm impressed. It's almost like being in a sound studio, only in a garage. Kade winks at me as he tunes his guitar.

Paxton counts out the beat and the band starts playing an original song Myles wrote. Each note shakes the stool, sending the vibrations right up my spine. Damn, I'm in awe. They were great last week on stage, but this, unfiltered and raw, is so amazing. Every so often they stop to adjust a chord, teasing each other as they strive for perfection.

This is what I've always loved about music. How it's formed, how it changes and adapts. Like a living being. That's where my passion lies now. Still with the music, just not what my parents had envisioned.

"So, Adrienne, how long have you been putting up with

this pain the ass over here?" Paxton asks me in between songs.

I smile as Kade and Myles play a few chords together.

"About a week now, I guess. We're not a thing or anything like that. Just friends."

"Friends?" Brecken says, coming up beside me. "That's not what I heard. If what you two are doing is friendship, you need to introduce me to some girls like you."

I raise an eyebrow while narrowing my eyes to Kade, who doesn't notice. "What exactly have you heard?"

"Just that you're the most beautiful woman who's ever graced the earth," Paxton says.

Oh, well, that's not so bad.

"And you have tongue skills that he's never seen before."

Ah. Now that sounds more like something he would say.

"Oh, really?"

Brecken laughs and winks. "Don't tell him I told you that. He may chop my nuts off for it."

"You idiot. Then why'd you say it?" Paxton pushes him back to his spot before taking a seat behind the drums again.

Did Kade really tell his friends about me? Now I feel like an ass. I've barely talked about him to Quinn, mainly because she was pushing us together in the first place. I didn't want to encourage her. Not to mention I could barely understand my own feelings for him. Sure, he's an amazing kisser, one of the best my lips have ever touched. But I can't start an entire relationship based on that, can I? Okay, yeah, we also have a common love of music and his talent rivals my own. I mean, he plays guitar and the piano, plus he sings. I wouldn't doubt a few more instruments lay hidden in his musical repertoire. All of it is rolled into this sexy rock god, who brings me to my knees every time he speaks.

"Adrienne?" Kade yells to me, snapping me from my daydream. "We need an opinion."

I start walking toward the guys. "Sure, what do you need?"

Myles and Brecken continue arguing while Kade hands me a sheet of paper.

"I'm going to assume you can read music." I give him a side-eye. "Right. So the bass guitar is here, the lead guitar is here. This is how it's written." He plays his part, skillfully dragging his fingers across the strings, making the guitar sing the few chords.

"Okay."

"And Myles' part is supposed to sound like this." Myles strums the chords, barely looking at the sheet music in front of him.

"Huh."

Kade looks to me with a curious grin. "What?"

"Well," I start, moving over to him. "What if you tried this? While you're playing the fifth chords, Brecken harmonizes with you a step higher. That way when Myles is playing his bass line, it'll sound fuller, maybe even giving it a little edge."

The three of them look at each other and shrug. "Worth a try," Myles says.

Paxton counts them down, starting a few measures before my suggestion. When they finally get to the part, the sound explodes, pulsing with a new feeling that the original version lacked. It's damn near perfect. They try it a few more times, tweaking it so the sound is just right, making sure one guitar is not heard more over the other. I sit again on their third try, this time playing right through it to the end.

"Fuck, I hate to admit it, but she's right. That made the whole difference in the song," Myles says, giving me a nod.

I flush and look away. "It was just a suggestion. Not a big deal."

"Not a big deal? That was amazing!" Brecken exclaims, placing his guitar back in the stand while smacking Myles's head.

"Really, it's nothing."

Kade drags me from the stool and brushes his lips over mine. Our tongues briefly twist together until the cat calls grow louder behind us. "You really are a prodigy," he says.

I've always hated that nickname. Hated what it meant to me, hated what it did to me. The prodigy label turned my love of music into something I resented. For years. Yet, when Kade says it, there's no expectations behind it, nothing that makes me despise my gift. Like everything else about him, he's making me believe in myself, believe in more than what I've become.

I focus on his shirt rather than meeting his eyes. "I'm just a pianist. I wouldn't exactly lay my talent to every form of music."

"Get a room!" Myles yells when Kade kisses me again.

"We're in a room, fuckwad," Kade says irritated.

I giggle and push him away. "Go back to being a rock god. Impress me with something other than your mouth."

He presses against me again, letting me feel every hard inch of him. "Where's the fun in that?"

I narrow my eyes and he laughs, kissing my nose before picking up his guitar again. They play another set, asking my opinion on the song placement, quality, and sound. It's been a long time since someone has asked my opinion on things like this. I kind of like it. Makes me feel important, needed even. Not just some girl playing notes off a page.

After a few hours, the guys call it quits. They make arrangements for their next rehearsal and to meet up later for drinks. "You coming with?" Brecken wraps some cords around his forearm.

I shake my head. "I'll pass. You guys have fun."

He finishes coiling the cord. "You'll have to come to the next rehearsal. It's nice to get an outside opinion sometimes."

Kade pulls me into his side, kissing my head in the process. "You can bet she'll be back."

"Oh really?"

Myles smirks. "Uh-oh. Trouble in paradise already? Well, when you get tired of him, come find me. I'll show you what it's like to be with a real man."

Kade increases the pressure on my hip. "Watch it, Myles, or you'll find yourself learning to play the harmonica one-handed."

Brecken laughs and waves him off. Myles returns his glare. "Fuck off, man." He walks away as Brecken comes up to us.

"Ignore him. He's all talk." He opens his arms wide and I walk right into them, surprised Kade even let me go.

"It was nice meeting you," I say when he releases me.

"Likewise. Take care of our boy. Don't wear him out too much. He's got a gig in a few nights and we need him to perform."

I laugh. "I'll do my best."

The three guys leave, ribbing each other on the way to

their cars. They act more like brothers than friends. I suppose in a way they kind of are.

"So how long have you guys known each other?"

We walk straight into the kitchen from the door leading from the garage. He flips on a few lights and opens the fridge door.

"We grew up together on this street, actually. I bought this house when my parents retired a few years ago, but the guys all have their own places nearby."

I sit on a chair at the small table in the corner and watch as he pulls various items from the fridge and sets them on the counter. "So this was your parent's house? That's awesome you were able to buy it from them. They must have retired early."

Kade pulls out a cutting board and starts slicing raw chicken breasts into chunks. "Well, my dad worked for the PD, so he was fully vested in his retirement by age fifty-five. Mom worked from home, so she could work from anywhere, but she stopped when he did." He places the chicken on a plate and washes the knife before slicing some vegetables. "Mom made him retire as soon as possible after he was shot during a traffic stop gone wrong. They had to wait another two years before he could, but they've never been happier."

"Oh my God, that's horrible," I say, cupping my mouth. "Obviously your dad was all right?"

Kade pulls a wok from a cupboard and pours some oil into it, letting it heat up while he finishes his prep work. "Yeah, he took one in the shoulder. A few more inches and it would have shredded a valve. After that, he took on more of a desk job and did some FTO work to keep him out of the line of fire."

"FTO?"

The chicken sizzles as soon as it hits the oil. Kade moves effortlessly around his small, galley-style kitchen, tossing in spices from the cabinet above him while constantly stirring the contents of the wok.

"Field training officer. Any new recruits were assigned to him, so most of his time was spent driving them around, being driven around by them, showing them the ropes while not really taking any calls himself. Don't get me wrong, he was still finding bad guys with guns. The odds were just less since he wasn't working too many night shifts."

The delicious aroma of garlic and ginger fills the air and I find myself moving toward him, wrapping my arms around him from behind.

"Your dad sounds pretty amazing."

He rests his arms on mine. "Yeah, both my parents are. My mom's a saint for putting up with it for as long as she did. Being a cop's wife isn't easy. It's a lot of lonely nights, filled with worry and anxiety. I spent a lot of childhood sleeping on her floor, just because she had terrible nightmares. It helped her when I was close. They seemed to stay away, or not affect her as much."

"So if you're living here, where are they now?" I let him go and hop up on the counter as he works his magic with the food.

Grabbing a box of lo-mein noodles from the cupboard, he fills a pot with water and resumes stirring the contents of the wok. "They're traveling across the country. Since my dad hardly ever took vacations, they decided this was how they were going to retire. See some family they haven't been able to see in years while driving across the country in their

RV. And before you say anything, it's basically like driving around in a little apartment. Hell, it's nicer than this tiny shack."

"Somehow I don't believe that."

His kitchen may be small, but it's all high-end appliances and newer, updated cabinets. The eat-in dining room has a nice, solid wood table, set up with four chairs and a lace tablecloth. I can't see anything else, but my curiosity has gotten the best of me and now I need to know exactly how he lives. It's definitely bigger than my apartment.

He plates our dinner and leads me to the dining room. My stomach grumbles loudly, not realizing I haven't eaten in hours. I dig into the delicious smelling food and hum my approval.

"Good?" he asks, taking a bite of his own.

"Amazing," I reply, shoving another forkful in my mouth.

I inhale a few more bites before realizing he's staring at me.

"What? Do I have something on my face?"

He shakes his head. "I kind of like you sitting here at my table."

"Oh," I say, wiping my mouth off with a napkin.

Truth be told, I kind of like it too.

After a few more bites, I take the opportunity to ask what's on my mind. "Why didn't you defend me when Myles was being as ass?"

He looks at me funny. "What are you talking about?"

"Earlier, when he said he hated to admit I was right. It was kind of an asshole-ish thing to say."

He places his fork down and gives me a sideways grin.

"That's just Myles. He's…an acquired taste. You'll get used to him. He didn't mean anything by it."

Somehow that doesn't make me feel better. "Okay, if you say so."

After dinner, he gives me a quick tour of his house. And he's right, it's tiny. Only two bedrooms with one bath. But it has plenty of character, something you can't always find in a newer house. Sure the hardwood floors have scratches and aren't polished to a shine. Just means they've been lived on. And the old-school shadow box built into the wall in the living room is something you don't see anymore. It's cute, and definitely a bachelor pad. Sports movies take up most of his DVD library, and his walls are decorated with music posters instead of art. A game chair and bean bag chair sit in the middle of the living room, and the spare bedroom consists of a clutter of clothes and furniture he no longer needs.

At least he doesn't have dead animals hanging from the walls.

"So what do you want to do?" Kade asks while pulling me onto his lap on the couch.

I check my watch. I can probably stay here for a little while. It's not like I've got anything planned or need to be anywhere tomorrow.

"How about a movie?"

He grabs the TV remote and flips through the channels.

"Stop, this one," I say, settling back onto his lap while laying my head on his shoulder.

"Really?"

I nod. "Oh yes. We're watching this one. Don't tell me you don't like *Anchorman*?"

"That's not it at all," he says. "I just didn't think you did."

I quirk an eyebrow. "Really? What do you think I watch? All Lifetime and Hallmark Channel movies?"

He laughs and kisses my forehead. "Hell no. I've heard your sailor mouth and know better than that. I just didn't peg you for a stupid comedy junkie."

"Well, my friend, prepare to be schooled."

We snuggle in close on the couch, laughing and reciting the movie. I lay my head on his shoulder and sigh.

This is the best friend-date ever.

Nine

DAMMIT! EACH NOTE I PLAY IS WRONG. I'VE SCREWED up this piece ten times already. Why is this so hard? The piano is second nature, easier than breathing. Yet with each key pressed, the discorded sound hits my ears. I shove away from the piano and walk to the windows. It's bright and sunny and still I'm holed up in this apartment like I'm on house arrest. What is wrong with me? Creating songs, making playlists…it's what I've done for the last few years. Now, now it's hard.

I need to get out of here.

With a sigh, I pick up my cell and dial Quinn's number, but stop. It's only noon. She's working, and will be for the next five hours. Fuck, I'm on my own. Maybe I can call Gabe, hang out with him. On second thought, maybe not.

I flip through the TV channels – twice – and skim over every trashy magazine Quinn's left at my place, and only an hour has passed. Jumping from the couch, I head to the bedroom and strip out of my pajamas. Shirts, dresses, and shorts slide along the closet bar but nothing catches my eye. Not that I have any plans. I just can't sit still.

I'll go for a run. Exercise would be good for me, along with some fresh air. I'm too pale as it is. I nod and grab a pair of running shorts and a loose-fitting tank top. Socks and sneakers on and laced, I pull my hair into a ponytail and grab the spare key, tucking it into the hide-a-pocket in the waistband.

"New Tattoo" by Saving Abel blasts through my earbuds. I blame Kade for my new music choices. The whole week he's dropped by randomly at work, watching me from the corner of the bar and walking me to my car. He also randomly text messages me throughout the day. Some brings a smile to my face—okay, all of them do. He's just so damn sweet and funny, I can't help it. Well, maybe sweet isn't the right word for him. Affectionate? Companionable?

Luscious.

Thoughtful.

Delicious.

Yeah, that's it.

My pulse kicks up but not from the exertion of pounding the pavement. It's from Kade. Always Kade. Everything about that man brings out pieces of me I didn't know existed anymore. It's refreshing, and scary as shit. For years I've lived in the dark and now the light is piercing through, forcing me to climb out of my shell. Last week when he forced me to go with him to the symphony, we didn't actually make it inside. I froze on the sidewalk, a cold sweat breaking over me. He didn't understand my panic attack and I wasn't about to dive into the mechanics of it. Kade just smiled, told me it was going to be okay, and took me to see the latest Melissa

McCarthy movie instead.

By the time I make my third loop around the block, my feet and lungs are screaming at me. Apparently I need to run more than once every four years. I bend over and brace myself against my knees, gasping and sputtering. If anyone stopped, they'd think I was dying. Maybe I am. The only time my heart beats this fast is when Kade's around.

Ugh, this stupid run was supposed to clear my head, not make it even foggier. Why can't I get him out of my mind for more than two minutes? He's just so frustrating, and cocky, and sexy, and completely perfect. Damn.

The hot concrete steps sting the back of my legs when I sit, taking a sip from the water bottle I remembered to grab before starting this terrible idea. This is just great. I'm flustered, and I'm sweating. Perfect.

But I'm still bored out of my mind. I can't call Quinn and Gabe is off the list completely. Before I talk myself out of it, I grab my phone and dial Kade's number. It rings twice before his gruff voice fills my ears.

"Hey, babe. What are you up to?"

I draw an invisible circle on the steps. "Oh, you know, just killing myself. Think I'm having my first heart attack."

A screeching chair assaults my ears. "Are you okay?"

With a laugh, I wipe another bead of sweat from my brow. "I'm fine. Just decided to go for a run. Hence, the dying."

"Ah, death by exercise. At least you'll die hot." He laughs. I catch his double entendre. Smartass.

"Yes, I'm going to melt into a puddle of boneless flesh and tissue because I'm certain there's nothing left of me."

"You know, no one has ever died boneless, right?"

The dirty rail helps to keep me upright. "Do you always have to be right? Can't you just play my silly-ass game?"

"Fine." I can hear the smile in his voice, making the corners of my lips turn up. "So besides dying, what else are you up to?"

"Well," I start, suddenly reconsidering the whole thing. I swallow thickly and sit on my hand. "I was actually calling to see what you were up to. Thinking about playing a round of mini golf. Feel up to it?"

It's not entirely false. I've wanted to go for the past few weeks. There just hasn't been a good time to go, and I refuse to go alone. Especially when I'll be surrounded by happy families and couples. Which is where Kade comes in. It's innocent enough. Two friends can go and not turn it into something more.

"Mini golfing, huh?" He pauses before clicking his tongue. "You've talked me into it. Should I come pick you up?"

I heave a sigh of relief. "Sure. Just give me twenty minutes. I need to shower first. I'm a little sweaty and gross right now."

"Don't tell me things like that over the phone. Now *I* need to shower, and I'm not talking the warm kind."

I laugh. "Perv. See you in twenty."

We hang up and I limp up the stairs and into the lobby of my building. I look between the staircase and the elevator. I know which one I should take verses which one would be better for me. I push the call button for the elevator. Yeah, maybe tomorrow.

Kade pulls up promptly twenty minutes later, dressed in those ass-hugging jeans and loose t-shirt. Today it's a

Nirvana shirt. Seriously, he has the best selection of music tee's I've ever seen. After my own cold shower and change of clothes, I feel better – more human. Though I'm wondering if my racerback tank selection and short shorts was a good choice. I run a hand over my shoulder, trying to cover up what scars are showing. Kade walks over and pulls my hand away, kissing the marred skin.

"Don't hide it. You're beautiful the way you are. Consider these kickass tattoos. Hell, I know people who purposely try to injury themselves in order to achieve these kinds of scars."

Why anyone would want scars? "You're crazy. *They're* crazy." I grab his hand and lace my fingers through his. "Come on, let's get our golf on."

Thirty minutes later...how in the hell am I losing? Okay, sure. I've only been here about two dozen times with Quinn since high school, but still. The actual mechanics of the whole thing is relatively simple. Put small ball into hole. Avoid hazards. Don't wrap cheap club around the nearest tree. I can't get any of it. I went three over par the first four holes, then a bogie on the fifth, two birdies, and a double bogie on the last hole. Meanwhile, Kade has sank shot after shot for birdie, and, just for good measure, a hole in one... or two.

Okay, hole nine. Halfway done. I look at the obstacles I need to avoid. There's a hill surrounding the hole. Nothing else. Looks like I just need to roll it up and sink it in. Simple.

I square up, shifting from foot to foot, and tap the ball. It rolls halfway up the hill and back down, landing right where it started at my feet.

"Mother–"

"Now, now." Kade barely contains his laughter with his

146

cough. He's not fooling anyone. "Try it again. Remember, this is a family place."

I huff out a breath and close my eyes. Okay, calm down, keep it simple. It's just a game. It's fun.

When the ball rolls back to me a third time, I almost throw my club into the fake river.

"Argh!"

Several people turn their heads, a few of them chuckling behind their hands. I'm failing to see the humor in this right now.

"Why don't I try?" Kade sets the orange ball down and I step to the side with a graceful bow.

"By all means, whack away."

He gives me a side-eye and I almost laugh. In a slow, methodical motion, he winds back and taps the ball. It sails up the hill, landing perfectly inside the hole. Another fucking hole-in-one. Goddammit!

With his hands in the air, he turns and tries to suppress a smile. "Okay, that was bad timing."

I shove at his shoulder, intent on pushing him on his ass, but don't. Instead, I grab his shirt and draw him to me, sealing my mouth over his. Kade's surprised gasp lights my insides and I drop the club from my hand, wrapping my arms around his neck. When his fingers trail up my sides, my whole body ignites with fire. Fuck the golf game.

A few throats clear behind us, pulling us apart. Kade moves some hair from my eyes and kisses my nose. "Didn't expect that sort of reaction."

I smile up at him. "Yeah, well, it was the heat of the moment."

"And speaking of this heat." A bead of sweat travels

down his hairline, tracing next to his ear. "Let's find a way to cool down."

"What did you have in mind?" I hope it involves a cold shower. Again. Only with him to warm me up.

"You'll see." He grabs my hand and we walk as fast as we can away from the game, leaving our clubs and balls where they were.

"You're kidding, right?"

He can't be serious. There's no way, *no way* I'm getting in that thing.

"What? Haven't you been pedal boating before?"

When Kade brought us to Blue Springs Lake, it wasn't exactly what I had in mind on how to cool off. Granted, it's beautiful and perfect for a nice, sunny day. Only work is on my mind instead of the blue and white pedal boat floating before me.

"Not the point. We don't have time to do this before I go in tonight."

"So call in. Tell Gabe you're sick or something."

I blow hair away from my eyes. "It's not that simple, Kade. I can't just leave. It's a busy night and he relies on me being there."

Has it been that long since he's worked? Playing gigs in bars isn't exactly a nine-to-five job. Not that bartending is either, but it requires a reliable employee in order to run efficiently.

"Call in a replacement. Get someone else to take your place."

If only it were that easy. The only replacement we have for the night shift is Melanie, and she's pretty useless with crowds. Or anything that involves actual work. I can't do that to Gabe. "I can't." I look down at my watch. "We've got five hours before I have to be at work. That's plenty of time for fun, right?"

My pulse kicks up as he stalks toward me. With the sun beating down on us, he couldn't be any hotter. There's nothing more I'd love to do than rip his shirt off and throw him in the water, splash around a little bit before getting dirty.

Wait, what? Where did that thought come from? Each time we're together, these thoughts keep getting stronger and more frequent. I'll fight it, but then he'll smile and turn my world upside-down. One simple action makes me weak.

I walk over and wrap my arms around his waist. "You're not mad, are you?"

Kade kisses my nose. "Of course not. You called me, so I'm at your mercy. I was just thinking we could spend the day here and then do something later. That's all."

"Rain check?" He pulls me closer, sending a shiver down my spine.

He nods. I open my mouth, but can't speak as his finger floats across my cheek. Each touch feels like he's caressing my whole body at once. Nerves come alive, along with my dark soul.

Maybe I should call in sick. I'd love to see what else he has planned for the day.

Instead, we climb inside, Kade following me as soon as I'm settled in the seat. The sun shade is up, leaving us in shadow as we pull away from the dock and head toward the middle of the lake. Children play and splash nearby, their parents watching from the beach or in the water with them. Their laughter is contagious and I find myself smiling as we pass. Maybe they're on to something. Kade and I could go swimming, with water dripping down his bare chest, hair slicked back, muscles on display...

Focus, Adrienne.

The boat slows and Kade turns toward me. I stop pedaling and tug at my shorts. A sudden bout of nerves hit me and I have no idea why. With everything that's happened since I've known him, I should be past this. He's grown into someone I can trust, a true friend. So why the sudden butterflies? He grabs my hand and brings it to his lips.

"Thanks for inviting me out today."

Heat warms my cheeks. "Anytime."

He grips my hand, placing it in his lap. "I know I wasn't your first choice, but I'm glad I was one."

I laugh. "Sorry, but Quinn will always be my first choice. When she and I settle down with someone, it'll change. You may have to deal with it until then. Chicks before dicks and all that jazz."

Kade pulls me over the divider onto his lap, the boat sloshing back and forth. I grip his shoulders hard; afraid I may tumble over the side.

"You wanted baby steps, right?" I nod. "This is me giving it to you. We'll go at your pace. Show me what you want."

How does he expect me to go slow when he says stuff like that? I lean forward, cupping his face with my hands. "Right now, I want this." Closing the distance, I run my lips over his, sealing our mouths together. He groans low in his throat before gripping my face too. We don't rush this time, not like earlier. This one is slow, sensual, and just as powerful as the other. It's a kiss you dream of while watching movies or reading books, where it consumes your existence and makes you forget everything.

I never want this kiss to end.

But it does. Kade lifts me off his lap and I'm assaulted with the sudden rush of cold water covering my body. I come to the surface, sputtering and gasping for air. The fucker on the boat laughs his ass off. I narrow my eyes. *Oh he's going to pay for this.*

"You look hot when you're wet." He's still laughing, practically crying tears as he holds his stomach.

"You are so fucking dead," I say, treading water next to the boat.

Whatever I was just thinking before is gone. Now it's war. Bring it on.

Kade reaches down to help me up. With my feet, I press against the boat and start to lift my body out of the water. When I'm almost fully inside, I twist and push his back, sending him falling down instead. He surfaces, not coughing like I was expecting, but laughing. Ass. He's enjoying this.

"If you wanted to get me wet, all you had to do was ask." He swims over to the boat and effortlessly pulls himself in.

My teeth chatter and I wrap my arms around my chest. Things are a little too *nippily* right now.

"You had to go and ruin a good thing, didn't you?" Even though I should be pissed, I can't help but smile. His shirt clings to his chest, outlining every muscle and giving me a good glimpse of what's underneath. It reminds me of the water fight we had in my apartment a couple weeks ago. I will not argue with getting him wet. Ever.

Kade runs his hands through his hair and grabs my chin, pulling me forward gently. "Didn't ruin it. Just made it better." He kisses my lips and I sigh.

Damn him for being right.

We head back to shore and return the boat. Kade runs to his car, instructing me to wait for him on the beach. I kick my sandals off and am about to sit when he returns with a blanket in hand. Spreading it out, he pulls me down next to him. We lie back, letting the sun warm our soaked bodies. I curl into his side and he kisses the top of my head.

What I wouldn't give to play hooky and spend the afternoon here with Kade, wrapped in his arms. We're treading dangerously now, drifting farther away from friendship and into something... more.

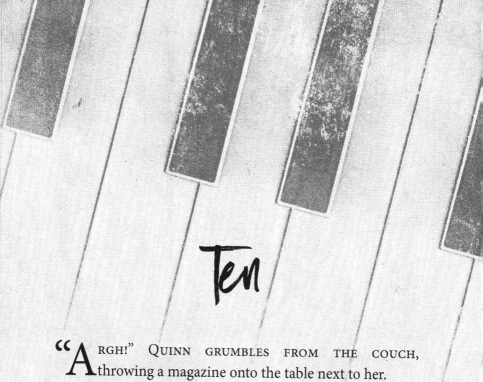

Ten

"Argh!" Quinn grumbles from the couch, throwing a magazine onto the table next to her.

It's rare I have Saturday night off, but dammit, we are so bored. "Oh my God, you have no life! How do you do this all the time? Sit around and do absolutely nothing." I look up from a book, laughing at the way her perfect little eyebrows draw together in a V while her lips turn down in frustration.

"I think I should be offended by that comment."

Quinn's head hangs off the arm of the couch, her blond hair almost touches the floor. "Pleeeeease? Can we go out and do something?"

Jesus, she's acting like a child. I'm almost afraid for her as she hangs off the couch. Any minute she could fall right off. Which she does, in a rather semi-graceful way. Quinn brings herself up to her knees and crawls over to me with clasped hands.

"Pretty, pretty, pretty please? I'm dying here, and you don't want to be responsible for my death, do you?"

"Fine," I say, rolling my eyes. "Let's go do something."

Quinn leaps to her feet and fist bumps the air.

"Yay! So glad you see it my way. I'd almost thought about slipping something in your drink to force you out." She grabs my arm and I drop my book. Quinn then proceeds to drag me to the bedroom. "Let's get you ready to go."

Now it's my turn to groan. "Why? What's wrong with how I look right now?"

She twists her face in disgust. "You're kidding, right? I refuse to be seen in public while you're in pajama shorts and ratty old t-shirt."

I cling to my shirt like she's going to rip it right off my body. "Hey! It's comfortable."

"Exactly. Comfortable doesn't get you a booty call."

I put my hands on my hips. "Maybe I don't want a booty call."

"I bet you'd take a booty call from Kade." A devious smile spreads across Quinn's face. "How is that going with him?"

My cheeks heat, spreading to my entire face and neck. I've avoided this conversation for as long as possible, and it's pretty amazing she hasn't tortured it out of me yet. It's just not her MO. Maybe she's just giving me time to adjust to the idea of Kade being in my life. Maybe I'm doing the same thing. As it stands, I really don't know what to say about Kade, even though I feel like we're so much more. All I know is that he's been a constant in my life these past few weeks, calling me daily and forcing me out of my comfort zone.

Quinn riffles through my dresser, tossing a pair of cut-off shorts and a white, gauzy boho shirt in my direction.

"You don't get a booty call from friends and Kade and I

are…it's…well…we…you see…" Shit! *Get yourself together, Adrienne.* All she said was his name and the idea of sex to-gether and I turn into a bumbling idiot.

Quinn's face lights up. "You like him, admit it. And you want more than friendship with him." I quickly strip out of my lounge clothes to put on the outfit she picked out. "Can you imagine how hot sex would be with him? I mean, your air conditioner wouldn't even cool you two down in this June heat."

I sit on the bed next to her and sigh. My thoughts are scattered as Quinn paints the picture that's been stuck in my head for the past few weeks. It's not that I haven't thought of it. Fuck, it's all I think of, and I know he wants it, too. Our make-out sessions are more frequent, and definitely hot-ter. Half the time, the only thing stopping us is our clothes. Well, and my brain.

Quinn grabs my hand, resting it in her lap. "You know you can be happy with him. Just try." She cocks her head to the side. "Why are you so afraid to be with him?"

"I don't want to hurt him," I say, sighing. "I know it'll end badly and when it does, I'll be right where I started: alone. Is it fair to bring someone into my fucked up life?"

She rests her head on mine. "Your life isn't fucked up and you really need to let go of the whole being alone thing. So you had a fight which ended badly." I pull back and scoff. "Okay, ended horribly, in the worst way possible. But, I be-lieve your parents would want this. They only ever wanted your happiness. Kade can do that, he can make you happy."

I shake my head, even though I know there's truth in her words. Maybe it's time to let go of the guilt and self-loathing I always fall into and give this a try. "I like him."

Quinn rests her forehead on mine again. "I know."

"But if it never starts, then it will never end."

In a sudden rush, Quinn leaps from the bed, dragging me with her. "Nothing in life is easy. Life is messy and throws curveballs at every opportunity. But you have a choice: either take the walk, guaranteeing you'll make it on base, or swing and take the chance at hitting a home run." She tucks some hair behind my ears. "And if you strike out in the process, it's not the end of the world. You always have another at bat."

I blink several times, a bit stunned and well, stunned. "When did you all of a sudden get so philosophical? Better yet, when did you learn about baseball?"

Her blue eyes twinkle with laughter. "I blame it on the guy I saw a few weeks ago. A baseball freak and apparently I learned a lot in a week."

"Subliminally, I'm guessing?"

She shrugs. "He liked to watch baseball while we fucked."

I laugh. "Whore."

"Recluse."

I nod. "Duly noted."

Quinn claps her hands. "Okay, enough of this deep shit. It's time for fun! What shall we do?" She skips, literally, over to my kitchen counter and grabs her purse and keys.

Grabbing my wedge sandals from the closet, I follow her to the kitchen and shrug. "No clue. What do you feel like?"

Her perfect pink lips twist in contemplation before she snaps her fingers. "I got it! You guys have karaoke night at The Warehouse, right?"

"Yeah."

"Let's do that. We haven't done karaoke in ages."

My shoulders sag. "I really don't want to be there on my night off. How about Mickey's instead?" I should be afraid of her smile. Nothing good ever comes of it.

"Perfect. They have the best drinks ever."

"Hey, I take offense to that." I pout.

She tosses my purse to me then drags me to the door. "Present company excluded. Come on, let's get our song on!"

"Don't you need to change first?" I look at her outfit, a short sundress she's paired with strappy heels. I shake my head. "Never mind."

She laughs all the way down to the street as we wait for the taxi to arrive.

Mickey's is a small, quiet tavern in the middle of downtown. It's also the only bar that does karaoke every night of the week. Technically it's a college bar since the drinks are so cheap. I mean, no one else offers a list of dollar shots and three dollar margaritas. The atmosphere is like nothing else. There is absolutely no rhyme or reason to what's hung on the walls or the ceiling. Old license plates decorate the wall around the front bar while signed one dollar bills are stapled to the ceiling above. The back bar, where the stage is set up, is in a giant U shape. Stuffed animal heads line the walls, along with vintage beer signs and several disco balls hanging down. It's Stephen King meets Saturday Night Fever.

There's already a pretty good crowd here, yet somehow we manage to snag a table along the wall. Quinn nearly threatens someone's manhood in the process, which I apologize for, stating she was recently granted a day pass from the mental hospital and hasn't been integrated back into society yet. He didn't argue. Before my ass hits the chair, Quinn sprints to the DJ booth.

"Gee, wonder what you're going to sing," I tease when she comes back.

She sticks her tongue out at me. "Well, some of us weren't graced with natural musical talent so we stick with what we know."

I shake my head the same time the waitress approaches. She's petite, dressed in the standard tuxedo shirt, bright red bow tie and short skirt uniform. Again, no rhyme or reason to anything around here.

"How's it going tonight, ladies? What can I get for you?"

Quinn doesn't hesitate. "Sex on the Beach."

The waitress turns to me expectantly. "Oh, ummm, I guess I'll have a rum and diet?"

Quinn rolls her eyes and sighs. "Oh, come on. Have a drink for crying out loud. Something that doesn't sound like you've never been in a bar before. Honestly, I'm a little surprised considering you *are* a bartender."

Only she doesn't know that because I'm a bartender, it's harder for me to decide what to drink. Hundreds of combinations run through my head and I can never pinpoint one that sounds good.

With a frustrated grunt, Quinn turns to the waitress. "She'll have a Sex on the Driveway."

The bubbly waitress smiles and leaves to put in our drink order. The noise around us is almost deafening, with the murmuring of multiple conversations and the drunken belting out of every song known to man. Quinn takes out her phone and texts someone while I start my favorite pastime: people watching.

A large group of girls take the stage, stumbling over themselves as they dish out the microphones between them. The first few notes hit and they scream the lyrics, making me cringe from the assault on my ears. Their drinks slosh while they sing "Girls Just Wanna Have Fun". The waitress comes with our drinks and I pay since Quinn is still occupied with her phone.

"Good, isn't it?" Quinn yells after I take a sip of the concoction she ordered for me.

"Surprisingly, yes. But I don't think I can have another, it's really strong and sweet."

A Cheshire cat-like smile crawls across her face. "That's the point."

The DJ calls Quinn's name and she pushes her way through the crowd to reach the stage. When the first few notes of "Genie in a Bottle" start playing, I roll my eyes and smile. So predictable. She never branches out, tries something different. She starts swaying her hips seductively, crooning out the soulful tune and capturing the attention of several guys standing near the stage.

While Quinn performs, a chill of awareness runs up my spine, like I'm being watched. I glance around, trying to make out the faces in the crowd, when two very familiar ones start walking my way. A slow smile turns the corners of my lips up as Gabe and Kade approach the table. Kade reciprocates my smile, giving me a glimpse of his dimple.

My mouth waters as I roam his body. He's wearing those jeans that hug his ass just right and a faded Seether t-shirt, showcasing his strong shoulders and narrow waist. How can he make a simple t-shirt do that? I don't know. However he does it, you won't hear me complain.

They pull out two chairs, Kade taking the one to my right as Gabe takes the one to my left. Kade leans forward, brushing his lips across mine. His uniquely sexy scent has my body springing to life, driving me crazy. He reaches his hand out to mine.

"Hey, babe," he rasps. I've never heard a voice ooze so much sex into only two simple words. Heat spreads throughout my body as my skin prickles with excitement.

"Hey," is all I can squeak out.

Gabe gives me a small wave and a wink, causing me to flush slightly. I know he can see how Kade affects me. It's nothing to be embarrassed about, especially considering we're all friends, but still. I'm not used to showing my emotions on my sleeve like this.

Their attention is brought up to the stage as Quinn sings the last part of the song. The crowd erupts into a deafening roar of cheers and applause. She raises her glass to them before making her way back to the table. The chair thuds loudly against the floor as she unceremoniously falls into it.

"Damn that's thirsty work." She wiggles her glass above her head, hoping to catch the attention of the waitress. "Hey, Kade! You made it." Quinn turns to her right and crinkles her nose in mock disgust. "Gabe."

"Nice to see you too, sweetheart," he says a little too sweetly.

"You kicked ass up there," Kade compliments. His thumb strokes the back of my hand, which he hasn't let go of since he sat down. The screeching of his chair as he scoots closer to me can barely be heard over the rushing blood coursing through my ears. It's taking every ounce of resistance I have to not crawl into his lap and let my lips roam his body.

The waitress, who has now noticed the two hot guys sitting with us, makes her way over. I watch as she pays rapt attention to Kade when he orders his beer. Unfortunately for her, his eyes never leave mine. Gabe orders the same and I watch his face soften at Quinn when she orders another drink.

"I'm good," I say, showing her the drink I'm nursing.

She gives Kade one last glance before turning to leave.

"So, Quinn," I say to get her attention. "Since you've dragged us here, you know you'll have to sing more than one song, right?"

She laughs it off as only she could. "Nope. You know I only sing one song when we come here. Learn to deal, lady."

The waitress sets our drinks down, letting her eyes linger on Kade a tad longer than necessary. Something churns inside me, making my stomach knot as she looks him up and down. I have no right to be territorial over him, but the carnal lust in her eyes makes me want to pull the hair out of her neatly placed ponytail and break her perfect little nose.

Kade is oblivious to her outright ogling. She clears her throat, trying to gain his attention, along with a not-so-subtle brush of her arm against his shoulder. Nothing works. He's still focusing on me, ignoring everyone around us. She lets out a frustrated huff and leaves, causing Quinn to break out into a fit of giggles.

"Man, she does not know the meaning of subtle."

I grab a binder of songs because I don't want to think about the waitress anymore, and start absently paging through it. There must be something here I can sing. I start looking for my usual songs, keeping a finger on the page so I can come back to it later.

Gabe and Kade start talking about his upcoming show at The Warehouse. Lightning Strikes have become a regular appearance there, drawing in larger and larger crowds with each show. It really is perfect for both of them. Gabe gets the business and Kade gets the exposure. Plus, to have a regular gig is always a good thing. And I get to see his sexy ass strut the stage. The extra tips are just an added bonus.

Quinn watches Gabe out of the corner of her eye while trying to look uninterested in their conversation. Maybe she isn't as immune to him as I previously thought.

I continue to thumb through the sticky pages before seeing a song jump out at me. It's been a while since I've sung it, but it's one of my favorites. I write down the song information, but tuck the slip under my drink. Not sure I'm ready to go up there and make a fool of myself yet. Kade grabs the book from me, flipping the pages and scribbles down his selection with a grin. He leans toward me and places a gentle kiss on my lips. It ends too soon and when I open my eyes, Kade's walking up to the DJ booth. I glance at the table and notice mine is gone too.

Sneaky little shit. "Ass," I say as he retakes his seat.

"Were you going to turn it in if I hadn't?" he counters.

"Yes…eventually."

He shakes his head with a laugh. Quinn and Gabe are debating the merits of Netflix over Redbox rentals. A really deep conversation that somehow Kade and I get drug into. Obviously Netflix is far superior. No rental or having to remember to return a disc, even if the selection isn't great or have any of the newest movies right away. The banter back and forth has us all laughing and clutching our sides. Who knew Gabe was such a die-hard Redbox fan?

The DJ calls my name, forcing me to perform "Like a Prayer" before I've had enough alcohol to sing this — or anything else for that matter.

The crowd loved it, swaying in their seats, even singing along to the chorus. I cheered them on, playing it up for them. It's amazing how a good crowd can change your mood when you're on stage.

Kade takes the stage after me, singing Robert Palmer's "Simply Irresistible." Several girls recognize him, screaming out his name as he plays up the crowd, being the rock god I know he is. His song selection is curious though, since almost everything he sings is alternative rock. This 80's selection surprises me. He nailed it, of course.

The waitress swings by as soon as Kade is back to the table. Shocking. Gabe orders water since he has to drive. Kade orders another Coors Light while Quinn orders a Long Island Iced Tea.

"Really? That's essentially all alcohol," Gabe says, raising an eyebrow to her.

Quinn narrows her eyes. "Hence the appeal."

Kade looks over at my empty drink, picking it up and sniffing it before turning his nose up in disgust. "What the shit is this? It smells way too sweet."

"It's a Sex on the Driveway. You'll thank me later," Quinn says. I kick her shin under the table, making her yelp. "Bitch."

Kade ignores her and turns back to me. "Babe, you want another one of those?"

The waitress's smile fades slightly at his pet name for

me.

"No, I think I need something else. Any suggestions?"

"She needs a Slow Screw Up Against the Wall," Quinn chirps. "Oh, and the drink, too."

Gabe snorts but then quickly covers it up by clearing his throat. Quinn's nose is still stuck in the song book, acting like she didn't just say that out loud. If only she could see the glare I'm throwing her way. "Could you possibly get any dirtier with my drink choices?"

She looks up, a devilish grin spreading across her face. "Add two blow job shots as well."

When am I going to keep my big fat fucking mouth shut? I shake my head. "No, no shots. Uh-uh. No way."

With a flick of her wrist, Quinn sends the waitress on her way, leaving me to groan in my chair. Kade's laughing next to me, enjoying Quinn's little show. Gabe shakes his head, choosing to stay silent for now. Smart man.

"There's barely any alcohol in those shots and you know it. It's not even enough to get a decent buzz." I hate it when she's right. It's just an utterly sweet shot that you can only do so much of without puking everywhere. I grab the book from her hands to keep myself busy.

When the waitress returns with our drinks, she gives Kade a wink. "Looks like you have an admirer, Mr. Rock God," I tease. That nagging, raw feeling doesn't go away in my stomach as I say the words.

He takes a pull from his beer and shrugs. "Whatever. She's not my type."

I sip my drink, still sweet but more tolerable than the last. "Oh, really? What is your type?"

Kade grabs the book from me after I finish writing my

selection down. "Well, let's see," he starts. He takes another pull from his beer and I watch his Adam's apple bob as he works it down. The stubble along his jaw has my fingers tingling again, aching to touch it, to feel it scratch against my skin.

"She has to have brains. Must have a deep love of music and be able to sing. She has to have a quiet side, as well as a side that no one else see often, adding to her mystery." My glass freezes mid-air, just beyond my lips as he continues. "She's sexy without knowing it or flaunting it. She has this draw I just can't get away from. A siren's call."

He writes something on the paper before placing the pen down and leans closer to me. I can feel his breath whisper across my cheek. "Her skin smells like coconuts and citrus. She'll have the most amazing honey-colored eyes that compliment her chocolate-brown hair, which falls in waves down her back." His hand reaches up to tuck a curl behind my ear, thumb gently brushing against my chin before igniting a trail of fire when his fingers graze down the column of my throat.

I try to swallow past the newly formed lump. "That's awfully specific," I rasp out. "Where are you going to find someone like that?"

His hand reaches around to the back of my neck, pulling me closer to him. The warmth of his breath tickles my ear. "All she has to do is say the word and I'll make her mine."

I try to pull back, needing to look at his eyes to make sure I'm not imagining what he's telling me. He doesn't let me move an inch, just keeps my cheek pressed to his, feeling the rough stubble against my skin. Everything fades away. Quinn and Gabe disappear, along with the drunken idiots surrounding us. All I see is him. All I feel is him, yearning for more of his touch. The whispered promise of more echoes through my head, awakening the deep-rooted urge lying low in my belly.

This is it. I can't fight it anymore. The need to be with him is too great, too powerful. Besides, it's all semantics anyway. We spend most of our time together. How is one little definition going to change us?

"Okay," I whisper so only he can hear.

Kade pulls back, his eyes searching mine. It takes mere seconds for a smile to crawl across his beautiful face. He must have found what he was looking for because he cradles my face in his hands, leans forward, and possesses my lips, branding me as his.

"Tonight," he murmurs.

Holy shit, tonight? Are we ready to take this next step? More importantly, am I? One look in his eyes and I know my answer.

Yes.

He tilts my head to the side, tracing my bottom lip with his tongue. I sigh and open for him, eagerly waiting to taste him, show him what's been building inside me for the past few weeks.

We consume each other, taking deep licks while gripping the other as if we'll float away. When he digs his fingers through my hair, I'm light-headed. Background noise slowly filters back in as our urgency slows, pulling us from the lust-filled haze.

"Get a room," Quinn yells. *Shit!* We're in a very public bar making out like a couple of horny teenagers. Why does he always fry my brain until I forget where I am or what I'm doing?

Kade releases me, but only slightly. He pulls my chair closer to his, wrapping a hand around my knee and tickling the soft skin behind it. All coherent thought is gone as I attempt to regain control of my body. Pandora's Box has been opened, something I've fought for ten years to keep shut. Emotions are sticky and get in the way. Now, they're fighting to get to the surface faster than I can contain them. It's a high, a rush, a foreign but welcome sensation.

"Earth to Adrienne? Are you still there?" Quinn snaps her fingers in front of my face. "Jesus, Kade, stop making her stupid with your tongue."

I shake my head and laugh. "Shut up."

She slides a shot in front of me with a smirk. "You better take this the right way."

"You're on," I say, curling my lips into what I hope is a sultry smile.

We bend over the shot glasses, filled with the sweet liqueur and topped with whipped cream. I wrap my lips around the rim of the glass, my hands clasped firmly behind my back. Holding onto it with my teeth, I lift the glass off the table, throw my head back and swallow the contents, trying not to let any slip out the side of my mouth.

Kade pulls the glass from my lips, his thumb brushing against the corner to catch a smidgeon of leftover cream. He brings it to his lips, wrapping them around the pad and humming his pleasure. If there wasn't already a pulse between my legs from his kiss, watching him suck cream off his thumb has just sent it into overdrive.

Holy. Fuck.

When my tongue darts out to catch any remnants of the

shot, he adjusts himself in his seat, sparks seemingly shooting from his eyes.

Gabe tries to help Quinn, but she's too mesmerized by Kade's performance to register it. She swats his hands away and orders a round of Washington Apple shots instead.

The drinks flow freely now. Quinn's defense system is down as the constant stream of alcohol runs through her system. I keep catching her trying to discreetly place her hands on Gabe's lap under the table. She plays it off as a joke, but I know better. Quinn may talk a big game, but really she's like me. Timid until she feels comfortable enough to show her true emotions, not that Gabe minds. However, he is watching her intake, making sure she doesn't drink so much that it throws her over the edge.

After yet another round, I can feel the heating effects of the alcohol on my cheeks. My teeth take on a pleasant tingle and everything moves just a tad slower. Kade wraps his arm around my shoulders, letting me lean into his body for stability. He hasn't had much to drink tonight, which makes me feel slightly guilty. But this blurry stage between buzzed and drunk feels good, something I haven't done in a while.

Quinn slaps her hand against the table. The glasses chatter from the sudden movement. "I have an idea. It's kamikaze time!"

"No way. No more shots, Quinn," I say, concentrating hard to make sure the words don't come out slurred.

She rolls her eyes with a smirk. "No, dummy. Karaoke kamikaze."

My eyes widen. "Only if you're involved, Ms. I-Only-Know-One-Song. And you *have* to sing whatever is picked for you."

"Deal." We shake hands before looking to the guys. "Okay, bitches, let's do this."

We each grab a sheet and agree to pick a song for the person seated to our right. Quinn whispers something into Gabe's ear, bringing a smile to his face as he nods.

"Hey! No cheating. He has to pick his own song for me," I whine.

Quinn sticks her tongue out and continues searching for a song for Gabe. When all sheets are ready, Kade takes them to the DJ booth and we wait our turns. Luckily the crowd has died down, leaving only a few tables filled with drunken patrons. Thank God. The less people to witness this train wreck, the better.

Gabe is called as the first victim. Quinn bounces in her chair as he takes the stage, looking nervous while waiting for the screen to show his fate. I'd be nervous too if Quinn was picking a song for me.

Quinn practically falls off her chair in peals of laughter, along with everyone else, as The Divinyls "I Touch Myself" begins to play. Gabe, in his good sportsmanship, plays along and completely makes himself a fool on stage, running his hands up and down his body during the chorus. He even moans a little like he's really getting into it. Quinn stops laughing and transforms before my eyes when Gabe comes back to the table. Her normally subdued eyes have lit on fire as she looks at him. Before we know it, her lips are on his, making him gasp in surprise, but not stopping him from grabbing the back of her head as they devour each other.

Kade dips his head low into the crook of my neck, nuzzling softly for a moment. I close my eyes and squeeze my legs together. He's really good at this whole seduction thing.

Ever since he made that promise about tonight, it's all I can think about. His hand climbs higher and higher on my leg, sparking a tingle with each inch more he takes.

Quinn is called next and she pulls away from Gabe, her lips swollen and red. She grabs the mic from the stand and laughs when she sees Kade's selection. The annoying sounds of Aqua's "Barbie Girl" fill the bar.

"You couldn't have picked a better song," I yell over the high-pitched squealing Quinn is doing on the stage. Unfortunately, it was one of her favorite songs when we were younger. Needless to say, she has the song memorized.

When Quinn sits down again, it's Gabe's turn to devour her, resuming their little make-out session.

I lean into Kade, my nose touching his cheek. "Alcohol apparently loosened her up. Maybe there's hope yet," I whisper.

He turns and runs a finger down the side of my face. "Hope is all us guys have when it comes to the beautiful women who drive us nuts."

I swallow thickly, my mind quickly sobering up. The DJ calls my name, but I barely register it as I stare into Kade's indigo eyes. He laughs and nudges me toward the stage, smacking my ass for good measure on the way up.

When the song "Stay the Night" by Zedd, featuring Hayley Williams appears on the screen, I glare at Quinn, who finally pulled herself away from Gabe just long enough to wink at me. She thinks she's so damn funny.

Bitch.

With a deep breath, I lock eyes with Kade's and sing. I know this was Quinn's plan all along. Joke's on her. We had already planned that before this song. As I sing, I can't help wondering what it'll be like tonight, feeling him against me, next to me, inside me. Everything will change. We'll be more than friends, giving in to the feelings we've been dancing around. The sudden revelation leaves me breathless. The song ends and I slowly make my way back to the table, Kade watching my every move. Each step kicks up my eagerness to leave, so it's just us. Alone. Together.

Kade greets me by crashing his lips on mine. My arms fly around his neck, pulling him closer, convinced that I could never be close enough to him.

When his name is called, we pull away while still keeping our eyes locked on each other.

"We're leaving after this," he whispers hoarsely into my ear before standing.

All I can do is nod since he just scattered my wits all about the dirty, sticky bar floor. I can't help but watch his ass as he walks away. The few remaining girls start flocking toward the stage, like the constant flow of groupies at his concerts.

The song starts and I instantly regret my selection for him. In my drunken stupor, I somehow thought having him sing Sam Smith's "Stay with Me" was a good idea. Now I just want to crawl under a rock and hide. Lighters fill the dark space as he croons the song to me. I sit, mesmerized by his voice, like I do every time he sings. His voice is so sexy, so smooth. So deep. So…perfect.

Why did I think I could fight this growing feeling for him? It's in the way he touches me, making me feel as if I'm the only person in the room. The way his eyes never leave mine, speaking all those words I'd rather leave unspoken between us.

When Kade reclaims his seat, he wraps his hand around the back of my neck, pulling me in close and pressing our foreheads together. My eyes flutter closed as we just stay there, feeling the pull between us, and building up the anticipation of what's to come.

Quinn and Gabe finally come up for air. At least I don't feel quite as foolish for the few times Kade and I have blocked out the rest of the world and done the same thing.

"So who's ready to leave?"

Kade never takes his eyes off mine. "It's definitely time to go," he growls.

My eyes flick down at his lap when he runs his tongue over his bottom lip. I can see the strain starting to form in his jeans.

He wants me.

We need to leave.

"Let's go then," Gabe says. He wraps an arm around Quinn's waist, helping her out of the chair. She stumbles slightly but clings onto Gabe's shirt as the four of us make our way to the front of the bar. Kade firmly grips my hip, pulling me as close as possible while still being able to walk at a normal pace.

The chill of the night air hits us, sobering me up even more. Gabe digs the keys out of his pocket while Quinn laughs about something. Not sure what it would be since no one has said anything. I give Gabe a sympathetic look and he just shrugs before scooping Quinn into his arms, cradling her to his chest.

"You two have a good night. Don't worry, I'll get her home safely." Gabe places a gentle kiss on her forehead as she snuggles into him, tossing an arm around his neck.

Kade slaps his back and nods. "Have fun, man."

"Night," I say with a small wave.

We watch as Gabe places Quinn in the cab of his truck, taking extreme care to buckle her in before climbing into the cab and driving away. I shove my hands into my pockets as a chill runs through me from the wind. Kade wraps his arms around my waist, pulling me into the safety and warmth of his body. It wraps around me like a blanket, making me feel safe and secure. Something new. His lips make contact with my ear, the stubble along his jaw rubs against my neck causing a spike of desire to run straight to my core.

"Let's get you home." His fingers flex on my hips, pulling me back against him. The bulge in his pants more pronounced, pressing firmly into my hip with a groan. I run my hand through his hair before taking his mouth, consuming him as he's done to me all night.

"Hurry," is all I say against his lips.

With a low groan, he grabs my hand and drags me to his car. I try not to sound too desperate, but I have some pent up sexual desire to burn off. Coupled with the fierce desire to have him inside me, I'm doing everything I can to not claw the clothes off his back as we make our way back to my apartment.

Eleven

WE TUMBLE INTO MY APARTMENT GROPING AT EACH other's clothes, all hands and lips moving franticly. The door shuts behind us and before I know it his hips have me pinned against the door, his hands running over every curve of my body. I fist his hair and anchor his mouth to mine. Tongues slide against each other, devouring. Owning. Each moan pushes the kiss further, into something possessive and desperate. And sexy as all fuck.

Kade grabs my wrists, pinning them above my head. I gasp at the sudden loss of control. His mouth makes contact with my neck, rolling it backward to give him better access. His knee presses between my legs, opening my body to him more, giving up that last little bit of restraint. It's been so long since I've felt this sort of passion, this sort of need, this sort of excitement.

Kade's expert tongue teases my collarbone before swirling into the shallow dip at the base of my throat. My hips have a one-track mind of their own, grinding against his muscular thigh wedged between my legs, seeking out any sort of friction I can find.

I take another long roll of my hips, eliciting a low moan from my throat. He moves both my wrists so he's only holding them in one while the other slowly descends down my body. Kade dips his head lower, taking a now hardened nipple between his teeth through my shirt and bra. I cry out at the slight pinch of pain his love bite evokes, struggling against his hold. Kade anchors me in place as he plays with my body.

While his mouth is on one breast, his hand mimics the movements with the other. It's a sweet torture with every nip and tug, pain mixed with pleasure. I need to feel him inside me, need to feel his body as close to mine as possible. I have to have him.

"Please, Kade. I want to touch you," I beg, but I'm beyond caring.

He shakes his head against my breasts and lets out a small laugh. "Don't worry. You'll feel me."

My shorts are deftly unbuttoned and easily slide to the floor. Kicking them off, along with my shoes, I focus my attention to his mouth as it plunders mine again. His erection digs into me, showing exactly how much he wants this, wants me.

I've never desired someone as much as I do Kade. My fingers flex with the need to trace the lines of his body, just as he's doing mine. His hand dips into my panties, allowing his fingers to lightly skim over the smooth flesh between my thighs.

"Oh God!" I cry out as Kade makes contact with the tight bundle of nerves at my pleasure center. Somehow, he manages to keep me upright as my knees threaten to give out. He fucks my mouth in time with his finger, slipping the digit in and out, drawing the aching need to the surface with each stroke. My body hums with electricity. I feel so…alive. Slow and steady yet fierce and powerful. It's a heady mix as he expertly strokes my sensitive walls, bringing me to the brink of madness.

He adds another finger while rubbing my clit with his thumb. I squeeze my eyes shut and my brain shuts down, crying out from the ecstasy. I don't even have time to prepare myself from the force it hits me with. Each wave tenses my body before relaxing it, pulsing around his fingers which are still milking out every last drop of my orgasm. I rock into his hand, drawing out every bit of pleasure he has sprung from my body.

I barely register his mouth by my ear, lightly sucking on the lobe as he drags my panties down my legs, allowing them to pool on the floor next to my discarded shorts.

"You are sexy as fuck when you come," Kade growls in my ear, gently clamping his teeth down on the flesh.

The more he plays my body, the more this desperate need quakes through me, dying for another type of release. I need him like I need my next breath. Need to feel what he can do to me, what I can do to him. Because the rock hard erection pressing into me tells me of the same desperation I'm feeling.

I can barely make out the rustling of his pants and belt as they hit the floor. With his free hand he wraps it around my waist, lifting me up to wrap my legs around his hips. My arms ache from being held above my head for so long, but the dulling pain is forgotten when I feel his swollen head nestling at my core.

"You want this?" If I thought his singing voice was sexy, it's nothing compared to this raspy tone, heavily laden with sex and lust.

I nod, unable to trust myself as need sweeps through my body once more.

"I want to hear you say it." The thick head of his cock rubs against my swollen lips. "Say it for me. Tell me what you want, Adrienne."

His body is tense against mine. Whatever control he has left is slipping. I know he's as desperate to be inside me as I am. Licking my parched lips, I tighten my legs around his hips. "I want you, Kade." A flash of light passes behind my eyelids as his cock rubs against me once more.

"You need to be more specific. I need to fuck you right now, but I won't do it unless you want me to."

I meet his heated gaze, letting all my worries, all my insecurities fade away into nothing. Nothing exists except us. Only the fire and desire he's burning into my soul. The sole thing I want in this moment is to get lost inside this man.

"Fuck me, Kade." My voice is so soft I'm not sure if he hears me or not. But I know he does. His pupils dilate with excitement as his lips curl into a slow, sexy smile.

"Hold on tight, babe. It's gonna be a rough ride."

He readjusts my position and I can feel him slowly slip inside, expanding me to fit his length. My head thumps against the door, a low, satisfied sound escaping my lips. His hand tightens around my wrists as he pushes the last few inches inside me. The feel of him, it's unlike anything I've felt before. Hard like steel as he begins to move inside me.

"Kade, I need to touch you. Please, let me go."

The minute my hands are free they fall to his shoulders, gripping him as if he'd disappear at any moment. With both his hands grasping my hips, he lifts me higher against the door, changing the angle so he's sliding deeper inside me. A bead of sweat trickles down his temple, his fingers dig into the flesh of my hips and ass as he picks up the tempo. Each thrust has me panting his name, a cadence of lust and desire rolling off my tongue as another orgasm builds inside me.

He's moving frantically, as if he's chasing away his own orgasm, trying to prolong this feeling for as long as possible. I want that too. I never want him to stop fucking me. All day, every day, this is what I want. I want him inside me, fucking me senseless until we don't know where one stops and the other begins.

Another roll of his hips sets off the bomb in my body. With a guttural yell, I cry out my release, milking his cock with everything I have. "Kade!"

His name echoes off the walls in my apartment, when the only noise that could be heard moments ago was the erotic sounds of our bodies colliding.

Kade's grip tightens, his body jerking in a frenzied rush to finish. I can feel his cock swell inside me before filling me in a rush of warm fluid. His movements slow as he strokes out the last of his orgasm, my name still falling off his lips in reverence.

I fall forward, exhaustion taking over. I've never had sex like that before. It's never felt so possessive, so fulfilling, so completely satisfying. My hair is damp, my skin showing a fine mist of sweat from the workout, my heart pumping wildly, wanting more even though I feel spent.

I trail my fingers lazily across his shoulders before

gripping the sweat-slicked hair at the back of his head. Tugging his mouth toward mine, I keep us suspended in our perfect bubble as we slowly come down from our high. He moves his lips down my neck, his hot breath bathing my skin, causing it to erupt in goosebumps even though I feel like I'm on fire.

As I ease out of his grip, he moves back, sliding slowly out of me. His eyes dilate as he watches the evidence of our lust trickle down the inside of my thigh. Holy shit, he cannot be ready to go again. No fucking way. Not after that performance. Hell, I'm not even sure I'm ready to go again. Two monstrous orgasms in one session is unheard of for me. Can my body handle three?

Kade bites his lower lip. "Now that's what I like to see, a little bit of me running out of you. You know what that makes you?" I shake my head. He grips the back of my neck and pulls me within inches of his face. "Mine."

As the wetness travels down my leg, I bite my lip as realization sets in. *What the fuck did we do?* I have never, *never*, been this reckless before. There just wasn't time to prepare or say anything. The only thing on my mind was sex with Kade, damn the consequences.

Kade drags the shirt over my head and tosses it to the floor. Not wanting to feel left out, I repeat the process to him. I run my hands up his toned, muscular chest, letting the shirt bunch up at my wrists until finally whipping it over his head. He truly is a god. The lines and definition of his chest and stomach, the roundness of his shoulders, all of it calls to me, begging me to run my mouth, my tongue, and my fingers over each and every inch of him.

The tattoo on his shoulder grabs my attention, along

with several others that haven't been visible before now. I trace the one on his side, showcasing his chiseled oblique, leading down into the inverted triangle of his groin.

While I explore his body, Kade's gaze travels to the swell of my breasts, still confined and aching to be released. He gently cups each one in his hands, lips seeking mine, making them pliant again, ready to do anything and everything he wants. The confidence Kade exudes while he manipulates my body is astounding.

"Yours?" I whisper, finally finding my voice to answer his question.

Suddenly he picks me up with a deep laugh. I wrap my legs around Kade's waist and he walks us to the kitchen, placing my naked ass on the counter. I yelp at the sudden assault of cold on my heated flesh.

He cups my face with his hands, dragging me down again getting lost in his sinful mouth.

"Fuck, you have no idea what you do to me."

I pull back and draw my brows together. What could I possibly do to him? It's nothing compared to what he does to me. He's so collected and self-assured. He doesn't fear anything and takes what he wants. Including me.

"You are…that was…just…wow." I can't bring myself to look into his eyes. He's so experienced and I'm so, well, me. My one-night-stands have been nothing of this magnitude. They pale in comparison to what I just experienced against my front door.

Kade tips my chin up with two fingers, forcing me to look into his eyes. "You. Are. Amazing," he says, kissing me roughly between words. The heavy scent of sex still lingers in the room, making me drunk on lust, drunk on Kade.

My breath hitches when his fingers skim down the sides of my breasts, traveling lower until he settles on my hips. Gripping them tightly, he pulls me forward until he nestled in the V of my legs. His cock jumps to life against my core as he reaches around to unclasp my bra. The cold air hits my nipples and the ache revs up once more. I'm aware of his position and how a slight change would put him right back inside me, where I want him.

"Hmm, I think someone wants to play some more," he says as I wrap my legs around him. "Not quite sated?"

The feel of his tongue against my bare nipple has my eyes rolling back into my head. I cry out when his teeth clamp down, but it's soothed by his tongue instantly, turning the pain into the most desirable pleasure. Rocking my hips into him, he repeats the process on my other breast. I can feel his cock thicken and lengthen against me. *There's no way he could go again.*

I lick my dry lips, feeling my heartbeat kick up a notch. "Lie back. Let me take care of you." The cold granite counter makes my back arch, but Kade gently guides me back down. "Do you trust me?"

As soon as I'm flush against the surface, Kade begins his slow torture. His fingers travel over the swell of my breasts, down my midsection until he is circling my navel, his mouth following the path.

I grab fistfuls of his hair, trying to decide if I should push him away or beg him not to stop. He widens the gap between my knees, his lips trailing dangerously close to where I want them the most.

Kade stops, pulling back to admire my exposed sex which is completely bare and open to him. A flash of a smile appears; the look of a satisfied man who's enjoying what he's seeing.

"Look at you, still weeping from before. Or is this a new wetness for me?" He slowly runs his index finger across my swollen lips, making my hips jerk upward. Kade pins me down with a hand.

"Uh, uh, uh. No moving. I need to clean you up since you decided to make yourself a mess."

I lift my head up slightly and rest my weight on my elbows. "I'm pretty sure I wasn't the only one who made a mess." He laughs before dipping his head lower, gently grazing the skin with the tip of his tongue. I feel drunk with pleasure as he repeats the motion again. And again. And again.

"Watch," he growls. The warmth of his breath hits me as I snap my head up. His eyes are so dark with desire they almost appear black in the muted light. *Thank God for always turning on the stove light.* "Watch what I do to you." He never once breaks eye contact as his tongue swirls and flicks over the sensitive bud, sending delicious shockwaves pulsing through my body.

It's erotic.

It's hedonistic.

And I want more.

I've never been one for pornographic things, but watching Kade pleasure me, tasting the combination of him and me on his tongue has me on the brink of insanity. As his tongue darts in and out, his thumb presses against my clit, rolling it with the slightest amount of pleasure.

"Oh fuck." Each flick has my arms shaking and my eyes rolling. I dip my head back with a low moan.

"Eyes!" Kade commands.

I force myself to watch as he continues his assault. It's too much, too soon, too good. Everything comes crashing down, spiraling out of control around me. I cry out his name between panting breaths. He lessens his ministrations before trailing his hot mouth up my stomach, between the valley of my breasts, and finally claiming my mouth.

"You are the sweetest thing I've ever tasted. Wouldn't you agree?"

I lick my lips at his command, feeling the buzz still circulating through my body. Suddenly I'm being pushed down, my back easily sliding across the counter. The heat rolling off him warms my chilled skin, blanketing me in a fresh round of goosebumps.

Kade settles between my thighs, feeling his renewed arousal press against me. The shockwaves are still traveling through me, but quickly get pushed aside when his mouth crashes against mine. He consumes me, dominates the kiss, letting me know he's in charge. And I willingly hand it over to him.

The thick head of his cock presses against my slick opening, slowly entering me inch by inch. He dips his head into the crook of my neck and a struggled groan escapes when he's fully inside. Curling his hands around my thighs, Kade lifts them higher, allowing his cock to slide in deeper.

"Fuck, you feel so good." He begins his tortuous rhythm, rocking his hips slowly, letting me feel every hard inch of him. Reaching up, I cling to his biceps and dig my nails into his skin on a sharp thrust. Kade looks down at me with intense desire. Why did we wait so long to do this? It's everything I could have ever imagined and more. More because

I can feel something change between us, growing stronger with each day that passes.

I match his thrusts, feeling the pressure build inside me, sweat slicking my skin again. He palms a breast in one hand, twisting the nipple while his other rests on my shoulder, holding my body down as he thrusts harder and harder.

"God, I love it when you squeeze my dick like that." And his dirty, filthy mouth throws me over the edge, shaking my head back and forth as I struggle to catch my breath. Only Kade has been able to hit the spot deep inside me. My thighs become a vice grip as they squeeze his hips, my toes curling from the shockwaves coursing through my body.

"Fuck!" Kade finds his release inside me after several jerks. The world blurs and then quiets as we cling to each other. He keeps most of his weight off me, resting on his forearms instead. I trail my fingers lazily up and down his back while his fingers play with the hair around my shoulders. When I come back into focus, I'm greeted with a very satisfied smile. My lips turn up, hopefully mirroring the joy and awe I see in his eyes as he stares down at me.

"Tell me, is that close to what those fucking rich boys do in your books?" he asks between kisses.

Embarrassment consumes me as my cheeks flame. He's talking about that damn book on my shelf. Has it been bothering him this whole time when I said no one has sex like the couples in those books? "You're definitely giving them a run for their money." I can barely put words together, surprised it's coming out as anything but breathy.

That cocky smile is back in full force. "I told you. You just haven't been with the right guy before."

"Well, you can prove me wrong anytime you want."

Kade looks at me with such devotion, possession, and power. Like I'm the sexiest woman he's ever seen. Yet I'm the one who feels in control. I'm the one who brought him to orgasm, twice. I'm the one who drove him wild enough to take me home and fuck the ever-living life out of me.

Kade pulls out, slowly extracting himself off the counter. He helps me sit up and I brace myself on my hands. "Stay there." He walks to the sink and grabs a clean cloth from the drawer while letting the water warm. That's when I get my first glimpse of his fully naked form. How in the hell did *that* fit inside me and not rip me to shreds? The ache between my legs says otherwise.

Kade runs the cloth over my sensitive parts, cleaning me with gentle care. I wince slightly as it runs over me again. "Sore?"

I nod and bite my lip. He presses his lips against mine and tosses the cloth into the sink. "Good. I want you to remember me in the morning, and every time after. I want you to remember that I was here and no one else can be where I've been."

"Possessive much?"

Can he see how much that turns me on? He can't know yet how much I enjoy his game; enjoy his body, his mind, and inevitably his soul.

I thought my teasing would be funny. When I see his lips turn down instead of up, I start to panic. Did I say something wrong?

"With you, yes. I don't play around with things like that. When I say you're mine, I mean it." He closes the distance between us, placing his hands on my knees. "We're the real deal. Got it?"

I nod. The real deal? Seriously? There's no way this beautiful man could possibly want me. He's barely seen the real me, only glimpses of what I've wanted him to see. He doesn't know what plagues me at night, what makes my pulse race and the panic to set in each time there's a storm in the area.

Kade deserves so much more than me. But after tonight? I'm too selfish to give him up. Not yet. I know the clock has already started counting down our demise. But until it stops ticking, I'm going to enjoy every minute of this ride.

With a light thud, I jump off the counter with Kade's help. A look crosses over his face, a sheepish look laced with panic. "Um, I know it's a little late to ask, but are you..."

I know exactly what he's alluding to. It's bad enough I was careless to let it happen once, but twice? There's something about him that scrambles my brains and makes me forget the basic rules. Not that pregnancy is even the least of my concerns. I know my history. What do I know about his?

"Don't worry. I've had an IUD in place for the last two years. No worries of an unexpected surprise from me." I fail to fully hide the contempt in my voice. Whether I'm pissed at myself or Kade has yet to be seen. We're both guilty of recklessness, but I'm not taking the fall for this one by myself.

Kade winces. "I'm usually careful when it comes to stuff like this." He shakes his head as he gets lost in thought. But when he looks up at me with regret in his eyes, instantly I feel ashamed. Does he regret what we've done? I look away, but Kade grips my chin, forcing my eyes to make contact with his.

"Look, I'm clean. I've never had sex without a condom. Ever. But with you...tonight was different. I can't explain it because if I try it's going to come out all wrong."

"Oh," I whisper.

He releases my chin and runs a frustrated hand through his hair. I sigh in relief, though there's still an unsettled feeling in the pit of my stomach. It has nothing to do with STDs, pregnancy or anything like that. No, I'm more worried about what his last statement could mean.

The shadows start creeping up the walls, slowly taking over what little light is in the room. These shadows I'm familiar with. They plague me nightly, holding my fears, reminding me to the mistakes of the past.

"Okay, let's leave it at that then. No explanation needed. It was earth-shattering sex and nothing more."

Can he hear the waver in my voice? Can he see how saying those words are ripping a fresh hole in my heart? I know what we did is more than just sex. No one in their right mind would say otherwise. Kade's passion and attention, his reverent worship of my body tells me I'm more to him than what my mind will allow.

"That's a load of bullshit and you know it." Kade's face falls, but says nothing more. Instead, he gathers up our clothes, dumping them in a pile on the couch before extending a hand to me. I take it, gnawing on my lower lip as he leads us to the bed.

Normally when I have sex with someone, they're dressed and out the door within minutes. This is new territory for me. Kade *wants* to stay. More importantly, *I* want him to stay. More than I ever thought I would.

Throwing back the covers, he pulls me down next to him and I snuggle into his welcoming embrace. For a brief moment, I pretend I'm normal and let him hold me, live in the fantasy that I can have a relationship with someone.

I listen to his steady breathing until I succumb to the sleep my body so desperately needs.

The loud crack of thunder shakes the walls, causing me to bolt upright in bed. Panic spreads throughout my body as light flashes across the darkened wood floors.

"No!"

Kade sits up next to me, but I'm already bolting across the room as quickly as I can. I fall into the bathroom, a cold sweat breaking out across my brow, and lock the door behind me. Sinking to the floor, I wrap my arms around my knees and hug them tight, rocking back and forth.

My fault. My fault. My fault.

Dead.

Alone.

Kade approaches the door and jiggles the handle, followed by a soft knock.

"Babe? You okay?"

The handle moves again, the knocking becoming more urgent. I swipe at the tears falling unbidden down my cheeks.

Alone. I need to be alone, but I know he won't leave willingly. He can't see me like this. I need to protect him, shield him from the terrors within me.

With a shuddering breath, I pull myself off the floor and take a long glance in the mirror. I turn away, seeing nothing but the broken girl with the scars. How could he want me? He can't.

He won't.

I pull on a robe and open the door. He's standing there in his boxer briefs; concern and fear are etched on his face, breaking my heart even more. He doesn't deserve what I'm about to do. It's not going to stop me, though.

I walk past him, straight to the kitchen to fill a glass with water.

"What happened?" Kade asks as he slowly approaches. He starts to wrap his arms around me, but I shrug them off.

"Nothing. It's just…you need to leave. I can't have you here right now. Please, just go."

My voice betrays the poisonous words leaving my mouth. They hit their mark, just as I intended them to. If his face is any indication, maybe it would have been better to have hit him instead.

"You don't mean that. What the fuck happened?"

He tries to move toward me again, but I skirt out of his way. It's like we're playing a game of chicken now. He moves, I back away.

"I told you. I'm fucked up."

He braces his hands on the counter, leaning forward. "And I told you you're not. Whatever delusions you have in your head need to get out now. You don't see what I see. And maybe I don't know the whole story. I don't know why you bolted up out of bed and started freaking out. Probably because you won't tell me." Kade runs a hand through his hair. "You're opening up slowly, but not fully giving yourself to me. What are you so afraid of? That I'll run?"

He strides over to me, easily pulling me into his warm embrace. "Not everyone who cares about you leaves. If that's even what you're thinking. But I don't know unless you talk to me. Please, let me in."

I shake my head. How do I explain this? Music is how we communicate best. With purposeful strides, I push away from him and head to the stereo to plug in my phone. Scanning my playlist, I find the song that conveys my feelings better than I can.

I wrap my arms around my waist as I bring my fearful eyes to his hurt ones. "This is my shit to deal with, not yours. Let me do this. Alone. I'll call you in the morning, okay?"

"Demons" by Imagine Dragons fills the room as I walk to the couch, picking up his clothes and holding them out to him. *Please just take the clothes, let me handle the darkness that's crawling toward me.*

Kade stares at the clothes in my hands. When he doesn't take them, I shove them into his chest. He's shocked. Backing away from him hurts more than I thought it would. I can't look him, see the disappointment and hurt swirling in his beautiful eyes. I can't bear to see his pain, knowing I'm the cause of it.

Another crack of thunder sounds and I jump. It's coming—the panic attack sitting below the surface, waiting to release.

Once he's fully dressed, he moves toward me, but I hold a hand up, stopping his progress.

"Just go."

This time he gives in to the anger brewing inside. "Fine. You won't let me help you with whatever the fuck is in your head? Have it your way. Call me when you get your shit together."

Grabbing his shoes, he slams the door behind him, causing the pictures to shake on the walls. He's gone. I've done it again. Pushed away another person in my life. I crumble to the floor, letting my tears flow freely down my cheeks this time. Pain wracks my heart as I heave on the floor, mourning the happiness I had experienced only hours ago.

Kade deserves someone better than me. Now he knows it.

Pulling myself off the floor, I slowly walk over to the piano and sit on the bench, playing the beginnings of the "Moonlight Sonata", the source of my constant torment. The shadows on the wall laugh at me for daring to think I could be normal, even just for a night.

A tear slips down my cheek as I hang my head and play my penance.

Oh God, what did I just do?

Twelve

MY FINGERS ARE NUMB. MY WHOLE BODY IS NUMB.
Tears sting my eyes, surprised my body is still able
to produce them. All in all, I feel weak, defeated, and very
much alone.

It's been four days since Kade stormed out of my apartment. Four straight days of thunderstorms taking over, forcing me to call in sick to work because I can't leave my apartment. Gabe understands though, trying to soothe me with
his kind and sympathetic words. Nothing will make me feel
better. Nothing will take away this pain or seal the gaping
chasm where my heart used to be. Instead it hemorrhages
into my broken body, filling me with every broken promise
ever uttered.

I start the song again, unable to stop, unable to continue, unable to think. Every time I close my eyes, all I can
see is the hurt on Kade's face as I pushed him away, trying
to save him from the torment I bring. It was foolish of me
to think I could keep him, have this one good thing. But I

won't be responsible for taking another life.

The ringing in the background starts up again, like it has for the past few hours. Quinn will get over it. I know she's concerned, but this is something she can't fix. No one can help me. It took her two days to finally stop coming over when I refused to answer the door, only speaking to her through it. She called me every name in the book while reminding me of how stupid I'm being. As if I needed the reminder.

Another stinging tear slides down my cheek. Every time I close my eyes, I see those indigo eyes burning holes into my soul, piercing me while we shared the most intimate of acts. His beautiful face and body, worshipping me as only he could, invade my waking thoughts with each second that passes. It was only one night, but it meant so much more. For those few hours I was at peace. My problems had been lifted off my shoulders as I lost myself in his arms. He didn't think I heard his hushed whispers as we lay in bed, leaving me broken inside.

I let him get too close.

The lone tear hanging off the tip of my nose falls silently onto the keys. My shoulders shudder with the sobs trapped inside. If they escape, this becomes too real and I don't think I can handle it right now.

Knock. Knock. Knock.

Ignoring the unwelcomed visitor, I play louder. My matted hair is plastered to my face, unwashed since Saturday. The rumbling in my stomach had ceased yesterday after I convinced it that food wasn't welcome. Not that I was really hungry anyway.

The wind howls as the rain pelts against the window.

Thunder rumbles low and steady, sending another shudder through me. At least the lightning has stopped. Thunder is bad enough, but lightning throws me over the edge.

I tune everything out as I close my eyes, effectively shutting down my senses. There are no sounds, no smells, no sight. Just pure and absolute nothingness.

A hand gently presses on my shoulder, causing me to leap with fear. A shrill scream escapes me, echoing across the room as I clutch a fist to my chest. Panic races through my body, keeping my eyes closed while gasping for precious air. And then it becomes too much. The blackness settles in and I crumple to the ground.

I'm vaguely aware of hands around me, pulling me off the floor. Soft clothing presses against my cheek as my head lolls back and forth limply. I can barely register my arms hanging lifelessly at my sides. It's almost as if I'm having an out of body experience. I can't open my eyes, they won't co-operate. Nothing moves as commanded, yet I feel like I'm travelling somewhere.

Cold sets in and my body shakes. The numbness has been replaced by body-wracking jolts. What's wrong with me? I want to open my eyes, but I'm too weak, too tired, too…everything.

Darkness comes and goes; muffled sounds and voices surround me in spurts. I do my best to focus on the sounds, but nothing registers. And then I feel it. Heat surrounds me with the gentle touch of a hand against my cheek. The blood begins to move again, bringing that precious heat to the extremities of my body. Something familiar hits me. That smell, the one I've been obsessing over for weeks. It's him.

Kade.

The muffled sounds turn into a male voice. His warm breath beats against my cheek as I try to blink back to life. The sexy tone I've come to know is replaced with pain.

Something warm hits my skin, slowly sliding down the curve of my cheek before pooling in my ear. Only my eyes don't sting like before. It's not my tear. This is pure agony, and all my fault.

With everything I have left inside me, I force my eyelids open. Colors blur together, everything unfocused. He speaks again, the words still lost in my ears, but slowly getting clearer the longer he holds me.

When everything clears, I stare into sad and panicked eyes. A few days ago they were happy, laughing, and dancing with amusement. Now, dark circles lay in shadows underneath them and at least several days' worth of stubble on his chin.

I reach out, trying to touch his face, but it's a feeble attempt. My body's still unwilling to fully cooperate. The ringing in my ears eases and I can finally hear clearly.

"Adrienne," he whispers.

Pain etches his face, twisting my heart with a new kind of misery.

Why is he here?

"Kade," I manage to squeak out. Strong arms wrap around me as we rock on the floor. He presses his cheek against my forehead, and every now and then his lips brush my hair. My strength returns and I wiggle my fingers and toes, feeling the prick of discomfort as if they'd been asleep.

"Shh. Shh. Don't move. Just stay here with me. I'll keep you safe."

Reaching up, I cling weakly to his bicep and squeeze

with as much force as I can muster until the darkness swallows me again.

"Quinn, I'm worried. Shouldn't we take her to the hospital?"

What? Take who to the hospital? The darkness fades, letting the voices around me filter into my ears.

"No, she hates hospitals. Refuses to go to them after..."

"After what? Someone needs to tell me what the fuck is going on! I'm not getting anything and have no fucking clue how to help her."

A whimper escapes my lips from the hurt laced in his voice. I slowly open my eyes, blinking in rapid succession as they regain focus. Turning my head to where the voices are coming from, I'm greeted by my best friend and would-be boyfriend fighting at the end of the bed. Their heads whip around so fast I'm surprised they didn't fall right off.

"Thank fuck you're awake."

Kade pulls me into the safety of his chest. My whole body still feels like gelatin and barely twitches when commanded.

"What–"

"Don't talk. Save your energy." Kade strokes my hair. "I'm just glad you're awake."

He rains kisses across my forehead, warming me. On the other side, the bed dips and a gentle hand strokes my back.

"You scared us, Adrienne." I can hear the tears in her voice.

I'm surrounded by the two most important people in my life. Guilt kicks in again. Oh God, what did I do to them?

Kade stares at me, but I quickly turn away. The redness surrounding his normally vibrant blues shatters my heart into a million pieces.

I try pushing out of Kade's hold but he pulls me in tighter. Quinn quietly sobs from behind. I cry out, but no sound escapes. There's nothing left to give as I limply fall against Kade, giving up the struggle.

"Don't pull away. I want to help you but I don't know how. Help me help you." He sounds defeated, hurt, and scared. I don't want to be this way anymore. I need help. I need *his* help.

I've missed him these past few days. I thought I was doing the right thing by pushing him away. But I was wrong. I always assumed my heart was shattered the night of the accident. I thought for sure it would never heal and be whole again. Kade showed me how wrong I was. He eased his way into my life slowly through friendship, picking up the pieces and gluing them back together without my knowledge or understanding. He did it so stealthily that I didn't realize it could break again until I forced him out with my selfish need to protect him. I took away his choice to help me, to be something more to me than just friends. And when he walked away, I felt it, felt the splintering pain as he took my heart with him.

Can I guarantee I won't hurt him again? No. But I need him more than I ever realized. For the first time in a long time, I don't want to be alone. I want someone to take care of me.

"Water," I croak softly.

I need to tell him these things, need to make him understand the broken shell of a person I've become. But I can't do that when it feels like the Sahara is lodged in my throat.

"I've got it." Quinn jumps off the bed and runs to the kitchen. Kade continues to stroke my hair, keeping his lips pressed against my forehead. After a moment, Quinn holds out a glass to me. Kade shifts me into a sitting position.

"Take small sips. You're dehydrated."

I nod as Kade tips the glass to my lips, allowing the cool liquid to flow down my dry throat. It burns slightly and I wince. He removes the glass briefly and I catch my breath. With a small nod, he lets me have more. This time it doesn't burn as much. In fact, it soothes the dryness a little.

Kade sets the glass on the table next to my bed. Quinn sits next to us, wringing her hands in her lap.

"I should have listened to myself and come sooner, whether you wanted me to or not. I knew better."

I twist my head and look into the sorrowful face of my best friend, riddled with a guilt she shouldn't feel.

"No." My voice is still weak and barely recognizable. I adjust to face her but don't get far. Kade pulls me into him, my back to his front. His legs encompass my body, holding me there so I can't get away. The notion that he hasn't released me since I woke up isn't lost on me. In fact, it halts the tremors still shaking my body with my unshed tears.

Quinn vehemently shakes her head. "No, it's my fault. I knew better. And then when the rain didn't stop, I knew what you were doing and ignored it. I let this get too far. I'm so sorry."

She clutches the blanket draped over my lap, hanging her head low. Her hiccupping sobs constrict my insides. I don't want her feeling this way. She's not to blame.

"No, I did this," I say with a labored breath. "I'm to

blame. Not you. Not either of you."

Kade's hands cross my body, holding my shoulders and pulling me back into his chest. Resting his chin on the crown of my head, he exhales a soft sigh.

"Let me take you to the hospital. You need medical care. Please let me do this since you won't let me do anything else."

I place my arms over his. "Hold me. That's all I want. No hospitals. No doctors. You know how to take care of me."

A reassuring look passes over Quinn's face. Her eyes flicker down to mine before meeting his again. I know she's torn on what to do, given the fact that she's a medical professional. But at the same time, she knows why I can't go.

"Kade, I'm sorry, but I have to agree with her this one and only time. We can't take her to the hospital." She places her hand on my knee and squeezes it. "What I can do is run to work and grab an IV bag and supplies to start a drip to get some fluids in her."

"Won't you get in trouble?" he asks.

"Only if I get caught." She gets up and gathers her purse off the counter. "Be right back. Remember, small sips." And with that she rushes out the door.

We sit in silence; Kade trails his hands up and down my arms, soothing the guilt and worry plaguing me.

"I'm sorry," I say finally.

Kade turns me in his lap, swinging my legs over his. I nuzzle into the safety of his body.

"No, I'm sorry. I shouldn't have left like I did."

I shake my head against his chest. His heart pounds a steady rhythm against my cheek, threatening to push me back to the edge of consciousness. But my lids are too heavy.

Must. Fight. Sleep.

"I'm so tired."

"Please, not yet."

"Tired." He cups my head, pressing me against his chest while wrapping his other arm around my middle, grounding us together.

"Can you tell me what happened? You and Quinn keep talking in code and it's freaking me the fuck out." He pulls back slightly. "Why can't I bring you to the hospital?" His voice is walking the thin line of fear and anger.

I close my eyes because I don't want to see the hurt in his.

"Later. Not now. I promise."

With a frustrated sigh, he relents. "Fine. But you will tell me. You won't run me off or scare me away. I'm here, whether you want me or not." He tilts my chin up, forcing me to look at his face. "You don't get to make those kinds of decisions for me. I'll decide if I don't want to be here anymore. Not you. Understand?"

I nod meekly. He brings his face closer to mine so we're almost nose to nose. "Not good enough. I want to hear you say it. You won't push me away anymore. You're going to let me take care of you." The pain in his voice causes my heart to lurch.

"Yes."

"Good," Kade says, exhaling loudly. His kiss is gentle, but it stings my dry lips. I wince and his face falls.

"God, I'm sorry, babe. Here, drink some more. This will help."

I take small sips of the glass he places at my lips. Once satisfied, he returns the glass to the table.

"So tired," I say again. My words are slurred and thick as I lose the battle with my eyelids, growing heavier and heavier by the minute. I just need to rest now that he's here. Now that I'm safe. He'll keep the shadows at bay.

"Okay. You rest. I've got you."

Sleep takes over as Kade strokes my hair again, his heartbeat beneath my ear.

"No!"

I thrash from side to side. A cry of agony fills the room as I clutch the blanket tightly around me.

"Dad! Mom! No!" I scream again.

"Adrienne, wake up."

He shakes me and I look from side to side. I don't smell the burning flesh anymore or hear the screeching tires. No crunching metal or bloodcurdling screams. It's only me and Kade, safe in my bed.

I take a few short breaths, pain lancing with each one. My throat burns still from before. I try to move my left arm, but can't get it very far. Quinn must have placed the IV in my hand while I was asleep. The cold liquid flows through my veins while my head throbs with the panic still sitting heavy in my body.

Kade wraps his arms around me, pulling me into the safety of his embrace. "Shh. I've got you. You're safe."

His soft, comforting voice washes over me. Tears prick the edges of my eyes. I don't want him to see me cry. My body trembles again and he strengthens his hold on me.

"Please, Adrienne. Let me in. Tell me what's wrong. Tell

me why you're shaking like a leaf, why you wake up scream-ing in the middle of the night." His voice drops low. "Tell me why Quinn and I found you like we did."

The dam breaks and tears flow freely down my cheeks, soaking his shirt beneath my face. He rubs his hands in soothing circles along my back as I cling to his shoulders. Memories come flooding back: the pain, the flashing lights, the storm, my parents' screams. The smell of the hospital in-vades my memory and I'm brought back to when I woke up, only to find out I was alone. They didn't make it and I knew in my heart I was to blame.

Kade lets me cry it out, never once forcing me to talk. He sits quietly, giving me his soft comfort, knowing it's ex-actly what I need. Somehow Kade always knows what I need.

After a few minutes, my sobs quiet down to just a hic-cupping cry. My face feels hot and I know it's a blotchy mess. I pull back, wiping at my face with the back of my good hand.

"I'm sorry," I whisper.

He leans down and places a small kiss on my forehead. "Don't be sorry."

I close my eyes and let out a struggled breath. When I reopen them, my eyes lock with his. The kindness and car-ing I find almost brings me to tears again. He raises his hand to cup my cheek. The pad of his thumb gently strokes over my lower lip, causing it to tremble again.

"No more tears. It's okay." I nod and he brushes a few stray tears away from my face. I look up and see his smile. "There's my beautiful girl."

I dip my head down and am surprised when a quiet giggle escapes. I can feel the vibrations in his chest as he laughs with me. The giggle erupts into a full-blown laugh, even though it's painful. Obviously delirium has hit us because nothing about this situation is at all funny.

After our sanity returns, I wrap an arm around his waist and pull him close.

"Thank you for staying with me. I know this must be driving you insane."

"You have no idea," he says. The seriousness from before returns as he looks me over. "I've never been so scared in my life. But when I saw you crumble to the floor, your face complete devoid of life…I thought…"

I tighten my arm around him, hoping it calms his fear.

"I didn't mean to scare you. But I didn't hear you come in. Then when the adrenaline stopped pumping through my body…I was so weak and tired. I guess my body just gave up."

Kade brushes a few tendrils away from my eyes. The concern shines through, piercing my heart and giving me the courage to finally tell him why I am the way I am.

With a nod, I start.

"For as long as I can remember, playing the piano has been my life. I was forced to perform and attend special schools and everything that comes with it. I know my circumstances pale in comparison to kids with harder situations than mine, but just because I came from some sort of privilege doesn't mean it was any easier. I've already told you about what how I grew up. Well, here's the unabridged version.

"There was a storm; one not much different than the last few days. Dad was trying to be careful, doing everything he could to keep us on the road. Mom sat in front, trying to ease his mind by keeping the conversation light. I had other plans. There was this concert I wanted to go to with my boyfriend, which meant I would have to skip an important performance with the orchestra. My dad got pissed, started yelling at me, telling me how stupid I was being and how it was going to ruin my career if I missed this performance. Then I decided to attack my mom, calling her a washed up has been, simply because she couldn't make it playing the piano like I could."

I close my eyes, trying to find the strength to go on. Kade holds me tighter, sending me his courage through the embrace.

"The car started sliding, my dad still yelling at me while trying to keep us on the road. I told them I hated them and wanted to be left alone so I could make decisions about my life." I swallow thickly, bracing myself for the blow. "We didn't even see the car cross the center line. All of a sudden, there was a blinding light. My mom screamed while clutching my dad's shoulder. He tried in vain to stop the collision, but he couldn't."

The memory knocks the breath out of me again. "I can still hear their screams in my dreams. Still hear the sounds of the car being smashed around me. Still feel the pain of waking up in the hospital room, not remembering why I was there. I asked the doctors about my parents, only to see the sad eyes of everyone around me as he told me they didn't make it, that I'd been orphaned and left alone.

"That's when Quinn's family took me in. I stayed with them until I graduated from high school. They still consider me part of their family and look over me, even though I'm an adult."

Kade is deep in thought, his eyes darting across my face. "The piece you were playing when I found you?"

I nod. "It was the piece I was supposed to play that weekend. I play it every time it rains, bringing me right back to the accident. It's my penance for killing my parents. They wanted me to perform, to make a future for myself. And I… well, I fucked that up when I killed them."

Kade cups my cheeks and looks deep into my eyes. A hundred emotions flash across his face, the most prominent one being understanding.

"You didn't cause the accident and you didn't kill them."

I look away. "But I did. I started the fight. If I hadn't yelled at them for wanting to be a normal teenager, none of this would've happened. They'd still be here and I…I wouldn't be broken."

He guides my face to meet his. I know he can see the regret in my eyes, the pain and loss that's always there. Our lips touch softly in a whisper of a kiss. His forehead presses against mine while both his hands snake around my neck.

"You are not broken and definitely not to blame. You didn't cause the crash that killed your parents. Which almost killed you. You can't say with certainty the other car wouldn't have crossed the line and avoided you." His thumb brushes along my jaw, trying to soothe my fears. "This is not on you."

A cry gets lodged in my throat and I blink back the tears burning my eyes. I want to believe him, but he wasn't there. He doesn't know about the fights I would wage against my parents just because I wanted to feel something. I knew they loved me, but they pushed me so hard I had to fight back. I had to fight for me because I was losing myself, becoming someone I didn't want to be anymore.

"I don't think you'll ever convince me it wasn't my fault. I'm just...so...hurt...and scared...I don't want to be... alone...anymore." Another round of tears falls. Clinging to his shirt, I bury my face into his shoulder and let it out. All the pain and fear I've kept with me for so long, all the guilt I feel for living while they're not here anymore. More so the guilt for not being what they wanted me to be.

Kade doesn't say anything. Just holds me and breathes life back into my weak body, continually stroking my hair, relaxing me even more.

I sit back and wipe my nose in the most unladylike fashion. I laugh when he gives me a disgusted look.

"Well, I was going to kiss your hand, but fuck that now."

It feels good to have that simple banter back, to have any emotion present that isn't sadness or remorse or guilt. For the first time in days, I give a heartfelt smile, a silent show of my thanks and appreciation for everything he's done.

"Wimp."

He picks me up with the ease of someone picking up a feather. Grabbing the IV pole next to me, he wheels it with us as he carries me to the bathroom.

"What are you doing?"

He sets me down gently on the counter and runs his hands down my arms.

"No offense, but you haven't showered in over four days. You're a little rank. I need to get my woman back."

I cover my face with my hands, praying he can't see the red creeping up my neck. Oh God, I can only imagine what I look like, let alone smell like. And he's been wrapped around me for...I don't even know how long I've been conscious.

He starts running water in the bathtub, checking the temperature before adding some bath salts he found under the sink.

"Kade?"

"Hmm?"

"How long was I out?"

He pauses and I can see his body tense. His face is grim when he turns. Kneeling in front of me, he unties the knot and slowly pushes the robe from my body.

"A few minutes that turned into a couple hours the first time. Then four hours the second time." He runs his hands over my naked shoulders. I look down at my arm and see it's unobstructed. Kade had the insight to pull my arm out before Quinn inserted it. It amazes me how he's always two steps ahead of where he needs to be.

"Six hours? I've lost most of the day."

He lifts me up, setting me in the tub with ease. The warm water swirls around me, relaxing my tense muscles.

"But we're not going to focus on that. Right now we need to get you clean and relaxed. Then you and I are going back to bed and you're going to do nothing but let me hold you."

I turn my head to look at him. My heart kicks up a notch as I realize what he said.

"You're staying here?"

Kade doesn't reply. Just guides my upper body into a reclining position so he can easily wet my hair, cupping the water and pouring it lovingly through the strands. "You're not leaving my sight again. Ever."

He pours some shampoo on my hair and begins massaging it into my scalp. I close my eyes and hum my pleasure as he rinses and repeats the process. I stay in the tub and allow my rock god to care for me like no one has done before.

Thirteen

"**B**ABE, CAN YOU GRAB THAT WIRE OVER THERE?" KADE adjusts the guitar strapped across his body.

I nod and walk in the general direction he pointed to, but stop and stare at the floor. There's a shit ton of wires here. Is he serious? I turn to see his shit-eating grin. He did this on purpose, the bastard.

"Okay, asshole, which one do you want?" I roll my eyes. Kade is so fucking adorable when he's playful and teasing. It makes me want to do dirty things to him. More than usual.

Kade sets the guitar in the stand and leaps off the stage. Pointing with his finger, he strides over to where I'm standing. "Blue one."

Blue wires litter the floor everywhere I look. He leans in close and rests his chin on my shoulder. One arm wraps lovingly around my collarbone while the other snakes around my waist. He nuzzles into my neck, which causes my eyes to roll into the back of my head before closing. A small hum of pleasure escapes me.

Kade teases my neck, nipping and sucking at the skin. He's definitely in a playful mood today. Each pass of his lips sparks something to life between my legs. *Would Gabe miss us if we disappeared for about ten to thirty minutes?*

"I don't think the wire you need is here." My voice is breathy, even though I'm trying in vain to control it. I look down again and laugh. "These are all computer wires for the boards, not your guitar."

I turn to meet his eyes, clearing enjoying this way too much. His sexy lips curl up in the corners, flashing my most favorite smile.

"I know. Just wanted an excuse to come down here and wrap my arms around you."

"As if you really need a reason."

He nuzzles into me one last time before stealing my lips in what I have now labeled as "Kade Says So" kiss. No matter what we're doing, if he wants to kiss me, it's going to happen.

Because Kade says so.

Such a caveman. But I love it.

The tip of his tongue runs over the seams of my lips, coaxing them to open. Sparks ignite again when I turn in his arms, pressing my body flush with his. The sounds of his band and everything else fade away when I wrap my arms around his neck and lose myself in the kiss.

Ever since that night four weeks ago when Kade found me at my lowest, he never left like I thought he would. So much about him has surprised me, but in the best of ways. Hardly a day goes by where we're not wrapped in each other's arms, or our legs aren't tangled beneath the sheets. Kade is so much more than a lover and a boyfriend. He's my whole world, which still scares me sometimes. The nagging voice in the back of my mind hasn't fully been silenced, reminding me that one day he'll leave and then I'll be alone again.

It hasn't helped that his band has been getting more and more attention in the entertainment scene lately. Their talent and energy make their show the best in town. Each time they play, the crowds get bigger and the venue gets larger. They were even asked to play at the Fourth of July celebration at the outdoor amphitheater. Kade and I go through the local newspaper daily, clipping out articles we find about the Lightning Strikes. I've amassed quite the scrapbook so far. He's going to make something of himself, and I'll be his biggest fan, even if it means I'm left here while he makes his fortune around the world.

After everything he's done for me, all I want is his happiness.

"Why don't you two get a fucking room already? Jesus, come on," Paxton yells from the stage.

We smile, reluctantly breaking away. Kade lets out a small chuckle and kisses the end of my nose.

"Fuck off, Pax. I can do whatever I want with my girl."

"Yeah, but we've got a show to prep for and you're not doing shit to help," says Brecken. The speaker he's carrying lands with a thud on the side of the stage.

Kade narrows his eyes. "Fine. But you fuckers are going to pay." He turns, flashing me a teasing grin. All I can do is shake my head and sigh.

"Okay, Rock God, you need to get ready and so do I." I slap his ass as he turns away. It's only fair. He does it to me every chance he can get.

Before I realize it, he slings me over his shoulder. I grab his waist, trying to keep myself propped up while squealing with a mixture of surprise and delight. "Kade!"

He laughs and smacks my ass. Hard. It sounds more painful than it really is. When he reaches the bar, I slide down his body before he places me on a barstool.

Kade leans in close, our noses barely touching. "Don't be making promises you're not willing to follow through on. I take my ass slapping very seriously. Because right now, what I've got running through my head would make your toes curl and have you screaming all night."

I swallow hard around the lump in my throat. Holy shit. His low growling voice combined with his dirty words has my panties soaked already. I press my thighs together and he gives me a knowing smirk.

Ass.

Well, two can play this game. "What makes you think I'll be screaming? Maybe I don't think you can follow through."

How does every female lead I've read about make this seem so easy? They'd probably laugh at my weak seduction attempts. Not that I need to seduce him or anything. We're pretty much a sure thing. In fact, we both know damn well that I *will* be screaming until I lose my voice. We've tested, and proved, that theory over, and over, and over again.

He glides his hand around to the back of my neck, pulling me so close there isn't anything between us except the constant humming of desire and lust. "Oh, I'll follow through. Don't worry." His free hand reaches down and slips between my legs, pressing with two fingers against my heated core. "This is mine," he says, bending to whisper in my ear. "You are mine. And tonight I'm going to show you exactly what that means."

I draw my brows together. Huh? "Don't you show me

every night?"

He shakes his head and kisses my nose. "Just be ready when we're done. I need you all to myself for the rest of the night."

I cup his cheek. "You have me. You know that, right?"

Why is he acting so strange? He's fidgety, more than usual, and his eyes are constantly searching mine. Not in a bad way. It's like they're trying to confirm whatever it is he's looking for.

"There was never any doubt." He slants his mouth over mine one last time before leaving me in a stupor. When I open my eyes, I'm graced with his retreating form and tight ass. He joins Brecken, Myles and Paxton as they haul everything off the edge of the stage and finish putting it together. Good thing too because they start in an hour.

All reasoning has abandoned me. I shake my head, heading to the bar to help Gabe.

"Finally able to pull yourselves away from each other?" he asks while scribbling something on a piece of paper.

I shove his shoulder as I walk by to wipe down the rail bottles. "Shut up. As if you're any better lately. Is Quinn coming in tonight? Figured you'd know since you see more of her than I do."

The slow smile crawling across his face tells me all I need to know. Why they fought it for so long beats the hell out of me. Nothing makes me happier than seeing my best friend happy.

"Yeah, she said she's got some family thing going on tonight, but she'll be in later."

I start loading the dishwasher and nod. "Oh, that's right. Her grandma's in town. Are you heading over tomorrow?"

When I turn to face him, the excitement is barely contained in his eyes. "Her whole family is going to be there so I'm a little nervous."

I wave a hand at him and polish the clean glasses. "They're harmless. Trust me, I lived with them for years. They may be a huge family when they get together, but they're also the sweetest people you'll ever meet."

The tension around his eyes eases and his shoulders relax. "Good to know. I mean, it's only been a few weeks, but when she asked me to meet her family, how could I say no?"

I laugh and lean against the bar. "As if you could say no to Quinn. She's been my best friend for as long as I can remember, and I have yet to tell her no. If I can't do it, there's no hope for you." I smirk. "Besides, you're kind of pussy-whipped when it comes to her."

He smacks my shoulder with the clipboard. "I am not."

I rub the abused spot and laugh. "So what did Quinn tell you to wear tomorrow?"

Gabe hangs his head and sighs. "My khaki pants and green button-down."

"Ha! Told you."

"Shut up." He shoves me once more for good measure before continuing with the inventory sheet.

"Hey, stop picking on my girl." Kade's voice booms through the speakers, startling me. I turn and stick my tongue out. He shakes his head and goes back to setting the stage up.

I tap my finger against my lips, as if I'm missing something. What? The glasses are polished, the liquor is stocked. I grabbed several six-pack backups and brought them to the front earlier. I turn and point things out around the bar.

Bar towels. Check.

Sanitizer. Check.

I snap my fingers and run to the dial on the wall, cranking it up until the room fills with music from my favorite satellite radio station. The collective groan from the stage makes me smile. Mission accomplished.

"Turn this shit off," Myles yells.

I flip him the bird. "Fuck you. My bar, my music. Until you guys start playing, you'll have to suffer through the 90's." Myles turns away from me to continue tuning his guitar.

Gabe walks over, trying really hard to look serious, but I can see he's holding back a laugh. "Pretty sure it's my bar."

I shrug. "Whatever. I'm the bartender and what I say goes." He gives me a sideways glance. "Love you," I say sweetly while dragging the words out.

"You and Quinn need to get a hobby outside of torturing me."

"Where's the fun in that?" *Oh Gabe, you should know better by now.*

The first wave of people parade in as I grab two pitchers and fill them with ice and water. Kade strides over and once again I find myself mesmerized by his movements, watching his muscles flex underneath my favorite white shirt and ripped jeans. God, I could eat him alive when he wears that stuff.

Reaching over the bar, he grabs me by my arms and pulls me over until my feet are barely dangling off the ground. His tongue sweeps through my mouth, sending a rush of wetness and warmth to pool between my legs.

There's no way I'm going to be able to work if he keeps this up.

"Thanks, babe." He grabs the stack of plastic cups next to the pitchers with a wink.

"Knock 'em dead tonight." He cocks an eyebrow and I laugh. "Sorry. Knock 'em dead, Rock God."

He pins me with a heated stare, and I forget where we are and what we're doing. I take in his mouth, needing it again, claiming me, owning me, branding me as his in front of all these people. Of course, thoughts of where else his mouth can go infiltrate my brain and my nipples tighten beneath my bra. I'm going to need a cold shower before the night even begins.

Kade senses my wayward thoughts because he bites his lip and peels back my clothes with his eyes. "Don't you forget it."

As if I could.

I lean over and frame his face with my hands, sending him off with one, sweet, gentle kiss. The complete opposite of what was just running through my head, but that's more for later than in public.

"Letting all the girls know I'm taken?" he asks with a smirk.

I glance left and right, noticing a few of the skanks staring at us. "Damn straight."

"Love it when you're possessive."

I have half a mind to kiss him like I want to, but Gabe shouts my name, grabbing my attention. "I could use a little help here."

Shit. When did all these people come in? Ugh, Kade is such a bad influence. Nothing ever gets done when he's around. If I wasn't Gabe's best bartender, I'm sure he' would've kicked me to the curb by now.

When I glance over again, Kade's gone, along with the pitchers and glasses. Probably a good thing since the crowd is getting thicker by the second and he's supposed to start in ten minutes.

Work is the best distraction I have, so I pop open two beer bottles and set them down in front of a group of guys who are calling out multiple drink orders. At least Gabe and I are a well-oiled machine when we work together. It's basically like the movie *Cocktail*, minus the fancy bottle flipping. I tried it once. Gabe banned me from doing it again.

As soon as Paxton pounds on the drums, I run over and turn off the music. Not that anyone could hear it anyway. The multiple conversations going on were enough to drown out even my own thoughts. Brecken joins in with his bass while Myles strums out several chords. The tech guy dims the main lights while turning on the colored spots. Girls scream excitedly and several howls erupt from the pit as the stage goes completely dark. It's brilliant really. Builds up the anticipation before the song actually starts.

Whistles and screams still fill the room. I can't help but smile, knowing it's my guy they're all here to see. One day, he's going to rule the music world.

My heart constricts at the thought, knowing he'll be doing that without me, but I shake it off when I see his shadow cross the stage to grab the microphone.

"What's up, KC?"

Another round of screams and whistles commences, giving Gabe and I our first little break of the night. The guys start off with "Paralyzer" by Finger Eleven, my favorite of theirs. I dance along to the music, tossing my hair back and forth while really getting into it. Kade stands center stage, hanging onto the mic stand and running a hand through his black hair as he sings. He is nothing but pure energy and sex up there. It's in the way he takes command of the stage, rocking out and making everybody scream until their lungs give out. It's also in the way he teases the girls, getting them all riled up to keep them coming back for more

Okay, that part I hate with a white hot passion. I don't want Kade looking at anyone other than me. But it's the nature of the game. He's going to look at other girls. It's in his personality to do so. As a rockstar and lead singer of the band that's going to make waves across the country, it's bound to happen. I've heard the rumors swirling around their YouTube channel and how many hits the videos of his shows accumulate daily. Soon he'll attract the attention of a music producer and the rest will be history.

He won't say it to me, but I know he's received a few phone calls already from interested labels. And who can blame them? They'd be stupid not to sign.

"We're going to take a quick break. Be back in fifteen," Kade says. Sweat drips off his forehead and temples, running down the sides of his face before picking up a nearby towel to wipe it off. A group of girls scream around the stage and he tosses the used towel to one girl, making them lose their minds even more.

The muscles deep in my belly clench as I watch him approach; all sweaty and hot, his shirt damp and clinging to his body. The outline of the black tattoo running down his side starts to become visible and I bite my lip when he sits in front me.

I finish pouring the Captain Coke for a customer and turn to give him my rapt attention, which he always has anyway. My fingers trail over his sweat-slicked forearms and I bite my lip. His eyes dilate and I swear I hear him growl at me.

"So what'll it be, sir? Can I interest you in something wet behind the bar right now?"

I drag my index finger down the column of my throat, feeling a little more bold than normal tonight. Maybe it's the fact there's so many women here and I want to prove to myself that I can drive him as wild as he's making them.

Kade grabs me suddenly, pulling me to his mouth. I moan against his lips as I open for him, letting him take control.

"Yeah, buddy. I'm next in line for some of that. She's fucking hot," I hear some drunk guy say.

Oh no. This won't be good.

Kade releases me, almost tossing me onto my ass before turning to the face the guy.

I grab his arm, trying to diffuse him. "No, let it go." My pleas fall on deaf ears. It's too late.

He grabs the asshat by the back of the shirt and drags him off the barstool. Kade is damn near foaming at the mouth while the drunk guy looks like a ghost, the color almost completely drained from his face.

"What the fuck did you just say about my girlfriend?"

His jaw clicks and tenses as he narrows his eyes into tiny slits. I run around the bar and grab his bicep. It's flexed so tight I swear his muscles are going to snap at any second.

"Baby, let him go. Please."

I move around, trying to get in his line of sight, but he's completely zoned in on the guy in his hands. Gabe has been patient, but Kade's possessive streak over me has been an ongoing issue lately as more and more fights happen when they're playing. I don't want him to get into another fight. I glance over at Gabe, who's ready to break them apart. If he does, it won't be good.

I tug on his arm once more, bracing my other hand on the guy's chest, trying to push him away.

"Hey, man, I didn't know. I'm sorry!"

"Kade, he said he was sorry. Stop this, now!"

His head finally swings to mine, locking me in his sights. He releases the guy, tossing him on his ass. Kade looms over him and snarls. "Don't you ever fucking say that about her again. Are we clear?"

The poor guy nods as he quickly scrambles to his feet, making a beeline for the doors. Great. Another customer gone because Kade can't keep his temper under control.

He turns back to me and grips the hair at the back of my head, forcefully kissing me in front of the crowd gathered around us.

I shove him away with a glare. "That was uncalled for. You need to rein your shit in now. You can't keep doing that."

Kade steps closer to me. "No, his comment was uncalled for. You don't say that to a woman, let alone mine. If I hear anyone disrespecting you like that, I will throw down."

"Ugh!" I throw my arms in the air. "I don't need a bodyguard and I sure as shit don't need a crazy-ass boyfriend beating up all of Kansas City." I cup his face, letting my eyes soften. "I need *you*."

The tension in his shoulders drop when he pulls me close, not forcefully this time, enveloping me in a sweet embrace. I rest my head on his shoulder as he strokes my hair, trying to appease me for his behavior.

"I won't apologize, Adrienne. But I need you too."

The music starts up again, Kade's not-so-subtle hint to get back on stage. With a final kiss on top of my head, he weaves his way through the crowd. Several girls throw themselves at him and I can hear their high pitched squeals as they attempt to kiss him. He smiles and doesn't stop until he jumps back on stage.

Taking my place back behind the bar, I throw myself into work. Only the crowd is busy going to the pit again, so we're in another lull. Gabe comes over, running a hand through his hair.

"You know he can't keep doing this. Something's got to give."

I sigh. "I know."

"Look, either you won't be able to bartend on the nights they play or I'm going to have to black list them from here."

Panic sets in as I widen my eyes. "No, please. Don't do that. If word gets out they're black listed, that could cause problems. We're the largest venue in the area. It'll kill their career."

My bottom lip quivers as I think about what that would mean for him and the guys. They'd never play around here again. Sure, there're some bars who don't mind fights. Hell, a few even encourage it. But The Warehouse is *the* place to come for entertainment. If he can't play here, he's fucked.

Running my hands through my hair, I hang my head and sigh. "Take me off the schedule when he's here. That should solve the issue."

Gabe nods. "Let's hope so because I don't want to lose them. He's got quite the following and we'd pay a heavy price without them."

"I know. I'll talk to him about it."

"Please do," Gabe says, squeezing my arm.

When "Next Contestant" by Nickelback starts to play, I turn my attention to the stage and narrow my eyes to Kade. His sick sense of humor is not amusing right now.

"He's a funny guy," Gabe yells.

"Don't encourage him." I try my best to stay focused while silently brooding over what to do about the rock god.

After three more sets, it's finally quiet in the bar. The last of the customers have been ushered out as I wipe down the round tables on the floor, placing the stools on top as I go. The guys are putting away the equipment, loading everything onto dollies and taking them backstage.

Strong arms wrap around me from behind as I wipe down the last table. I stop, hang my head and loudly exhale.

"Still mad at me?" Kade nuzzles against my neck while his lips trail from my ear to my shoulder, igniting that ever present need deep within me again.

I elbow him in his side and step away. "As a matter of fact, yeah, I am. You were a dick tonight." He tries to hold me again, but I put a hand up, halting his movement. "And seriously? That fucking Nickelback song was uncalled for." I sigh and shake my head. "What am I going to do with you?"

He pulls me close and this time I let him. I trace his muscular back while resting my head on his shoulder. The tiny patterns he's drawing on my lower back and hip ease my tension a little.

"You're going to let me take you home is what you're going to do with me."

His intense blue stare pins me in my place. That strong, commanding voice has my stomach flipping again, causing tingles to travel all the way to my toes.

I huff out a breath through my nose. "We need to talk when we get there. I'm not letting this go."

Kade runs his nose down the length of mine before kissing the tip. "I know you won't. Meet me at the back door when you're finished."

I back away, needing to put some distance between us and grab the rag from the table. He helps me flip up the last few chairs before disappearing to finish loading up the truck.

Quinn's at the bar, talking to Gabe with a swoony look covering her face. I sling my arm around her shoulder and rest my head on hers.

"He's nuts about you. You know that, right?" she asks.

"He's nuts all right. He can't keep doing this shit. It'll put me in the looney bin for sure."

Gabe finishes locking everything up behind the counter and glances over at us. He winks at Quinn and her face pinks up in the most adorable way.

Why can't I have a boyfriend like him? Gabe never gets into fights when Quinn gets hit on at the bar. They trust each other enough to know nothing will ever come of it. Why can't I have that with Kade?

"You ready?" Gabe asks us.

"God, please get me out of here," I whine.

The room goes dark, leaving the security light above the bar to show us the way out. When we walk through the back door, Kade's leaning against the building, just where he said he'd be.

"See you tomorrow?" I call out to them.

"Don't forget!" Quinn yells back. She laces her fingers

with Gabe's as they walk to their cars.

And that leaves me and my Neanderthal boyfriend standing here in the empty parking lot. He pushes himself off the building and wraps his arm around my waist, pulling me to my car.

"Come on, let's go home."

I laugh because I don't know what else to do. He always calls my place home. It's not surprising. We spend the majority of our time there. At this rate, he might as well just move in.

Flicking on lights as we walk through the door, I kick my work shoes off and drop my purse and keys on the counter. Kade's kept a watchful eye on me since we left the bar. I think he's afraid of my reaction, which he damn well should be. Grabbing his hand, I drag him to the couch and throw my feet over his legs. He begins massaging the life back into my feet one at a time. Oh, God, that feels so good. For the first time since the fight, I relax.

"Kade." I close my eyes and take a deep breath. "Gabe's pulling me from the schedule the night's you play."

His fingers stall briefly, but continue working their magic. "I figured."

"It was either that or ban you and I couldn't let him do that. Your career would suffer."

"I don't care."

I jerk my head back. "What do you mean you don't care? Isn't that the point of playing all these gigs? To make a better life for yourself and get discovered?"

Kade releases my foot and walks over to the stereo, hooking up his phone to the dock. After scrolling through the list, he taps the screen with his selection. Soft music fills the air. Okay, now I'm lost. He's not one who actively listens to Top 40 music, but Justin Timberlake's unmistakable voice is coming through the speakers.

With purposeful strides, he joins me back at the couch. He stretches an arm to me, helping me to my feet.

"Dance with me?"

The smile gracing Kade's face makes my heart skip a beat. How can I deny him this request? Leading me around the coffee table, he pulls my body close to his. Our hearts beat in time as I lower my head to rest on his chest. Kade bends his head low, singing the lyrics of "Not a Bad Thing" softly in my ear.

I freeze, halting the impromptu dance. *He can't. Can he?*

When I look into his eyes, I see my answer. His breathing has picked up and I watch him swallow thickly. I'm not sure I want to acknowledge what he's trying to say to me. Words were never necessary with us. Not as long as there are songs to say it instead.

"Adrienne, I know I'm a pain in the ass and I fly off the handle when other guys look at you. I can't help it. I've tried. Honestly, I have. But the need to show everyone in the world that you belong to me is so strong, I can't deny it." Kade lifts his hand, running the back of it down my cheek before wrapping around my neck and pulling me closer.

"You have to trust me, Kade. Nothing will come of guys hitting on me. I won't let anything like that happen. Just like I trust you when you're up on stage and women shamelessly throw themselves at you. Have faith in the strength of our relationship to know I'm not going anywhere right now."

Fuck, why'd I add the last part? I cringe, wishing I would have kept that thought internal, but it's too late. He pulls back and bends to put us at eye level.

"Why do you keep saying we're not going to last? You've written us off before we've even left the ground. This right here," he says, waving a hand between us. "This is why I act the way I do. Because I never know how you're feeling, if you still want me around, or if you're going to run away because that's what you do. You've got some issues. We all do. And yours are a little more complex, having been through a horrible tragedy at such a young age." He traces the scar by my ear. "I told you before, you don't get to make the choice for me to stay or go. That's my decision to make."

My lip quivers again. "I'm not trying to push you away. Not on purpose. But let's face it. Your career is important. You'll be going places that I can't follow. You have so much talent to give and I don't want to be the reason you stay behind and waste it. I've done that once. I won't do it to someone else."

He grabs my chin between his thumb and index finger, pulling my face up. "I don't give a fuck about sharing my talent with the world. Yeah, a few months ago my answer would have been different. Things have changed now. You think I'm doing all this for a career? That it's my life's mission?"

I nod and blink back tears. "You have so much to give and I…I'll only keep you behind."

"Adrienne." He lets out a frustrated growl while running a hand through his hair. "I don't care about fame and fortune. Not anymore. Do you know why I do this? Why I put myself out there every night? I do it for you. I do it so I can start making a life for us because you are my future. Not this crap. *You* are what I want in my life." He grabs my hands, holding them against his heart. "My priorities have changed. You take center stage."

A quiet gasp escapes my lips. How does he always know the right things to say to completely take my breath away? I honestly thought his passion lies with his music. Now he's telling me it's running for…me.

"It drives me crazy when you don't have enough faith in us, in you, that we'll survive anything. You're always looking over your shoulder, taking a cautious step and waiting for the other shoe to fall. Life doesn't work that way. If you're always looking behind you, you'll never see what's in front."

"Kade–"

"Sometimes you have to take the chance and let go of the past, let someone else take the lead because they want what's best for you. That's what I want, to take the lead for us. Sure, I'm a selfish asshole with a temper around other guys, but it's because you don't give me any other choice. I don't want you to slip through my fingers. So I'm going to hold on tighter until you're ready to figure it out on your own."

He reaches up and cups my cheek. Tears fall from my eyes. He's right. I know I'm a head case, yet he still wants me. What did I ever do to deserve him?

"I'm done talking for tonight," he says, swaying to the music again. "I won't apologize for my actions, but now you know the reasons why. You're the most important thing in my life and I'm fighting for you, trying to knock down the last barrier you keep sliding into place." He dips his head low to meet my eyes. "You say I need to trust you? Well, I need you to trust us."

Kade surprises me at every turn. Nothing he's said is

wrong. He pretty much nailed it right on the head. But the fact that he said I'm his future has floored me.

And even though he didn't outright say it, the songs playing in the background, and his little confession, give away his admission of love. The question is can I say it back?

Scooping me into his arms, he carries me across the room and lays me on the bed. "Now get naked because I'm going to drive my point across again, and again, and again, until all your doubts are gone."

Our mouths seal together as we get lost in each other's body the rest of the night.

Fourteen

"WHERE ARE WE GOING?"

The silk blindfold covers my eyes, put on the minute I opened the door to him. The last thing I saw was his bright, beautiful smile, the one that melts my insides. Things have been easier between us since the "Come to Jesus" talk we had a few weeks ago.

Ugh! I've no idea where we are. We've taken so many turns I lost track of where we could be. Sneaky little shit. He probably drove around the block several times to really throw me off. I wouldn't put it past him.

"I told you, it's a surprise. You just sit there and look pretty."

Those long, rough fingers I love run lazily up and down my thighs, leaving tingles in their wake. It's a little scary not being able to see, but I trust my life with Kade. Besides, it's definitely heightened my other senses. He's driving me mad with each caress of my body. And when he swats my hands away, it only increases my need.

Unfortunately, I'm not a patient person. I want to see him, run my hands up and down his body and pull him so close it's almost like we're one person. Fingers brush the side of my cheek before trailing lightly over my bottom lip. I shift restlessly in my seat. It doesn't help when Kade laughs.

I love the sound of his laugh. The gravelly timbre of his voice, the way his Adam's apple bobs up and down sends me into a frenzy every time. What I wouldn't do to be able to see that now.

After what feels like an eternity, he finally parks the car. When my door opens, the warm summer breeze hits me. Kade glides his hands down my arm, and tugs me from the car. The sundress floats across my thighs as the wind picks up.

"Where are we?"

Gravel crunches beneath our feet as he guides us. I bask in the warm sunshine. The heavy scent of wild flowers and trees float through the air, as well as the various sounds of nature. Birds chirp and flutter above our heads while bull-frogs croak somewhere in the distance.

I have no fucking clue where we are.

Listening, I note each of his movements before Kade wraps his arms around my shoulders, pulling me into the safety of his chest. He nuzzles into my neck and I tilt my head to the side, giving him better access. Needing to feel him too, I reach behind me and run my hands along his lower back, feeling the muscles tense then relax beneath my fingers. Slipping my hands into his back pockets, I rest my head against his shoulder and sigh. We stand there in the warmth of the sun, listening to nature all around us, while feeling isolated and free of all responsibilities for the moment.

"Are you ready to take this off?" He tugs on the blindfold. I nod and squeeze my eyes shut to help against the sudden onset of light. After my eyes adjust, I look around and gasp.

"Kade, it's beautiful."

Obviously I figured we were somewhere in the country, but this was not what I was expecting. Acres and acres of green, grassy hills, filled with purple and pink flowers bending in the breeze. Green, leafy trees surround a clearing along with a few weeping willows. Somewhere in the distance, I can hear the faint sound of a stream or brook running through it all.

It's breathtaking; almost like it's out of a picture book or some expensive painting you'd see hanging in a museum.

"Do you like your surprise?" He presses his lips to my ear.

I nod. "It's amazing. Where did you find this place?"

He turns me in his arms and runs a hand down my cheek before cupping the back of my neck. Tingles run up and down my spine as he strokes the vertebrae's.

"Well, a friend of mine actually pointed me here." His eyes soften and almost glow in the sunlight. The adoration shows in his smile, threatening to make my heart stop beating.

"It's perfect."

I reach up on my tiptoes and press a kiss to his lips. Kade won't have any of it and pushes the kiss farther, opening me up and possessing my mouth.

"What would you think about waking up to this every day?"

I tilt my head to the side. "What do you mean?"

He turns me around so my back is pressed against his front again and wraps his arms around my waist while my fingers trace small patterns along his tanned forearms.

"The friend who told me about this place was Gail Lawry."

I furrow my brows. "Why does that name sound familiar?"

Kade rests his chin on my shoulder, letting me feel the steady beat of his heart against my back. My senses feel like they're on overload between the soft steel of Kade surrounding me and the picturesque nature around us.

"Gail is a real estate agent, one of the best in the area actually. She was at our last show and we started talking. I mentioned that I wanted to place some roots of my own somewhere. When I described what I was looking for, she said she had just the spot."

"But what about your parent's house? I mean your house? You're just going to sell it?"

He nods. "It's too small for what I have planned. I talked it over with my parents and they said whatever I choose to do is fine with them. A house is just a house. What you do with it makes it a home."

What he has planned? I look around, finally seeing the sign by the road with a giant red SOLD plastered across the front.

My breath hitches in my chest. "You bought it?"

I feel him nod against my shoulder and my legs threaten to give out underneath me.

"Sixty acres and it's all mine. The trees, the flowers, the meadow, the brook, everything."

"This had to have cost a fortune. Are you sure you want to live out here? I mean, wouldn't you be happier in the city, closer to all the entertainment?"

He tenses beneath my hands before pressing another kiss to my ear. "All I want is to be near you, all day long. I don't care about the rest of it. Besides, I'd like to think of this as more of a summer home for us."

Okay, now he's officially lost his shit. I wiggle free and face him.

"Why are you talking in code?"

His lips curl into a smirk. "Doesn't feel so good, does it?"

I place my hands on my hips and attempt a menacing glare. "That was a different situation. Not even comparable."

"Either way, you were holding something back and so am I." He closes the distance between us. "I want to build a house here and I want you here with me."

"But you said summer home. Where else are you going to be?"

"That's another surprise, but it's not ready. I'm working things out with that one."

I groan and turn my back to him, taking a few steps before facing him again. "Did you already sell your house?"

He nods. "Myles bought it. He's essentially moved in since we spend most of the time at your place. It only made sense. Don't worry, I gave him a good deal. Band discount." He winks.

"Don't you think this is something you should have discussed with me? Especially considering this affects both our lives? Plus, you're basically homeless right now."

He takes a step forward. "Are you kicking me out of

your bed?"

My cheeks heat up. "No. That's not what I'm saying. What I *am* saying is we should have discussed this first, not just assumed you'd be moving in with me."

Another step forward. "Okay. Let's discuss. I'm moving what little things I have left into your loft, we're going to build a house here, and live happily ever after. There. Discussion over."

"Ugh!" I walk toward the meadow, yelling over my shoulder. "You are the most frustrating man ever!"

"That's rich coming from you!"

I laugh and halt in my tracks. He's right. I'm not exactly the easiest person to deal with. I know it. He knows it. Hell, the whole world knows it. But this gnawing feeling eating at my stomach won't go away. Can we live here like he's saying? Wake up to this, to him, every day of my life? The smile pulls at my lips before I can stop it.

Kade catches up, walking beside me before grabbing my arm and gently pulling me back.

"Tell me what you're thinking?"

Worry lines appear around his eyes as he chews on his lip. I sigh and hold his hand. "It's beautiful. And the thought of spending any time here with you seems too good to be true. But it's too soon, don't you think? I mean, yes, we're in a really good place right now, but we're still discovering each other. It hasn't been enough time. Not to mention the fact you just admitted you're holding something back from me."

"This is a good thing, though. There's still some fine tuning to do and I've been sworn to secrecy until it's finished." He presses his forehead against mine.

I love it when he does that, looking deep into my eyes. I

can almost feel them go liquid with need and an overwhelming emotion that's getting stronger every day. It doesn't matter where we are; all we really need is each other.

That's because you love him.

What the hell was that? The other voice in my head is gaining strength each day we're together. I'm not sure what love feels like or if that's what I feel for Kade. I do know I have strong, deep feelings for him. I would do anything to see him happy, even if it means stepping away so he can follow his dreams. But isn't that what love is? Putting someone else's needs before yours?

I don't know the answer to that.

Kade patiently waits as I war with myself. What's he hiding? And why would we only be here in the summer? He must be leaving. It's the only solution I can come up with.

I clear my throat and meet his eyes. "I can't say yes right now. It's too soon." When his face falls, I place my hand on his cheek, bringing his gaze back to mine. "But I'm not saying no, either."

He narrows his eyes. "What are you saying?"

I let out a puff of air through my nose before speaking. "I'm glad you've found your own place. You have no idea how excited I am that you want to share this with me. It's going to take months to build a house out here and it's already late July. The earliest it'd be ready would be mid-fall?"

"Yeah," he says warily.

The smile appears before I can stop it. Getting on my tiptoes, I brush my lips against his. "If, in three months, you still want me living with you, I may consider it."

I want to capture the smile on his face in a photograph so I can remember it for years to come. You'd think I told him he won a million dollars instead of moving in with him. He pounces, lifting me high in the air and spinning us around.

"Three months is nothing compared to what I have planned for us," he says, letting me slide down his body. "So if you need this time to work it out in your crazy head, then I'll wait. Besides," he says, pulling me in so close that our legs are entwined. "I'll always want your ass, even when it's sagging to the ground in a few years."

I gasp and shove him away. For good measure, I smack him. Hard. Right on his shoulder. He barks out a laugh as I stomp away, giving him the finger. He thinks he's so damn funny. And my ass will not be sagging in a few years.

At least I hope it won't.

Note to self: make sure I go to the gym more often.

I walk into the clearing and find a spot in the tall grass. Kade's still laughing behind me, but I don't care. The scenery is enough to make me forget about things for a while. It's amazing how beautiful it is out here, how quiet and tranquil everything seems. I sit down and run my hands over the flowers, inhaling their light fragrance.

How could Kade afford this? I mean, yeah he probably used the profits from the sale of his house, but he doesn't exactly have a steady paying job so I can't see him qualifying for a loan. Maybe he has some money stashed away somewhere, oodles of it just earning interest every day that he's living off of. Or maybe he had rich grandparents who left him a sizable trust he can only now draw from.

This is all stuff I still don't know about him. And he wants to move in together? Shouldn't you know at least these basics before that happens?

I need to lie down.

The sun feels good as it warms my body. But a shadow blocks the rays and I cup my hand over my eyes. He's still smiling from his not-so-funny joke as he lowers himself to the ground next to me. I turn my head away before I start laughing with him.

"Come on, Adrienne. It was a joke. You know I love your ass."

"Humph."

I roll over onto my stomach, resting my head on my folded arms. Kade starts drawing circles on my lower back, something he usually does during foreplay or just after sex. It eases my muscles and ebbs the tension from my body, making me pliable in his hands. An involuntary hum of pleasure escapes. It's hard to stay mad at him when he's doing this, even if it's only pretend.

Soon his fingers tangle in the hair around my shoulders as he curls his body around mine.

"I'm still mad at you." It's a muffled response, but I'm so relaxed that even turning my head to face him seems like a chore. A hand wraps around my waist and tugs me toward him, making me flip over on my back.

"Look at me." I shake my head, but let a small smile twist at the corners of my lips. "I want to see those bewitching honey eyes." A kiss over one eyelid. "The ones with the specks of gold around your pupils, that dilate when you're aroused and sparkle when you're happy." A kiss over the other eyelid. "The ones I get lost in every time I see you and ache for every time I'm away."

Damn him. Using his words to woo me. It's like he knows exactly how to speak to my heart. Almost like he has the other half of it.

Kade places a finger under my chin, tilting it to the sky. Squinting against the sun, his black hair comes into focus first, moving with the breeze. On instinct, I reach up and run my fingers through it. I could do this all day. And he'd probably let me. The look of pure contentment on his face every time I do it tells me so.

"Where's your phone?" I ask.

With a puzzled look, he reaches into his back pocket and digs it out for me. Unlocking it, I find the playlist labeled "Adrienne" and hit play, laying the phone on the ground next to us. The list of songs he's put together is impressive just to tell me how much he cares. Once again he shows off his music knowledge, getting a mish mash of songs ranging from classical to oldies to pop and everything in between.

This playlist goes both ways, though. It easily could be used as my expression to him.

The sparkle returns to his eyes as "Everything" by Buckcherry plays in the background. His hand travels down my neck, between my breasts before resting firmly on my stomach.

"Are you trying to tell me something?"

How do I admit to him I feel the same way without giving him some sort of false hope? I can't guarantee I won't fuck this up any more than I can guarantee I'll wake up in the morning. But looking into his eyes, feeling his adoring touch, I want to try. God, how I want to try.

My breath hitches when his hand caresses the inside of my thigh.

"What are you trying to say?" he asks again. His fingers graze against the silk of my panties. All coherent thought is gone. I can't think when he's touching me like this.

"I'm saying I like you."

Lame. So fucking lame.

Am I twelve?

Two fingers press against my heated core, drawing out a moan and making my hips jerk forward.

"I think it's more than that. Don't you?"

Twisting my fingers harder in his hair, I have half a mind to drag him over me just so we can drop the conversation. The hard erection pressing into my hip tells me he wants the same thing. But the amused grin says he's enjoying my discomfort more.

"You know I'm not good at verbally expressing myself." Lifting my head up slightly, I lick at his bottom lip. A hum of pleasure leaves him; a low, sexy sound that rumbles from his chest. At this point, the panties are useless. They're thoroughly soaked and should be tossed to the side.

Reading my thoughts, Kade pushes aside the scrap of fabric, guiding two fingers deep inside me. I gasp at the sensation while he swallows my moans with his mouth. With another tug of his hair, he practically crawls on top of me. Our tongues keep tempo with his fingers, driving my need to have him inside me higher. His fingers briefly leave me, only to peel the panties down my legs. I drag my nails down his back, trying to find the smooth skin I know is underneath the cotton of his shirt.

When I tug the shirt over his head, he deftly rolls us over and I straddle his half-naked body. My hair hangs over my shoulders, shrouding us in a curtain of curls. Making quick work of his belt, I slide his pants and boxers down his legs until his cock springs free and lays thick against his abs. I lick my lips ever so slowly, feeling the sexual desires building around us.

"What are you going to do? You're in charge." The thick, gravelly voice has come out. It's music to my ears. Rough and needy, it's the second sexiest sound he makes. The first being the noise he makes when he comes.

Licking my lips again, I let my gaze fall onto his stomach. "I skipped breakfast today."

He raises an eyebrow in silent challenge. "And what are you hungry for?"

I lean forward, pressing my lips roughly against his, like he always does to me.

"You."

Oh, how I love the taste of his skin, savoring every inch as I slide down his body, nipping and sucking all the way to my prize. He takes a fistful of my hair, holding it away so he can see. I know he loves to watch me suck his cock, so I get in the best position for the show.

The first flick of my tongue has him jerking in my mouth. I love the salty taste of his skin, how smooth it is against my tongue. His grip tightens on my hair as I bob up and down, switching it up between long drags and short licks. Every groan, every instruction on what feels best drives me wild. I reach a hand between my legs and let my fingers slip through my folds.

"Fuck, I need you. Right. Now." Kade's barely hanging onto his control as his cock slips out of my mouth with a small pop.

Gliding up his body, I shift to straddle him before sinking down, taking him inch by glorious inch. It's always so much deeper this way, filling me to the brink. Once he's fully inside, I stay immobile, letting my body adjust around him. His hands caress my hips, sliding up my sides before massaging my breasts.

"Move." The light command has my hips moving slowly at first with my face hovering over his.

"I thought I was in charge," I say in a breathy voice. He drags the dress over my head and pinches my nipples, rolling them between his thumb and index fingers. I cry out with a mixture of pain and pleasure. Always the perfect mix.

He grunts as he increases the tempo. "Now it's my turn."

Bracing my hands against his chest, I sit up higher, grinding my hips and feeling the first jolt run through my body. Each thrust brings me closer and closer, squeezing him as he guides me.

"Fuck I love it when you ride me like this. I want to feel you come all over my cock."

Like a good girl, I follow his command, letting his words undo me. My muscles clench and release at once, wracking my body with spasms while digging my nails into his shoulders.

A few deep thrusts and a guttural yell, he comes inside me, milking out every last drop. Sweat glistens our bodies from a mix of the summer heat and the earth-shattering sex. He brushes away a few tendrils from my face and places a loving kiss on my lips.

"You look so sexy right now." He plays with my hair and I sigh against his chest, pressing a kiss on his pec.

"Yeah right. Pretty sure my hair's a mess and I have grass in places I don't want to think about."

The song switches, playing "1, 2, 3, 4" by the Plain White T's as I stare into his eyes. The words sink into my head as they float around the air. I've never felt such contentment, such perfection in my life. Being right here with Kade is what I want. I've never been so sure about anything before, even with my music career. What we share is beyond anything I've experienced and more than I ever thought I'd want.

Our lips brush against each other once more as Kade looks straight through to my soul.

"I love you, Adrienne."

He said it. He actually said it. Out loud. The words echo through my head as I try to process this information. I've had an inkling he felt that way for a while. It was in the way he touched me or picked out songs to play for me, even in the way he'd make love to me. But hearing it out loud, putting it out there, makes it real.

A lump forms in my throat as I trace his lips with my finger. I should say something. He'll start to panic if I stay silent any longer. And I don't want that.

"I–" The words get stuck and I chicken out. "Ditto."

He leans up and sweeps his tongue through my mouth as he pushes his fingers through my hair.

Sitting up, I rest my hands on his shoulders as he pulls away. "Ditto works for now, but mark my words, you will be saying them to me."

I get lost in his eyes as I nod. He's not wrong. I am falling in love with him, but I'm still afraid of screwing this up.

"I know. Just be patient."

He nods. "Get out of your head and everything will be fine. You'll see."

Reluctantly, I move off him, missing the intimacy already. Kade grabs his shirt and gently cleans us up before we get dressed. I arch an eyebrow while looking at the fabric in his hands. He laughs and shakes his head.

"I have another one in the backseat. However, don't get any ideas about washing this shirt. It smells of your sweet pussy, my favorite."

Heat rushes through my body as I think about him bringing that shirt on the road, smelling it when he gets lonely, possibly even jerking off to it while thinking of what we've just done.

"So do you really like it out here?" His voice brings my dirty thoughts back to the present. Bending down, he picks up his phone to shut off the music before sliding it into his back pocket.

The slight edge of worry surprises me, but I lace my hands with his and smile.

"I love it out here. It's the perfect spot to build a home for you."

"For us," he corrects.

"Don't put the cart before the horse. It's a marathon, not a sprint. We have plenty of time to reach the finish line. Let's just enjoy the moment before you have me running down the aisle."

Kade picks me up, carrying me back to his car with ease. As I wrap my legs around his waist, he lets out a laugh. "Baby, when we get to that point, you'll be racing me to get there first."

Fifteen

"**S**O HE BOUGHT LAND AND WANTS YOU TO MOVE IN with him?" Quinn asks around a forkful of fried rice.

I hover my hand over my mouth as I chew. "Yep. You should see it. Green hills, a meadow, lots and lots of trees, and I'm pretty sure there's a stream somewhere."

She nods and takes a large bite of her eggroll. "And your hold up is?"

I wipe my mouth with my napkin and sigh. "It's too fast. I mean, we've been together almost two months. Don't you think it's a bit extreme to move in right now?"

I've missed girl nights. Quinn's been on call twenty-four/seven since a weird strain of the flu had sent several kids to the hospital. This is the first opportunity we've had to veg-out in two weeks.

"Are you kidding me? When you know, you know. Since when is there a time schedule on how to do things in a relationship? Are you afraid your feelings may change once you live together?" She eye's the room. "He's practically a permanent fixture in your apartment now," she says, pointing to his guitar sitting next to the piano.

I shrug. "So, he keeps some stuff here. We mess around with the music he writes, doesn't mean anything."

Quinn quirks an eyebrow and darts to the bathroom, returning with two bottles in her hand.

"Okay, he has body wash and shampoo here, too. So what?"

She slams the bottles onto the counter and marches to my closet, pulling out several shirts from the rack.

"Oh. My. God, fine! He's basically, sort of, mostly moved in here. Will you stop?"

She laughs, siting back on the floor next to me in the living room. "No, but I'm proving a point. You two are already in a committed relationship. What's the harm of taking the extra step?"

The fork clangs loudly against the plate as it slips from my fingers. "You know why."

Quinn sighs. "Stop for a moment. Let's try something new, shall we?" She gives me a sympathetic smile. "Shut everything else off and think with your heart. What's it telling you?"

It's telling me nothing good will come of committing myself to Kade. That he'll be ripped from my life because I want something for myself. What will happen once he leaves? And he will. Now that the walls around my heart are gone, what's to stop it from breaking again?

"It's telling me things would be different."

"You're right."

Okay, I wasn't expecting her to agree. I open my mouth but she holds a hand up. "Tell me, if your parents were still alive, would you be in this apartment talking about this? No, you wouldn't. It also means you wouldn't be with Kade, either. This is what you're missing: a miserable life, doing something you'd grown to hate. You can't fool me. I saw it for years. The light in your eyes was fading with each performance your parents forced on you. Every night I prayed for it to come back." She looks down. "Maybe I'm to blame, not you."

I scoot over and clasp her shaking hands. "Praying for my happiness didn't cause the accident."

"And neither did your tantrum. It's the same thing. I didn't cause it any more than you did." Quinn catches my eye and smiles. "But you know what I see now? I see Adrienne Evangeline Carmichael, the talented pianist with the highest rated performance in the city every Thursday night. The woman who is dating the hottest up-and-coming rock star in the area. Sure, your path is different than what was paved for you as a kid. That's the beauty of the future. It's always in motion. You're living a life you want, doing things you enjoy, and being with a guy who thinks you're his whole world."

I blink back a few tears. "You think so?"

She scoots closer, grabs my shoulders and nods. "Because so help me, if you fuck this up, I'm going to kick your ass from now until the day you die. And then continue kicking it in the afterlife."

I laugh, blinking a few tears down my cheeks. "But–"

"Oh, my God, no buts!" She throws her hands in the air. "If I hear you ever utter that word again I will rip your tongue out. You deserve to be happy and to be loved by the sexiest man on the face of the planet. So shut the fuck up and move in with him!"

God I love her. She always knows how to simplify everything so it makes sense to my jumbled brain. Even if she does it in the most brutal way.

A smile slips from my face. "He told me he loves me."

Quinn's lack of response is rare. Rendering her speechless isn't something I'm used to. Minutes tick away as she stares blankly until confusion finally crosses her face.

"And?" I look away, but she forces me to look at her, impatience plastered all over her face. "You didn't. Please tell me you said something."

My heart slows as I recall how scared I was to say three little words out loud. "I said 'ditto.'"

"Ditto? Like the fucking movie, *Ghost*? Are you going to wait until he's dead before you say the actual words? Did you learn nothing from that movie?"

"Yeah, it taught me Patrick Swayze made a really bad choice in trying to pick a fight with a guy holding a gun."

Quinn sighs and takes her plate to the kitchen. She's not the only one who's disappointed in my answer. Three simple, easy words. Words I can say separately but freeze when they're strung together.

The feelings are there. They always have been, stronger than anything I've felt before. But the words…

The loud slap of the dishrag gets my attention and I look into the angry eyes of my best friend. "Okay, I can't keep quiet about this. Why won't you tell him you love him? You do, don't you?"

I scrape my bottom lip between my teeth and nod. "Yes, but it's still too fast."

"Enough with the timeline. Your heart knows what it wants. Just humor me and answer a few questions."

I carry my plate to the kitchen, leaning against the counter opposite to her. "Fine. Shoot."

"What's his favorite movie?"

I roll me eyes. "That's easy. *Die Hard* and *Bull Durham*. What does that have to do with…"

"What's his favorite shirt?"

Heat slowly rises up my face. Up until a couple weeks ago, I knew which one it was. But I'm not about to tell Quinn it's actually the shirt he keeps in the backseat of his car.

"His faded black Seether shirt. You know, the one he wore that night at Mickey's."

She smiles and nods. "If you had a normal life and saw him in a bar, would you approach him?"

If I thought my face was warm before, it's positively on fire now. Yet I can't seem to stop smiling. "Would I have approached him? Hell no. I'm not exactly the assertive type. Would I have objected if he came on to me?"

The memory of the night we met creeps in and pinpricks spreads through my body like wildfire. The way he smiled at me, the way he tucked my hair behind my ears, and how alive I became with very few words.

"There," Quinn says, pointing a finger at me.

I blink a few times before furrowing my brows. "What?"

"That, right there. The stupid smile on your face. You thought about the night you met."

"I was a hot mess that night. Who hits on a girl wearing a hoodie when he's surrounded by half-naked bimbos practically throwing themselves at him?"

She closes the distance and bumps my shoulder with hers. "A man who fell in love the instant he saw you. Don't you see? He saw you over everyone else, before he even really knew you. That's love. And he kept seeking you out, never giving up until you finally let him in."

"Only because *someone* had a hand in making sure he was everywhere I was going to be."

"Guilty." She grabs two bottles of water and hands me one. We walk over to the couch and sit on opposite sides.

"Okay, I will admit I was silently excited to see him at Copperfield's that night. One, because he saved me from Shane."

"And boy did he ever," Quinn says, waving a hand at her face. "That kiss was smoking hot. Hell, even I believed you two were a thing."

I smile. "It was pretty powerful."

"Powerful? You should have seen Shane's face when you two were basically fucking each other's mouth. He was fuming. It was awesome!"

"Anyway," I say. "The other reason was because later that night, when he brought me home, we really got the chance to know each other. It was a slow process, but it helped me open up to him." I chew on my thumbnail. "Did I tell you I played him a classical piece?"

Quinn's mouth pops open. "You did? Which one?"

"Not the one you're thinking, although I almost did. I played him one of my favorites. Very powerful and a little sad. I was hoping to scare him away. Obviously I failed."

"I'll say because that man is attached to you at the vagina."

"He is not!" I laugh and slap her knee. "But that night I made the choice to open up, like I couldn't help myself. We've always had a strong attraction, but that night, it was the first time I admitted to myself I could fall for him."

Quinn clutches her hands over her heart. "True love."

I run a palm over my face. I give up.

"Okay, I'm sick of talking about me. It's gossip night and I don't remember it involving my love life." I waggle my brows at her. "Tell me all about you and Gabe."

Quinn tucks her feet beneath her and smiles. She's practically glowing with just the mention of his name.

"He's an animal in bed. Holy shit. I've never had anyone make me come so many times in my life."

"Eww! That's not what I meant."

The pillow hits her in the face, making us both laugh like hyenas. "I know. I just wanted to see your reaction. It was classic." Her face turns serious. "But really, it is true."

"TMI. Anyway, how'd it go with your family? Sorry I had to miss it. Stupid Melanie getting sick."

"Good. It was a little shaky at first. He was so nervous. He knocked over my mom's vase in the front entryway, shattering it to a million pieces. Then he tripped over the hall rug and put his hand through one of the paintings. At dinner, he somehow managed to choke on a piece of bread. And once he coughed it up, it flew across the table, hitting my grandma in the head."

Tears stream down my face and while I clutch my stomach, nearly rolling off the couch. I think I may pee myself. "You call that a little shaky? How in the hell do you redeem yourself after something like that?"

Quinn wipes away a tear. "Needless to say, he was a little embarrassed and was ready to ditch me and my family. I thought for sure he'd run and I'd never see him again. Instead, he made massive brownie points with my mom by clearing the table and washing dishes, including the pots and pans. And when I say clean, I don't mean load them into the dishwasher. He hand washed everything. Mom told me I'd be stupid not to marry him one day."

"So all he had to do was wash the dishes to get back in her good graces?"

She takes a sip of water and shakes her head. "Oh, no. He has to come back and mow the lawn, weed the garden, and cook dinner every Sunday for a month. Then he'll be good."

"Poor Gabe," I say with a sigh. I knew he was nervous but wow. "He failed to mention all of this when I asked him. I'm so sorry I missed it."

"Mom was disappointed you couldn't make it. She understood when we told her why. But I'm glad you volunteered so he could meet my family. All in all, I think they loved him."

I stretch my arm over the back of the couch and let my head rest on it. "What about you? Do you love him?"

Her cheeks flush and she nods. "I think I do. He's not like any other guy I've dated. And I'm not just talking about the toe-curling sex." I scrunch up my nose. "He makes me laugh. Plus, all the sweet gestures he does like holding the door open or making sure I get the last soda in the fridge or the last Oreo in the package. He's always putting my needs before his. I've never had that before from a guy. Kind of a nice change of pace, right?"

Kade does the exact same things for me. Sure, he gets insanely jealous and starts pissing all over to mark his territory. He wouldn't do it if he didn't care.

"You're thinking about him again," Quinn says, nudging my arm.

"What?"

"You've got that look again, the 'Oh my God he's so hot and I'm totally in love with him' look. Why can't you admit it to him?"

I roll my head over and press my face into the cushion. "Because he's going to leave and it'll hurt that much more if I say it out loud." Not sure if she heard me or not. "Ow!" Guess so.

"Dammit, Adrienne! I love you. I do. You're the sister I never had. But Kade loves you. He's not going to leave. He will never throw away the best thing that's happened to him."

I rub my arm and draw my brows together. "How in the hell would you know that?"

A creepy smile crawls across her face. "Because he told me."

"Huh?"

"I have my ways."

"So, let me get this straight," I say, straightening up and facing her. "You've been talking to my boyfriend behind my back. About me?"

"Yep."

I run a hand through my hair and pull at the roots. "Why am I not surprised? What else do you know that I don't?"

"Stuff."

I raise a brow. "Just stuff?"

"And some shit."

I roll my eyes. "You're a shit."

"Bitch."

"Whore."

"Cleopatra."

"Huh?"

She laughs and sits up. "Yeah, because you're the queen of denial."

I shake my head and jerk Quinn to me, hugging her tight. "You know me too well. I do love you, even though you're a huge pain in the ass."

Quinn squeezes then pulls back. "Just do me a favor?"

"What?"

"Don't fuck this up."

I give her a weak smile. "I'll do my best."

Quinn leaves a few hours later and I head into the kitchen, cleaning up the mess before making my way to the bedroom with Kade on my mind. As if he knew I was thinking of him, my phone starts blaring "Smile" by Avril Lavigne, his designated ringtone.

"Hey, babe," I say.

"That's my line." I've missed hearing his voice. It's been, what, three days? I can't believe I miss him as much as I do. Something else that's new for me.

"Well, I'm borrowing it for the night. How's it going?"

He sighs into the phone. "It's hectic that's for sure. Definitely one of the biggest shows we've done. You wouldn't believe the size of the crowd last night. Five thousand people. It was insane. But the energy was huge and kept us going through two encores. We played a lot of our newer stuff and they ate it up. Wish you could have seen it."

Lightning Strikes are on an Up and Coming Bands tour, going to several venues in the tristate area. All five bands won their way onto the tour from the fan votes over the last few weeks. It gets them into the public eye, able to play in bigger venues, and expand their fan base exponentially. All of it helps get them to the end game: record contract.

I rub the space above my heart. "Wish I could have seen it, too. I knew you'd blow everyone away. You guys are the best. Soon, you'll be more than an opening act, signing the big contract, then you'll be–"

"What did I say about talking like that? Just stop right the fuck there. I'm not going anywhere without you next to me." His tone is angry, even though I know he's not. Annoyed? Yes. Maybe even a little frustrated.

"Yes, dear."

It brings a smile to my face, loving how comfortable we are with our banter back and forth. And I know that if I'm smiling, he is too. He keeps telling me about our strange connection, never really believing him until things started happening when he's gone. Last week, there was a huge thunderstorm. Lightning was streaking across the sky like crazy and the thunder was so loud it woke me from a dead sleep. Before I could even run to the piano, my phone rang and Kade was there to talk me down from my panic attack. Even in St. Louis, he knew I needed him. Said he had to call me, couldn't explain why.

"I'm serious. Don't make me say it again." Now I'm in trouble. I need to bring back the cupids and hearts again.

"I'm working on it. I'll do my best to lock up the insecure bitch inside me."

Success.

"Quinn was over tonight, wasn't she?"

"How'd you guess?"

I smile when he laughs. "Mmm, so sassy. These next few days need to speed up so I can have your sass all for myself."

"How many are a few? You've already been gone so long."

God, I miss him. Miss the way he hogs most of the bed and practically sleeps on top of me. Crave the way he holds me as I brush my teeth or makes breakfast because he knows I suck at cooking. These past few days, I've curled up on his side of the bed, hugging the pillow because it smells like him. Or wearing one of his shirts I find lying around, just to feel close to him.

"Another three days, possibly four."

"You're killing me, you know that, right?" I swipe a hand down my face and groan. "We haven't been apart for a week since we met. And I miss you. So much."

Tears well in my eyes. This is stupid. I shouldn't feel this lost without him here.

"I miss you, too. But it's only another few days, then I'll be home for a while." His voice gets low, more seductive. "Be prepared to call in sick when I get home. We have some lost time to make up. Pretty sure you won't be walking straight for days."

Everything south of my navel contracts, and I press my thighs together to stop the throb from progressing into a full blown need. "Promises, promises."

One of these days I'll learn not to poke the tiger while in his cage. "Just for that, make it three days of calling in sick. And don't think I won't talk to Gabe about it."

I roll my eyes. "Geez, don't get your boxers in a bunch. I'm teasing. What else am I supposed to do without you here?"

"Phone sex."

My jaw drops open. He did not. "Hanging up now."

"Come on, just a quickie?" He so damn cute when he begs.

"It's not the same. I don't get off as easily anymore by myself, unlike when you're with me."

I squeeze my eyes shut. *Stupid. Stupid. Stupid.*

"Soooo," he says, dropping his voice even lower. "You've tried it then?"

Ugh, walked right into that one. I pinch the bridge of my nose, letting out a puff of air.

"If I say no you're going to call me out, or badger me until I admit it, so I'm going to take the wind right out of your sails. Yes, I have tried it and no, it's not the same. Not even close. Before you, it was great. Since you, not so much. Happy now?"

"The thought of you touching yourself makes me very happy," he says, the phone going muffled for a moment. "Come on, humor me. Just slip a hand between your legs and tell me if you're wet. Don't bother with telling me what you're doing or wearing because I already know."

Twisting my lips to the side, I scoff. "Okay, smartass, if you can tell me what I'm doing, where I am, and what I'm wearing, I'll humor you."

There's a pause over the line before his quiet chuckle fills my ear. "If I know you, and I do, you're lying on my pillow, wearing my favorite shirt with nothing on underneath. And you're twirling your hair around your finger while biting your lip, secretly hoping I'll get the answer right because the thought of me listening while you touch yourself excites you."

How in the fuck does he do that? Is there a hidden camera somewhere in the apartment that he's watching me from? It's kind of scary how well he knows me.

"Am I right?"

My breathing spikes and I press my legs together, the pulse too strong to ignore any longer. And fuck if it doesn't excite me, thinking about what we're going to do.

"I hate you."

"No you don't. You love me." He tsks. "Wait, sorry, you 'ditto' me."

I know it drives him nuts I can't muster up the courage to say it, even though I do feel it. But right now, I have more important things to think about.

"I believe I was promised something."

"Are you joining me?" I ask.

"You want me to?"

Before I realize it, my hand starts moving down my body, floating over the well-worn shirt. "Yes."

The loud, telltale noise of his zipper being undone has my heart skipping a beat. We're really going to do this. Holy shit, are we ready for this? Am I?

"Where are your fingers?" he asks. I swallow thickly and play with the hem of his shirt.

"On my right thigh."

"Move them up slowly and tell me if you're wet thinking about me."

Obeying his husky command, I seek out the soft flesh between my legs. As soon as I hit the slick folds, I gasp. His responding growl is music to my ears.

"Tell me." He's breathing faster, more labored. A sound filters over the line, and I close my eyes, knowing exactly what he's doing.

"Yes, I'm wet for you."

"How wet?"

I slip a finger inside, feeling the walls clench around it as I slide in and out, the same way Kade does it for me.

"Dripping for you. God, you feel so good."

This should be embarrassing, but it's not. I should be ashamed of the way my hips move in time with my finger, of how I can picture Kade's hand replacing mine, caressing me, and cherishing me. His scent is everywhere, from the pillow and shirt, making it feel as if he's truly here, loving me with his body in the way only he can.

"Is your finger inside your slick pussy?"

"Yes," I pant out. Another moan falls from my lips, slipping a second finger inside, rubbing my front wall, finding the spot Kade always hits to drive me over the edge.

"Oh, babe, I can feel how tight you are. So fucking good."

I can hear him working his hand over his cock, probably imagining the same thing I am: his body over mine, hands brushing across every inch of exposed skin. Bringing each other to the brink of sanity.

"Kade, I need you so bad. Right. Now."

"Work your thumb in circles around your clit. I need you to come hard," he grunts.

He must be as close as I am. It's been days since we've had sex, days since I've felt him, kissed him, held him. I'm beyond desperate, needing to finish what we've started.

He's right about one thing. Listening to him, to the sounds he's making over the phone sets my nerves on fire with desire and my pussy begging for more.

I follow his commands, each and every one bringing me closer and closer. Until it all becomes too much. It's intense, real, leaving me emotionally raw. I know I said it's not the same. This time it's different. This time it's him doing it to me, just how I need it. Just how he knows how to give it to me.

"How close are you?"

He hisses through his teeth, sucking in air as fast as it's leaving his body. My own lungs feel tight as I try to match his pace.

"There. I'm there, Kade." I cry out, feeling the first wave crash over me, pulling me underneath the current. Everything stills as I pulse around my fingers, whimpering his name as I ride it out.

On the other end, I hear his strokes becoming faster; listen to the familiar hitch in his breathing. The same sounds he makes right before he empties into me.

"Fuck!" He repeats my name, a litany of reverence and adoration. It makes my eyes, and heart, flutter once more.

I feel spent, worked over as if I ran a marathon and beat my fastest time. Pulling my fingers out, I inspect them and smile. What Kade can do to my body amazes me daily, even if he's not in the room with me.

"If you want to go out of town more often, I'm okay with that." I smile and listen to his breathing. "That was intense and hot and…and…holy shit."

My stomach does that fluttery drop thing when he laughs. Mild aftershocks still pulse through my body, doing my best to ignore them. He's not here to stroke them away like he usually does.

"Just wait until I have you do that in front of me next time."

Holy. Fuck.

"Always so bossy."

Him and his dirty, filthy mouth. I love it.

And him.

"God, I fucking love you," he says.

I bite my lip. "Ditto."

Chicken.

He sighs. "One of these days, Adrienne."

"I know, I know. For now, it's ditto."

A yawn escapes as I stretch an arm above my head. We should be going to sleep; only I don't want to hang up. I want to cling to his voice, keep him with me as long as possible. Do anything to keep him on the line so I don't feel alone.

"It's late, and you need sleep. But I do love you," he says sweetly in the voice reserved for me.

The more appropriate responding words are right there on the tip of my tongue, only they won't come out. I've barely admitted them aloud to myself. Saying them to Kade may take a little longer.

"Hurry home please. I miss you."

"I miss you, too. Just a few more days, I promise. Sleep tight and I'll call you tomorrow."

We say goodnight and for the first time in a few nights, I fall right to sleep.

Sixteen

GABE SNAPS HIS FINGERS, TRYING DESPERATELY TO GAIN my attention, but it's futile. My focus isn't where it's supposed to be.

I haven't seen Kade in eight days. Eight days! It's been too long since I've felt his hot breath on my face as we slept, or snuggled with my ice-cold feet against his legs, then laugh as he flings the covers off the bed. His livid rants only increase the laughing until we finally settle down.

I swear I'll never understand the concept of getting naked to warm up, though his proven theory is effective.

"Huh?" I shake my head in order to function, but my brain is too focused on counting down the minutes until I see Kade again. If I talked to him I would probably be somewhat functioning, but the silence is putting me on edge.

"I asked if you had cut up the spare fruit tray yet. But judging by your space cadet capabilities, I don't think putting a knife in your hands is a wise idea. I'd rather keep all your body parts intact. A hospital run is not something I want to do tonight."

"Funny. You're a regular comedian," I quip back at him.

Gabe turns and cocks an eyebrow. "I'm damn hilarious, considering you've wiped down the same spot for the past five minutes. It's clean now."

I blink repeatedly at him then look down at what I'm doing. Sure enough, my hand is working in circles around the same spot while staring at the empty stage in front of me. Once realization hits, the rag falls from my fingers, landing in a pile. I run my hands over my face and groan loudly, much to Gabe's amusement.

"Fuck, what is wrong with me?"

With an arm over my shoulder, he laughs. "You're in love, that's what's wrong with you."

I shove him away and feign a scowl. "It was a rhetorical question. And who said I'm in love?"

He backs away with his hands up in defeat. "Hey, I'm just calling it like I see it. You two are all over each other and this is the first time you've been apart. Believe me, everyone has noticed how miserable you are."

Just to prove him wrong, I plaster a fake smile on my face, beaming with emotion I don't feel. "There. Bright and sunshiny happy. Better?"

He grabs his clipboard and starts working through the inventory sheet. "No, now it's just creepy."

I scoff and pick up the rag again. "Seriously, though. It's just, you know, I miss him. And he hasn't called yet today so I'm starting to get nervous."

Gabe glances at me out of the corner of his eye. "Maybe he's traveling." A faint smirk plays on his lips. "Did you ever think of that?"

"Maybe he owns a cell phone and he's driving, not flying. Ever think of that?"

He laughs. Not a small chuckle but a full-on, snorting laugh. Bastard.

"Okay, okay, fine. Maybe he's in a dead zone or maybe there's no service where he's at. I don't know why he hasn't called. But since you're living in la-la-land, why don't you go out on the floor and wipe everything down. You know, give the bar counter a break, save on the Formica a little?"

I huff out a breath and head to the main floor. Not because he asked me to, but because I wanted to.

Since no one has been here for a while, cleaning the tables is a breeze. But the closer I get to the stage, the heavier my heart sits in my chest.

If I close my eyes, I can see him when he was on stage a couple weeks ago. His energy astounds me; the way the crowd pushes him forward, the cheering fans, the cat calls from the women, the drunken guys spilling their beer while forming a mosh pit. All of it is a part of him. It's who he is and what he lives for. And the smile he wears on stage is real, but it's not his smile. No, Kade's true smile is reserved only for me. I see it every time we're together, even when we're fighting. It's a part of who we are. Opposites yet similar. Yin and yang. Sweet and sour, although if you ask anyone, I'd be considered the sour one.

The monotony of wiping down the tables has blanked my mind, easing it into a state of relaxation. Thinking of him is enough to ease me into a happy place. But I still crave his touch, his scent, just…him to bring me back to the real world.

When the hairs on the back of my neck stand on end

and a rush of tingles travel through my bloodstream, I gasp. My heart speeds and I still my hand on the tabletop while my eyes remain downcast. I may be mistaken, but I don't think I am. It happens. The first brush of fingertips along my spine. Starting at the base of my neck, his touch travels slowly down until he loops a finger into the back of my jeans. My breath hitches and my mind races.

"If you keep bending over like this, I can't be responsible for my actions. It's been too long as it is." The low, sexy growl of Kade's voice invades me as his breath beats against my ear. His chest presses into my back, causing my skin to prickle with heat.

Kade, my Kade has made it home. I flatten my palms against the table and press my ass against his hard bulge. Kade's surprising gasp excites me more, and my nipples tighten.

He's right. It's been way too long.

Kade leans further into me, leaving nothing but clothes separating us. And if I knew there weren't people around, there wouldn't even be that right now.

"I'm about to throw you down on this table and fuck you senseless if you don't stop teasing me with your tight ass, my little temptress. Exhibitionism is not my thing when it comes to you."

Every muscle south of my navel clenches turning me into a rigid pile of hormones and need. My already dripping sex is throbbing with its own pulse, beating solely for the pleasure that Kade brings. Fairly positive he'll need to carry me out of here because my knees will buckle the instant I unlock them.

"The same goes to you."

Kade grabs my hips, anchoring me to his body in a rather intimate pose. One I'm hoping we'll recreate later.

I can feel his smile against the bare skin of my shoulder, kissing near the roadmap of scars left on my imperfect skin. He traces each line with his lips, his silent way of kissing away my past.

"Kiss it goodbye," he told me one night. "You can't live in the past. What's done is done. All you have is the future and that means us."

I straighten, not wanting to give the few people in the bar a show. I'm sure we've become the center of attention as it is. Granted, it's only Gabe and Quinn, maybe a few early arrivals. I have no need to draw any more attention to my rock god. He does it well enough on his own.

Kade's mouth moves from my shoulder to my neck, licking a trail to his favorite spot behind my ear. "We need to leave. Now."

I wiggle free from his grip and turn to face him. Once my eyes fall to his body, I can't help but fling myself into his arms. A soft beard covers his cheeks, like he hasn't shaved in a few days. I have half a mind to tell him not to. I want to feel it scratching against my skin. Everywhere.

His lips find mine first, then his tongue sneaks out, gently pressing against my mouth. Need floats hot and heavy around us as my fingers tangle in his hair, pulling him closer to me. He rests a hand at the back of my head while the other travels down the length of my spine before firmly resting on my ass.

"Get a room you two," Quinn screams from the bar.

We smile against each other, slowing the kiss to a more appropriate level for the public eye. I can't let him go, though. Not yet.

"Fuck off, Quinn," I yell. "How about you go away for eight days and then try not to maul Gabe on your return. When that happens, you can have an opinion."

Kade smiles. I think he's proud of my response.

"Whatever. Just go fuck in the back room so we don't have to watch it."

We laugh together before peeling apart. Kade cradles my face, placing the gentlest kiss across my forehead before we walk to the bar.

"So we good?" Kade asks Gabe.

What in the hell is he talking about?

"Yeah, we're good," Gabe says, shaking his hand.

The tennis match my eyes are playing is beginning to give me a headache.

"Code," I simply say, drawing Kade's attention.

"You'll see, babe."

Just then, Melanie walks out of the back room, giving me a bright smile and a wave. I'm about to open my mouth, but Kade covers it with his hand, shaking his head at me.

"No talking. I'm kidnapping you for the next few days. Already worked out all the details with your boss."

He did what? What the hell! I honestly didn't think he was serious about that. My thighs press together, pushing away the urge below the surface. My bad boy rocker knows how to keep a promise.

Kade flings me over his shoulder and I scream out a surprised laugh, clinging to his back in the process. I won't complain about the up close and personal view of his perfect ass. In fact, I give it a playful smack as he strides us to the exit, laughing along the way.

"Kade! Put me down. I can walk." My breath is short between fits of laughter. The gravel crunches beneath his feet as he crosses the parking lot. I brace myself against his waist, expecting to fall into his sports car. When I'm flung upward into the cab of a truck, I blink several times and try to figure out where I am. The loud *thunk* of the door closing has me scrambling upright in the seat. It's definitely an older model due to the bench seat I'm sprawled across, not to mention the two-tone dashboard and non-digital dials.

"It's Myles's. I asked to borrow it for a few days," he says, answering my silent question.

"What do we need a truck for?"

The slow smile appears across his face, lighting it up instantly. "You'll see. I've got plans for us."

I cross my arms and huff out a breath. "I'm not having sex with you in the front seat of someone else's truck."

The transmission clunks as he pulls out of the parking lot, steering us out of town. He laughs then places his hand firmly on my thigh, pulling me closer to him. Of course, I don't hesitate, needing to be as close to him as possible. If only this truck could drive itself. I'd crawl into his lap…

Leaning my head against his shoulder, he drapes an arm over me, securing me to his body. His lips brush against the top of my head and I melt into him.

The scenery blazes by, not that I've noticed. The days have been getting shorter, signaling the end of summer soon. I close my eyes as I listen to his breathing, riding in complete silence otherwise.

The truck bounces a little. We must have gone off-road somewhere. I straighten up and look out the windshield, twisting my head from side to side. All he does is smirk when he parks the truck.

"Here?" I ask.

Nodding, he opens the door which is in desperate need of WD-40. "Here."

Kade pulls me to his side of the seat, helping me out of the cab before closing the door. With his body, he presses me against the side of the truck, nuzzling his nose into my hair.

This is what I've missed the most the past week. The intimacy of being together, the way he knows my needs before I do, giving me everything I could ever want.

"So why are we here?" I ask, breaking our silence.

Dusk falls around us, giving Kade a glow as the sun sets behind him. "Because I want to show you what's been going on with our house."

Grabbing my hand, he pulls me toward a cleared out section of trees. It's then I notice the giant construction trucks and piles of lumber lying around. A large cement slab occupies the middle of the space, pipes and tubing jutting up in what seems like random places. It looks huge, like a mansion is being built. But my sense of area isn't the best, so there's a good chance it could be a moderately-sized house.

"Your house," I reiterate.

The low growl coming from him stiffens my spine as he pulls me in front of him. Kade dips low, resting his chin on my shoulder and nips at the skin.

"Ours. And I don't want to hear otherwise again."

I wrap my arms around his, tracing the lines of his forearms while resting my head on his shoulder. "When did you start all of this?"

"A few days after I first brought you here. Blueprints

were finalized the next day and the construction company had an opening. The tentative day we can move in is the first of November, but I'm sweetening the deal if they can make it happen sooner."

I turn in his arms, placing my hands on his firm chest. "What happened to baby steps?"

He presses his forehead to mine and looks deep into my eyes. "Fuck baby steps. How about we go straight into making a baby?"

And just like that, a bucket of cold water is dumped on my fragile psyche. Whatever heat I was feeling is gone. I try to pull away, shaking my head while wrapping my arms around my waist. "Oh hell no. Nope. Uh-uh. No way. You are not getting me pregnant."

Kade's head tips back with a quiet laugh. "I can't think of anything sexier than seeing you pregnant with our child." He stalks closer, forcing me to retreat from his advances. "You'd looking hot as shit with that pregnancy glow women get, your boobs will be huge, which is an added bonus for me, and then being able to place my hand on your stomach and feel *our* baby move inside you. He'll probably be one hell of a guitar player."

Is he serious or trying to creep me out? Either way, I need to keep this buffer space between us. "Kade, you better be joking."

He moves fast, pinning me to the side of the truck, my hands above my head. The sheer force of his stare has me unable to look away. "I'm not joking, but I don't want it right now. Well, I do, but you don't, so I won't push it."

With each gulp of air, my chest presses into his. He wants to have kids with me? I never would have imagined those words coming from his lips. Not in a million years. To me, he's still this rock god always doing this own thing, never answering to anyone and not giving a fuck. The thought of him running around with a little kid never crossed my mind. Even if the image is sexy as hell.

This was never in my plans. Okay, so I don't actually have a plan. I'm sort of flying from moment to moment due to my history. Things happen to derail plans all the time. Cars crash. People die. Dreams get broken so there's no point in planning for something that may or may not happen.

"Kade." I breathe out, suppressing the urge to push my hips into him when I feel the hard ridge of his jeans press into me.

He releases my arms but holds me close. "Just know I'm making plans for us. Big plans. Life changing plans. And when you're ready, we'll start them."

"Can we please revisit this conversation later?" My palms start to sweat as I cling to his shirt.

"It's not up for discussion, so whatever you need to do to convince yourself, just go ahead and do it."

Then his mouth falls onto mine, silencing my fears as to whether or not I'm doing the right thing by staying with him. The fears I thought he'd buried start coming to the surface. My insecurities whisper in my ear, telling me not to worry about this because we'll never get to that point.

Kade picks me up, cradling me to his body as he carries me to the back of the truck, placing me on the lowered tailgate. I cradle his face with my hands and he smiles against them before pulling away.

"I need to get a few things first. Just sit tight and keep looking sexy."

Wrapping my fingers around the edge, I swing my feet carelessly as if I were a child. Glancing around, I take in the beautiful scenery before my gaze settles on the construction site. It really would be a great place to live with Kade. It's so peaceful and picturesque, a perfect place to raise a family. The onslaught of images fills my head as I picture a yard full of kids, screaming while playing on a massive wooden playground. Something Kade would go overboard in building for them. He's chasing them around while I'm swinging in a hammock, a small infant cradled against my chest, sleeping soundly.

An ache begins to form around my heart. A family was never in my plans. My parents never once mentioned anything about getting married or settling down with the standard two-point-four kids. But now Kade has given me that hope, a guide for the future. I don't know if I can shut it down.

He returns with a blanket and several pillows. Obviously my focus was too much on him to notice what was in the back seat. I watch as he crawls into the bed of the truck next to me, his muscles flexing and relaxing. The small back window is open and the soft sounds of a country song fill the evening air. Now, I'm not a country girl. Never have been, never will be. I know very few songs in this genre, most of them having been performed in the Nineties. But somehow, he manages to find a song I recognize. Kade sets up a makeshift area for us to lie down as Brad Paisley's "We Danced" plays in the background.

Without hesitation, I crawl next to him, curling my body into his as we look up at the stars peeking through the darkened sky.

"I've missed this," he says, whispering into my hair.

A hum of pleasure sounds in my throat as I press into him more. "Me too. Don't leave for that long again."

"I can't promise that, but I'll do my best. I swear."

And I know he will. I trust him. He does so much for everyone in his life, making sure they have what they need and are taken care of. I feel guilty for not being able to give him the one thing he wants the most. Those three little words that I feel but still get hung up when trying to say them aloud. Fear is a nasty bitch sometimes, even though I have nothing to fear when Kade's holding me tight.

The late summer air is still warm, but even if a cool breeze hit us, I'd never feel it. Kade shields me from everything except him. I trace circles over his heart as I tuck my head under his chin.

"What are you thinking about?" I ask.

He shifts to his side, facing me with a protective hand on my hip. "You."

Cupping his cheek, I feel the stubble against my fingers. "What about me?"

His hand wanders up and down my side, brushing against my breast before smoothing over my ass and pulling me into his body. "Thinking about how much I love you and can't wait to see you here next to me, by my side every day and night."

I worry my bottom lip between my teeth. "We're basically like that now. Not a whole lot is going to change."

Kade tilts my chin up, forcing me to look into his serious eyes. "You're right. Nothing major is going to change. Yet. But this house is a new start for us. It's not mine or yours. *It's ours.* No more leaving things behind or having a drawer at each other's place. Once we finish this project, it'll be ours. Together."

My heart beats frantically as his words swirl in my head. I don't know why I'm so amazed at his conviction to be with me, wanting to build a life together.

"I know nothing will change between us. It's only been a few months. But don't you think we're moving kind of fast?"

The pads of his fingers glide over my spine, sending a shiver up and down. "If I could have convinced you the first night to do this, I would have. But then circumstances were different and this wasn't a possibility yet. Now that I'm so close to the goal, I want you to share in it. I need you with me at every turning point down this road. Without you, it's not worth it."

What is he trying to say? I draw my brows in. "You're speaking in code again."

He laughs, the sound warming my soul. "Just a few more days and I'll clue you in."

"I don't like secrets." I purse my lips, which makes him laugh.

"And neither do I. Trust me, I'm dying inside from not sharing this with you. But I have to keep it quiet for just a bit longer. And when I finally get the green light, you are the first person I'm telling."

I can't help but mirror his smile. "Okay, fine. I'll let you have your way this time. But in the future there can be no more secrets, even if you're sworn to it."

The soft kiss he leaves on my nose causes my eyes to flutter. "Deal."

Crickets begin playing their melody in time with the other woodland creatures as nature fully surrounds us. In the dim moonlight, I trace his features with my eyes and fall further into the indigo hue I love.

"There's one more thing I want to talk to you about," I whisper.

"What's that?"

I throw my leg over his hip, practically crawling on top of him. "How much did you miss me while you were gone?"

There's a fire glowing in his eyes as his body sets off a blaze of heat against me. "We're all done talking now," he says in his low, sexy voice.

With that, he rolls over me, slowly stripping away our clothes. Sweet and gentle, we make love beneath the stars.

Seventeen

"**H**URRY UP, WE'RE GOING TO BE LATE," KADE grumbles from the kitchen. I scramble through my apartment, throwing clothes around in a desperate search for my shoes.

"They're not here. Have you seen them?"

He joins me with his hands shoved in his pockets, laughing. "Just put on another pair. I need to get there early to help set shit up. The guys haven't forgiven me from slacking off the last time you were around before the show."

That night I remember well. It's also the night I was told I couldn't work during his shows. Technically, Gabe never said anything about not attending them. Maybe if I sneak in quietly, he'll never notice. As long as the green-eyed monster stays contained, everything will be great.

"They're my lucky shoes. I need them." Another shirt sails by his head. For some reason, I have this need to wear these shoes tonight. There's a lump in the pit of my stomach, gnawing at me, telling me something bad will happen tonight. I can't explain it other than the nightmare that woke me last night. And for once it had nothing to do with the accident.

"Babe, just put something on. You don't need your lucky shoes. You've got me. Now hurry up. We have to go."

He hands me a pair of heeled sandals and I cringe. But I don't want to argue with him over this. It's the last night of my so-called captivity and I promised to watch his big show. He, in turn, promised something special for me, which means I probably shouldn't piss off the almighty rock gods above by jinxing anything.

Hence the need for the lucky shoes.

Once the sandals are secured, Kade wraps his arms around me. His hard body presses into me as he nuzzles near my ear, lightly sucking the lobe into his mouth. "God you look fucking amazing. I have half a mind to make you keep those shoes on later while I fuck you against the wall."

Oh, his dirty mouth. How I love the lascivious thoughts, picturing my back hitting the wall over and over while my shoes dig into his ass, pressing for more. If he keeps this up, I'll have to change clothes. Again.

"Promise?"

A devilish grin is all he responds with. It's never enough, though. I always need more from him, taking everything he has to give. The same for him, too. Kade can never get enough, sometimes leaving small marks and love bites across my skin. Normally, I would argue about being marked, but he never does it distastefully. It's not noticeable at first, only if you look closely can you tell the difference. It's the fact we know they're there.

"If you don't detach yourself we're never leaving my

apartment. And you said you're already in deep shit with the guys regarding your less-than-stellar work ethic."

Kade grumbles something into my neck, but I can feel the smile there as well. The way he makes my skin light up with that one simple sensation is enough, at least for now. Unfortunately, it also makes my nipples tighten beneath my tank top as he presses into me.

When he pulls back, his eyes run over my body, clad in the new ripped skinny jeans he just bought me. Another growl escapes him. "How am I supposed to concentrate when you're turned on right now?" He licks his lower lip and I suppress a groan.

"Do you need a cold shower? Or better yet, I can stay home and entertain myself so you can concentrate."

He scowls and grabs my hand, dragging me to the door while adjusting himself. Apparently I'm not the only one aroused.

"We need to go. Now."

I laugh all the way to the car, even though he scowls. Kade chants different phrases, ones I've heard before when he tries to get his mind away from sex. I don't help his cause when I place my hand on his thigh on the way to The Warehouse.

I have a new nickname now: Devil Woman.

When we walk in the stage entrance, the place is packed. Luckily, Gabe hasn't noticed me yet and I'm half determined to stay in the shadows so Kade will behave. It'll be safer behind the curtain, away from people so he can keep his protective eye on me.

The guys set everything up, moving speakers and tuning instruments, performing sound checks and the general bullshitting with the groupies flocking around the stage. Half-naked women with long hair curled to perfection and the full fuck-me pouty lips are all I see when I look over at Kade.

Of course they would be there. I mean, he's dressed to kill with those damned ripped black jeans and tight gray shirt, showcasing every muscle on his hard body. Hell, even I'm getting a little damp between my legs looking at him.

He turns his head, giving me a smile, reassuring that I have nothing to worry about. My heart skips and I blow him a kiss, my way of telling him I got his message loud and clear.

The phone in my back pocket buzzes, pulling me from my thoughts. An unlisted number appears on Kade's screen. Who in the hell is calling him from a blocked number?

I wave the phone in his direction. He quickly apologizes to the bimbos as he places his guitar in the stand and walks my way.

"Thanks, babe," he says, kissing the corner of my mouth before taking the phone. Kade stalks off to a corner, away from earshot.

He's never done that before, taken a call so I can't hear it. Every day he preaches about no secrets and having an open and honest relationship, forcing me to talk about things I never talk about or want to face. Yet here he is, taking secret calls and keeping something from me but I'm supposed to trust him. How can I when he doesn't seem to return the favor?

Doubt. I haven't missed you.

When he returns, there's a bounce in his step, giving me the biggest smile I've ever seen on him.

"You're chipper. Good news?" I ask.

He grips the back of my neck, pulling me to his mouth, scorching me with his kiss. I'm breathless and panting when he finally releases me, pressing his forehead to mine.

"The best news ever. Well, at least so far." He winks and my cheeks heat up. I know he's referring to my lack of response to all his requests: me loving him, me moving in, me having his children, and I think there was even a reference to us getting married in there somewhere.

Something is holding me back from answering him though. The nagging voice I've tried to put back in its place gets stronger every day. I want to give him the answers he seeks. God, I want that so much. And yet…

"That's great, Kade." It's hard to get excited when I don't know what I'm getting excited about.

"You know that secret I've been keeping from you?" He nuzzles into my neck.

A hum of pleasure sounds from the back of my throat. I nod, unable to do anything else when he pulls away from me. My skin cools at the lack of immediate contact, but heats again when he cups my face with his hands.

"So, here's the deal." He takes a deep breath, opens his mouth, but closes it quickly when Myles comes running backstage, grabbing his attention.

"Dude, you need to get up there. The crowd is going wild and Gabe says we need to start."

Kade's eyes flare, excitement and annoyance warring within them. "I need to talk to Adrienne first. I'll be up in a minute."

"No way, man. It's borderline mayhem out there. We need to go. Now."

Kade sighs and presses a kiss to my lips one more time. "I'll tell you at our first break. It's big, babe. Brace yourself."

They leave, making the crowd roar to life when they take the stage and sling their guitars over their shoulders. I slump against the wall, feeling as if my knees will give out at any time. Kade turns to the guys, telling them something, which makes them slap each other on the shoulders, followed by a round of high fives.

That's new. They've never done that before a gig. I wonder if it has anything to do with his phone call.

The first song blares through the speakers, rattling the walls and my body with the beat. It's a new song, one I've never heard before. Kade has been busy writing new songs; trying desperately to stay away from the covers they used to play all the time. The amount of talent he has astounds me. I'm waiting for the day he makes it big, playing in front of tens of thousands of people, winning numerous awards and being showcased on TV. The thought leaves a dark hole in my chest, knowing if he's doing all that then I won't be with him anymore. There's no way he'd want me when the whole world would be begging for his attention.

The flashing lights engross me, along with the screaming women as Kade walks to the edge, leaving his guitar in the stand before dropping to his knees and grinding his hips. Hands grab at him, placing their manicured nails over every inch they can get to. He flashes them a smile before standing and going over to each of the guys, playing up the crowd like he always does.

And I'm frozen, watching Kade in his element, seeing the joy on his face and even slightly turned on as the sweat drips down his hairline. It reminds me of sex. *He* reminds me of sex, in everything he does, every move he makes, every note he hits.

I rub the spot he marked before we arrived, still feeling his teeth scraping over my flesh while his tongue lapped and his mouth sucked. My skin pebbles as I drag my hand down the column of my neck, thankful no one can see me. No one, that is, except Kade, who just happens to be looking my way when my fingers finish their trail. Even in the bright spotlight, I can see his eyes flash with need. I press my thighs together as he continues to watch me, not paying attention to the screaming crowd anymore.

I point to the pit, tsking and shaking my head, reminding him where his attention is supposed to be. He gives me a panty melting smile and returns to the fans.

After a few more songs, he pauses, taking a moment to catch his breath and drink some water. Then I hear Brecken over the speakers, addressing the crowd about future gigs, listing the different venues they'll be playing. A few screams sound when they list some of the bigger cities. The strumming of guitars sound again, and they play one more song before retreating off the stage for their first break.

"You rocked it! God, you're so hot up there." I throw my arms around his shoulders, pulling him closer to me. His sweat-slicked face grins as he plunders my mouth once more, tasting and licking every inch he can find. I tangle my fingers in his damp hair, anchoring his body to mine.

"This crowd is amazing! There's so much energy out there it's almost visible." His body hums with excitement and I can't help but mirror his smile.

"Yeah, and did you see that chick who grabbed your dick? I've never seen fuck-me-eyes like those before," Paxton says.

What? How did I miss that?

"Oh, really?" My voice wavers slightly.

"I didn't notice," Kade says coolly.

Myles laughs and slaps his back. "Whatever. You turned so damn quick to hide your dick I thought you needed a break for a second."

I whip my head around as the first stab of jealousy sits heavy in my chest. "What the fuck, Myles? I'm standing right here."

At least he has the decency to appear ashamed. Brecken comes up behind me, placing his hands on my shoulders. "She may have fuck-me-eyes for Kade, but we all know he's got those same eyes for you." He jabs his thumb toward Myles. "Don't listen to him. He hasn't been laid in weeks. He's just jealous."

A friendly shoving match ensues, followed by name calling before grabbing their waters, draining them quickly. Soon the guys disperse into the crowd to mingle, leaving me and Kade alone. He cups my cheek with his hand.

"Don't listen to those assholes." I chew my lip, but he quickly releases it with his thumb. "I love you. I don't give a fuck about those girls out there. You're who I go home to every night. You light my soul on fire with the simplest of glances. It's you, not them. Just remember that."

I run my fingers down the side of his face, wiping away the drops of sweat as they trail down his neck. The amount of love he has still amazes me, even though I don't understand why.

"So what's your big news from before?" I ask, wanting to change the subject to a hopefully safer topic.

He grins widely, obviously excited to share his news. "You're going to go ape shit when I tell you." Paxton's voice cuts him off again. "Fuck." He sighs and runs a hand down his face. Lacing his fingers in my hair, he plays with the scar by my ear. "We keep getting interrupted. It's starting to piss me off."

I laugh and wind my arms around his waist. My nipples pebble again even though he's throwing off enough heat to warm the entire city. "Don't worry. Go be my rock god and we'll talk after the show."

Kade smiles, pulling my face to his before feeling his tongue invade my mouth once more.

"I love you," he whispers against my lips.

"Ditto."

I can't help the giggle when he growls at me. "You're going to be the death of me if you don't fucking own up to it soon."

"Baby steps," I remind him.

"Yeah, we talked about that, too."

Fuck. I had to remind him.

"Yeah, and my answer is the same there too. Patience."

He slants his mouth over mine one last time before taking the stage. When the first few chords sound over the speakers, I get antsy. I can't stay back here anymore. I'll develop claustrophobia if I do. The question is do I chance pissing off Gabe or go crazy?

Before I know it, I'm pushing my way through the sweaty bodies to the bar.

"Adrienne!" Quinn squeals.

I run over and throw my arms around her. "Hey! Some show tonight, huh?" It's hard to hear over the noise on the floor.

Quinn's face lights up and pulls me to her spot on the corner. The noise isn't quite as deafening back here and I'm still able to see what's happening on the stage.

"He's killing it. I can't believe how on fire they are tonight. And all these songs are just amazeballs! Did he play you his new demo yet? I was so excited all these songs made the cut before he mailed it out."

What. The. Fuck.

Maybe I heard her wrong. She must have said something else. There's no way Kade made a life-changing decision without talking to me. Especially after saying he no longer wanted that dream.

The transformation of Quinn's face answers all my questions as the color drains from her cheeks, looking suddenly ashen and guilty.

"I thought you knew. Oh God, I mean, Gabe's known for weeks."

The room goes silent. Blackness creeps in, giving me tunnel vision. He's leaving, probably going to L.A. for a huge contract. Then it hits me. The call he got earlier. But why would he keep this from me? Why would he clue Gabe and Quinn in before the girlfriend he supposedly loves? Did I push him to it through my paranoia?

Bile rises in my throat as the world slowly comes back into focus.

"Adrienne? Are you okay?" Quinn's voice vaguely registers over the pain lancing through my heart.

"I don't know. He kept it from me. Why wouldn't he tell me?" I whisper. A tear slides down my cheek, the track burning against my skin.

Quinn's blurry figure moves in front of me as I try to fight the anger and confusion.

"Honey, it'll be okay. Maybe he didn't want to get your hopes up. Or maybe it slipped his mind."

"But he told Gabe. He told you," I whimper, bringing the hurt closer to the surface.

She shakes her head, clutching my shoulders tight. "No, he never told Gabe. Paxton told Gabe accidentally. He was so excited about the demo that it slipped one night when he was drinking. But then he said something a couple weeks ago about Kade meeting with an executive. And their manager, Don, has been getting the final negotiations together while they've been on the road."

Even if Kade wasn't the one who said anything to Gabe, the fact is he never once discussed it with me, the supposed love of his life. The one he insisted he wanted to get pregnant less than seventy-two hours ago. How am I supposed to take this? Be happy for him? Which I am, knowing his dreams of being a star are coming true. Where does that leave me? I can't follow him to L.A. I can't go down that path because I have to stay here, where my parents are, where my life essentially ended ten years ago, damning me to a life in purgatory.

"I need to go." I pull away, feeling numb. She shakes her head and forces me to sit back down.

"No, you're staying here and going to act like a grown-up about this. You can't run away from him because if you do, if you push him too far, he won't come back. Is that what you want?"

Blankly, I stare off, unable to process her words. I can feel myself slip into survival mode, shutting down except for the vital functions, like breathing, even though it feels as if all the life has been sucked from me.

"I can't. He's going to leave and I'll be alone. I'm losing him."

Quinn bends down to my level, placing her hands on either side of my face. "You'll only lose him if you don't stop fighting your feelings for him. Why do you always do that? Have you even told him you love him yet?"

Something catches my eye by the stage. Kade found me in the crowd, a frown forming on his face. The energy in the room dims as his enthusiasm wanes. He knows something's wrong. During a guitar riff, he talks to the guys, indicating with his hands he wants to cut it after the song.

"I need to go." I spring to my feet, regardless of what Quinn says. Something else catches my eye as I stand. The blond that was all over him before rushes the stage, pulling him into a heated kiss and full-on gropes him in front of everyone. Her red nails run up his shirt before she grips his hair tight, pulling him closer.

Anger clouds my vision, red replacing the black. Quinn doesn't stop me as she witnesses the situation on stage. The woman's hand brazenly grabs the front of his jeans and I watch him roll his hips slightly, causing the crowd to erupt in an ear-splitting cheer. No one would notice it but me because no one knows how he operates. No one knows how his body moves when he's aroused.

But I do.

And right now, the feeling of betrayal is enough for me to not want it in this moment. Betrayal for his secret and for this display on stage, even if he's the supposed victim in the scenario.

I press through the crowd, needing to get as far away

as possible. Several guys try to stop me, grabbing me while trying to get my attention. Out of the corner of my eye, I see Kade leap off the stage, security dragging the blond away by her arms as the crowd cheers for her again.

I can't face him right now. Not until I have my shit together or calm the storm brewing inside me.

Another hand grabs my elbow and this time I turn to face the body I'm being pulled toward.

"Hey, baby, where you off to?" the guy asks. He's not bad on the eyes and I'm sure if I wasn't already lost in Kade I would have been all over him in another life. But my fragmented heart belongs to someone who's destroying it with lies and omissions.

Kade appears a few feet away. Maybe I should repay the favor.

I grab the stranger by the shirt, dragging him to me and kiss him hard. He gasps in my mouth but quickly recovers by grabbing my ass and pulling me closer. He tastes of beer and cigarettes, a mixture that has bile rising in my throat again.

I don't have time to process what's happening before I'm pulled back into Kade's hard chest. He tries to lunge at the guy, rage blazing in his stare. Fire burns in his eyes and I shove both my hands against his chest, pushing him away and continue walking toward the exit.

"Adrienne!" he calls out to me.

My steps falter at my name and the pull his voice has over my body. I want to stay, confront him on what I saw and what I know, but I'm hurt and confused and have the overwhelming urge to run.

"Dammit, stop!" He pulls my elbow, spinning me

around when I'm several feet out the door.

"Get the fuck off me."

There's panic in his face as his arms fall limply to his sides. "Babe, it's not what you think. I swear to God I don't know who she is."

I flex my hands at my sides before balling them into tight fists, turning the knuckles white. I grit my teeth as my jaw locks. "That's not what it looked like to me. It wasn't like you were fighting her off."

He runs a hand through his hair. "What the fuck did you want me to do, huh? Punch her? It's all part of being on stage. Girls throw themselves at me all the time, but I never give them another look."

I deepen my scowl as we continue our standoff in the middle of the sidewalk. "Are you fucking kidding me? You can push her away! And I sure as fuck don't expect you to kiss her back or roll your hips into her hand when she grabs your dick."

Kade's face reddens as he looks around. The scene we created inside was embarrassing enough, and this isn't helping. Tension's evident in his shoulders before he speaks again. "I did not kiss her back and I sure as shit didn't roll my hips into her. I don't know what you saw but that's not what happened."

"I was right there, Kade. I saw the whole fucking thing. It was a slight movement, but I'd know it anywhere because I've been on the receiving end of that move when we're in public."

He starts pacing, swearing up a storm under his breath. "You're reading too much into this. *She* was the one who came to me. *She* was the one shoving her tongue down my throat. *She* was the one grabbing me. And where were my hands the entire time? Not on her. Not one. Fucking. Time."

Thankfully no one is around to witness this debacle. He's slipping through my fingers. Actually, I'm pushing him away, saving myself from a pain I knew was going to come sooner or later.

"Fine. Let's say how you remember it is true. What about Myles's comment earlier? How many other times has this happened when I wasn't around?"

Kade lifts his face to the sky. "Fucking Myles. Can't you just ignore him like everyone else does? He doesn't know what he's talking about half the time and the other half is complete bullshit. You can't take him seriously."

"Then why do you let him say shit like that? Especially to me. Never once have you stuck up for me, told him to fuck off or shut his mouth when he hurts my feelings. Why do you always brush it off like it's no big deal?"

"Because it's not! He's a goddamn idiot. But he's one of my best friends so I'm used to brushing him off. I've never had to defend anyone to him because everyone knows how he is."

That hurts. "So I'm just supposed to sit there and take it because it's his personality to be a douche?"

Kade sighs. "Of course not."

I cross my arms over my chest. "Would you let anyone else speak to me like that?"

Realization hits him and he hangs his head, shaking it. "You're right, I'm sorry. I'll talk to him after the–"

"So when were you going to tell me about your record deal? Were you going to call me from L.A. when you made your first million? Or perhaps when I'm watching you on TV and another woman put on the same show I just witnessed?"

Yeah, that hit the mark. He cringes and shoves his hands into his pockets. "How'd you find out?"

I laugh spitefully, something not even recognizable to me as mine. "It sure as shit wasn't from you. No, I had to learn about my boyfriend's ambitions through my best friend. Why the fuck didn't you tell me about the negotiations?"

He takes a cautious step toward me, but I retreat, keeping him at arm's length. When he reaches for me, I hold my hand up and shake my head. The crushed look on his face breaks my heart even more.

"I didn't want to say anything because I wasn't sure what was going to happen. Didn't want to get your hopes up in case it all fell apart." He turns his head away. "I tried earlier when I got the news from Don that everything was signed and waiting for us tomorrow in his office. That we could finally start our life together."

I scoff. "How can I start a life with someone who can't even trust me with his plans for the future?"

"That's not it and you know it."

"Really? Gabe and Quinn knew. Hell, so did your entire band. All without speaking to me – about my life, *our* life." I grit my teeth. "I'm giving you a piece of me, and right now that's a hell of a lot more than what you're doing. I can't make decisions for you, but it's okay for you to do it to me?"

He blows out a frustrated breath. "You've known my plans all along. I've told you time and time again that I want you right here with me, by my side. I've never hidden that from you. Where the money was coming from to give you the life you deserve was inconsequential at the time."

My back stiffens and I take a step forward. "I never

wanted material things and you know that. I never wanted anything other than you."

"Talk about fair? You gave me only a fraction of you, fuck not even that sometimes. And you got me, all of me!" An angry tear slides down my cheek. "I love you and what do I get in return?" His jaw ticks as he takes a quick breath, anger flaring in his eyes. "You can't even say you love me back. I get a fucking copout instead."

My palm stings as an angry red mark colors his cheek. If his aim was to destroy what's left of my heart, he just hit his target. The stinging of my palm doesn't come close to the pain he's caused, even though he's not wrong. All we're doing now is hurting each other. We'll never recover if we keep this up.

I break our stare down first, turning away. "Then what are we doing, Kade? Why are we putting ourselves through this?" My voice trembles as I try to keep everything in check.

He turns his back and drops his head on a sigh. When he faces me again, pain and regret show in his eyes as he searches for some sort of answer.

"I know why I'm putting myself through this. And I'm looking right at her. You are my reason for everything, Adrienne. I would move heaven and earth to make you happy. But it's becoming obvious that you don't even know how to make yourself happy. How can either of us expect me to know if you don't?"

"So what are you saying?" I wrap my arms around my middle, trying to swallow past the lump in my throat.

He closes his eyes briefly before finding mine. "I fucked up, yes, but I'm not the only one to blame here. I want you in my life but living in constant limbo with you isn't working for me anymore." My heart slows as Kade swallows hard. *Please don't say it.* "I want it all, with you, and if you can't do that, I'm done."

All the air leaves my lungs in one swift whoosh. I knew it. He's leaving me. He couldn't handle my darkness. Even knowing it was coming didn't prepare me for the hurt. And it does hurt. So much so that it's like a thousand knives stabbing me in the chest. This is what I get for pretending I could have it all. But I'm not the only one going down. Kade's devastated look puts the final dagger in my heart.

A sob escapes as a hot tear rolls down my cheek. "I'm sorry I couldn't be everything you need."

Kade shakes his head and pulls me to him, placing his lips softly on my forehead. Something wet hits my skin, but it's not my tears. I stare into his red-rimmed eyes, wanting to take everything back. All the crap I just spewed, all the intentional pain I just caused, everything. His Adam's apple bobs again. "You're my world, Adrienne. I'm just sorry I couldn't make you see it."

And just like that, he turns and walks back inside, leaving me broken and sobbing on the sidewalk. I clutch my chest as I crumple to the ground, gasping for air. Every emotion, all the pain wants to leave at once. All I can do is cry.

He's gone.

And I'm alone.

It's what I wanted.

What I knew would happen.

I should have learned my lesson from before.

I should be careful what I wish for.

Eighteen

It's been one week since my world shattered to pieces. Seven long, punishing days. Kade left me standing alone on the sidewalk, my heart bleeding open for the world to see. It's my fault. I pushed him away, my darkness too much for him to bear.

Each time I walk into the apartment, it feels cold and desolate. Missing the usual spark and warmth only he brings. Everything is wrong. The bed's too big, the pillows too cold, the blankets not enough. I wake in the middle of the night; hopeful I'll feel his warmth but find emptiness instead.

He's gone.

The piano has been my savior. The haunting melodies ground me, keeping me a prisoner to the pain I've caused. The hurt I feel. The loss I bear. Kade was right to let me go. The devastation swirling in his eyes is something I will never forget. It's what I do, deliver destruction wherever I go.

I know I should cut the ties, find resolution in my

music, but without Kade, music has no meaning. No life. Without him...I'm not me. Once again I'm dead on the inside, but the thought of reverting to my old self is worse. So much worse. I can't keep doing this, living the way I have. Not after I've tasted what nirvana is like. Because that's what we had, our own piece of heaven.

Chopin's "Prelude No. 20" is on repeat, my fingers effortlessly gliding over the keys. My cracked lips and swollen eyes a testament to the torture I've created. How can I remove him from my thoughts, my dreams and memory...or my heart? A slow tear slopes down my nose, splashing onto the ivory key.

This time there is no end to the amount of salt water pouring from my eyes - my soul.

He left me. He was supposed to love me.

He lied.

No, that's not true. He didn't lie. I lied, to myself and to him. Every day without telling him how I felt was just another dagger to my heart. It wasn't fair to him. He was the innocent bystander, thinking I was someone whole, someone worthy of his love.

"I miss you. So much," I whisper to the air, praying the words will find their way to him.

The memories won't stop: making love under the stars, waking up tangled around him, the way my body fit perfectly against his side, the tender way he touched my face when I was feeling down. The way his smile would illuminate my world, bringing me from the darkness and into his light.

His kiss. I miss that the most. If I close my eyes, I can still feel his lips on mine. Claiming me. Owning me. Cherishing me.

Loving me.

Few things I regret in this life. One being the last words I said to my parents before they died. The other is not living my life to its potential. In doing so, I destroyed the vision my parents had for me, and destroyed myself in the process. But Kade saved me, whether he knew it or not. He showed me where I've gone wrong, forced me to face the hard truths, even when I didn't want to.

I don't regret loving him.

I regret breaking him.

The ringing cell in the living room draws my attention, pulling me from my reveries. I swipe my fingers under my eyes, brushing away the tears before answering on the third ring.

"Hey, Quinn."

"Hey." Her soft, gentle voice is barely above a whisper. "How are you?"

I shuffle to the couch to sit, leaning my head back and tossing an arm over my eyes. "Well, I'm here, so fine I guess?" It's hard to answer in anything other than a question because at this point I'm not sure what to feel.

"Do you need me to come over? We can play cards or watch really bad movies."

I shake my head as if she could see it. "No, I'm good. Thanks for offering, though."

She clears her throat and I dread the words I know will come out of her mouth. "Have you heard from him?"

Pain rises again through my body. Tiny pinpricks crawl over my skin, ripping open the wounds that refuse to heal. "No."

The phone rustles in my hand as I adjust into a supine

position. "He loves you," Quinn says over the loud pounding of my heart in my ears. "I know."

"And you love him."

A fresh tear slides down my left cheek, pooling into my ear. "I know." A silent sob rips from my chest as I attempt to beat back the hurt from resurfacing. "I miss him and I fucked it up beyond repair."

She consoles me with silence, knowing this is something I have to work out inside my head. My conscience has to be clear of all my wrongdoings before I can begin to step forward with a future. A future that was so bright and perfect only a week ago.

"You can fix this. Your relationship is not completely broken. Tell me again what he said to you."

Blowing out a trembling breath, I close my eyes and bring myself back to that night. "He said as soon as I figure out my shit to let him know."

"No he didn't and you know it."

"He basically did. I can read between the lines."

"Okay, and what do you think that means?" she asks.

"I don't know. I mean, yes I know I'm fucked up, and toxic, dark and tormented. I get it. And I knew I'd drag him down to my kind of hell. But at least he was smart enough to let go and allow me sink to the bottom while he floated safely back to the top."

"Stop right there," she interrupts. "That toxic shit, that darkness and solitude you've resigned yourself to is what you need to figure out. You don't see what we see: a beautiful soul capable of having everything you want, including love."

"But I killed them."

"No you didn't. Even if you hadn't fought with your

parents, there's no way to know if the outcome would have been the same. Life is unexpected, and not everything goes as according to a plan. You have to ride the curves and pray for a straight and narrow to eventually show."

More tears fall down my cheeks as I take in what she's saying. Perhaps my selfish ways didn't cause the accident. Maybe the outcome would be the same and I'd still be alone.

"You still there?" she quietly asks.

"Yeah." I clear the thickness from my throat. "I need some time to think for a while, okay? I'll call later," I whisper. Hundreds of possibilities flood my brain, causing an ache to settle directly in the middle of my forehead.

"Okay, sweetie. Call me if you need me. Should I stop by later to check on you?"

"No. I want to be alone for right now."

Her soft sigh hits me directly in the heart. "If you say so. I love you."

"Love you too, Quinn."

I hang up the phone, tossing it onto the coffee table. Her words are still jumbled inside my head, pulling me in many directions as I think about the last ten years. Is it possible she's right?

Thunder rolls in the distance, making my muscles tense. But the urge to play isn't there. The piano doesn't hold the same refuge for the storm anymore. Only one thing can do that now, and he's a thousand miles away.

Kade told me that I only allowed him the pieces of my heart. He was right. I let fear and guilt dominate my existence. As Quinn's words still linger in my head, mixing with words that Kade always said to me, a feeling of peace comes over me, blanketing me with a warming embrace.

My parents would be ashamed if they saw my life now. I survived the past ten years the best I could, but now that I'm older and able to make the choices for myself, they'd be disappointed. I know they would because I'm disappointed in myself.

I have things to finish, to put back together in order to be worthy of loving Kade. I spring from the couch, grab my keys off the counter and race outside into the pouring rain, heading straight for my car with a newfound determination on my life.

Nineteen

"**Y**OU DID WHAT?" QUINN SCREAMS AS I HOLD THE phone away from my ear. She about blew out my eardrum.

"I quit. I need to fix my shit, right? Well, this is a start."

This change is completely out of the norm for me. I knew Quinn'd be upset and was anticipating her call, just not ten minutes after giving Gabe my notice. Surprisingly, she hasn't said a word about quitting Copperfield's. But we both knew getting out of there was inevitable—only a matter of when. Today.

"What the fuck? You can't just quit. What are you going to do?"

A smile plays along my lips. "I need to find me and I can't do it there." My voice is soft and light. "You'll understand soon."

She's silent for a moment. So quiet I check the phone, making sure the connection wasn't lost. Cell reception isn't the greatest here.

"I hope you know what you're doing," she finally says. She knows better than to fight with me after I've made my mind up.

"I don't, but I have a good idea. I'll still be around, just taking some time to reflect on things."

"Like Kade?"

I laugh for the first time in days. It actually feels good to do it. "Like life in general."

"Just be careful, okay? Love you."

"Love you, too." I smile. "I'll call in a few days."

Hanging up before she gets the chance to respond, I shove the phone into my bag and sit against the fallen tree, staring at the construction site. Hammers and drills wail in the background as a breeze carries the smells of late summer. It pulls at my heart and soul while watching my future being built in front of me.

I don't really have a plan, more of a general outline on how to feel better. And somehow, I find myself here, watching the future Kade offered weeks ago. More trucks occupy the space each day, shaping it into something to fight for, rather than against.

Twirling the pen through my fingers, I chew on my bottom lip. So many thoughts travel through my mind and I write down each one as they appear: ideas on how to achieve my goal without failing.

With a few last scribbles, I close the notebook and shove the pen into the spiral binding. All this planning and waiting has a purpose. It's going to take time, but the more I spend here, the more everything feels right.

I dig my keys out and walk to my car, waving to the guys as I pass by. They've grown accustomed to my presence over the last few days, as long as I stay out of their way.

The hum of the engine doesn't drown out the thoughts streaming in my mind. My grip on the steering wheel tightens, and my pulse kicks up. Maybe I should abandon this idea and beg Kade to forgive me? But what good would that do? He would take me back and I would feel like shit because I didn't work out my issues, instead covered them up with a Band-Aid. No, I can't do that to us. Today I fight. I'll find my way back to life...to Kade.

There it is. Mile marker 159. I swallow hard and pull off to the side of the road. The clear blue sky is calm, quite the difference from ten years ago when the heavens opened and unleashed their torrent on the earth. I walk to the makeshift memorial, still standing after all these years.

Two simple white crosses, each decorated in purple and yellow silk flowers, sit off to the side. A testament that two people lost their lives here. Quinn and her parents put them there while I recovered in the hospital. They should have put three. Each step gets harder and harder. Sweat covers my palms and my throat dries.

Breathe. Just breathe.

A few fallen leaves cover the grass as I sit next to the crosses, hugging my knees to my chest. On a deep breath, I close my eyes, unable to stop the memories of the last time I was here.

The screeching tires, the crunching of glass, emergency crews twisting the metal from my body, attempting to save me. The silence in the front seat as I hovered on the edge of consciousness. Chills run down my spine, along with a tear down my face.

"Mom, Dad," I whisper, resting my cheek on my knee as

sleep takes me over.

"Dad, can I please skip the performance and go to the concert with my friends? Just this once? I promise to practice extra hard and even squeeze in more time with the orchestra, if they let me."

Rain pelts the windows as lightning flashes across the sky. Dad is quiet as he tries to maintain control of the car.

"Adrienne, your mother and I have gone over this with you. We're not comfortable allowing you to go on an overnight trip with your friends, especially when that boy will be with you." He sighs. "This performance is important for your future. We're only trying to keep your best interests at heart."

"Sweetie, the timing isn't right. There's so much that's planned for you already and performances cannot be changed. You understand, don't you?"

I look toward the darkened sky and sigh. "I know you want what's best for me. Can you try to understand where I'm coming from? This is all I've been doing since I was three years old. I've never had a normal day to myself. All of my other friends go to the movies, or have sleepovers, or just hang out at the mall. I've never once experienced that. My whole life has revolved around the piano." My voice grows quiet when I face the front again. "Just once, I want to be normal."

Another bolt of lightning dances across the sky, followed by the hollow sound of thunder as it shakes the car. Mom looks at Dad, a silent exchange passing between them.

"Adrienne, we..."

Tires screech, followed by the blinding lights from the oncoming truck.

Mom screams. Dad holds his arm out to shield her, his final attempt to protect her.

Helplessness fills me as I watch the two people I love most take the brunt of the impact.

Pain radiates through my head, blurring my vision to the point of blacking out. A car horn sounds in the distance, barely recognizable. I feel light, lifeless, like I'm having an out-of-body experience.

Am I dead? I don't feel any pain, just the sharp chill of dread covering me. When I open my eyes again, I see them, standing in front of me as if no time has passed.

"Adrienne," Dad calls while extending his hand to me.

They're just out of reach. I try and try, but I can't touch them. Something's holding me back, stopping me from joining them on the other side.

"Dad! Mom! I'm here." I try in vain but still can't move. "I'm sorry."

Mom shakes her head as a tear slips down her cheek. "Don't be sorry. It wasn't your time. We didn't want to leave you behind, but it wasn't our choice. Please don't blame yourself for what happened." She smiles, her eyes shining with love and peace. "This is your time now to choose your own path, to find what makes you happy. It's what we've always wanted. Find someone who loves you and will take care of you. Make sure he shares your interests and will encourage you to always follow your dreams."

Tears flow freely, wetting my cheeks before falling to the ground. "Don't go. I'm so lost without you."

Dad wraps his arm around Mom's waist with a smile. "Make sure he's worthy of your love because you're worthy to receive it. We'll be looking over you, helping you when you need it."

A sob escapes. Cold numbness still consumes me, but I

find my voice through the tears. "I love you."

Mom rests her hand over Dad's heart. "We love you, too. Go and live your life. Find your happiness and make your life into something you're proud of. Just like how proud we are of you."

She blows me a kiss and their forms float away, carried by the breeze up to the clouds.

I startle awake and clutch my chest. Tears stain my cheeks while taking in slow, shuddering breaths. It was a dream, not a memory for once. What does it mean?

A hand presses down on my shoulder and I yelp. "Are you all right, Miss?" a voice says.

Flecks of dirt and grass fall from my clothes as I stand. Shielding my eyes from the sun, I reply, "Um, I think so."

He smiles and my breath catches in my chest. The resemblance to my dad is striking. A little grayer on top, and slightly taller, but has the same strong facial features.

"Are you sure? You look a little lost."

I chew on my bottom lip before nodding. "I am. Was." I smile. "But I think I know my way now."

He shoves his hands in his pockets with a smile. "Then I best be on my way. Just wanted to make sure you weren't hurt. Not often you see a young lady sleeping on the side of the road."

I let out a quiet laugh. "I suppose not. Thank you for stopping."

With a nod, he returns to his car and drives down the road until his tail lights are no longer visible. Opening my own door, I glance back at the white crosses and whisper my love to the sky. With a newfound peace and purpose, I head back to the city, knowing exactly what I need to do.

It's been weeks since my heart left me. Even though he's not here physically, Kade is always in my dreams, reminding me of what I'm working toward. I smile as the last piece is put into place, amazed at how easily things have happened.

Kade was right about one thing. Sweetening the deal to finish the house before November definitely made them work faster. I shake hands with the construction crew, thanking them for humoring me these past few weeks as I stayed on site, trying to make sure everything is set up and ready to go.

Since she's an expert, I enlisted Quinn's help in my stalking efforts, even going so far as asking Gabe to set up a meeting with Kade during open mic night at The Warehouse. Kade was happy to accept since he was in town anyway now that the house is finished. I was lucky enough to get the time off from my new employer, who has been more than pleased with my dedication to the orchestra. Apparently old habits die hard.

My heels click against the wood floors of the open-concept living room, which I've decorated in soft, neutral colors. The late October breeze floats through an open window. It's chilly outside, but I have to get the new paint smell out. Nervousness sets in as I wring my hands together. God I hope he likes it.

I walk to my prized possession next to the giant floor to ceiling windows overlooking the meadow. Kade really did well designing this house. Everything has a place for his stuff and mine, creating a space that's ours. It's times like

305

this I'm grateful for his foresight as well as his strength in our love.

Glancing at my watch, I grit my teeth and grab my keys off the table in the hall. Locking the door quickly, I climb into my car and drive back to the city, toward the place where my heart waits for me.

I pace the floor backstage, chewing on my lip and feel the first drop of sweat form on my brow.

"What if I'm too late? What if he rejects me like I rejected him?"

"Impossible," Quinn says, trying to calm my fears.

It's been two months since we last saw each other and not exactly leaving on the best of terms. A lot has happened since that night. I've changed, thanks in part to the revelation on the side of the road. It allowed me to see the path I want, unsurprising that it leads straight to Kade.

Quinn's phone buzzes in her hand. "He's here." Her bright smile eases my fears some, but it doesn't make my heart slow down any.

I give her a weak smile. "Do you think he knows?"

She shakes her head. "I doubt it. Gabe's been really great at keeping Kade in the dark. You're just lucky Kade put him in charge of overseeing the house plans while he was away."

"Can you see him?" My stomach rolls, threatening to spill today's lunch all over the place.

Quinn peeks her head around the corner. "He looks good, better than I remember."

"Am I crazy?" I need reassurance, someone to tell me everything will work out.

"I think it's extremely romantic and long overdue." She tucks a stand of hair behind my ear and smiles. "Gabe is going to call a few people up first then he'll give you a nod to come onstage. I'll keep Kade distracted so he won't see you until you're ready."

I smooth a hand down the blue silk dress, brushing away a few wrinkles. This dress is his favorite, holding so many memories of our first night together. And he says it makes me look sexy as fuck.

Always the romantic.

Quinn's phone buzzes again, and she bounces on her toes. "It's time." She hugs me tight, placing a small kiss at my ear. "Good luck."

After Quinn leaves, my nerves kick into high gear. The first two singers take the stage, using the house karaoke machine rather than playing their own instruments. The next singer uses a guitar, which should ease the transition to my performance.

A round of applause sounds as she takes her bow, quickly exiting on the opposite side. Gabe nods his head, dimming the lights low as I approach the baby grand piano that's been moved to the middle of the stage.

Even though the room is dark, I see Kade and Quinn talking at the bar. His attention is to her, just like we planned. Sitting on the bench, I close my eyes and whisper a silent prayer. It's now or never. The voices disappear as I blow out a calming breath.

Kade whips his head around as my voice travels through the speakers, pouring every ounce of love I can into the lyrics of "All of Me" by John Legend. The stage is still dark, but through it all, I pick him out in the crowd. I always could.

When I start the chorus, the lights brighten, letting me really see the confusion and surprise on Kade's face.

Everyone fades away until the only thing in front of me is Kade stares. A smile creeps along my face as he rises from the chair, slowly making his way to the stage and up the stairs. The string that binds us is as strong as ever when he lowers himself onto the bench next to me, gazing at me with the same love and adoration he used to.

He still loves me.

Our legs brush against each other, sending a round of tingles through my body. My heart continues to flutter in my chest when I sing the last few lines directly to him.

There's nothing but us as we stare into each other's eyes. Eyes I have dreamed about every night and missed with every bone in my body. I yearn to touch him, feel his warmth beneath my fingers, and re-familiarize with his body.

Kade makes the first move, reaching over to cup my cheek while threading his fingers through my hair. I lean into his touch, letting my eyes close as I take a deep breath.

"That was beautiful," he whispers. I open my eyes and see nothing but my future, seeing the house and kids, and the laughter and tears. I see my life being lived the way I want; with the person I want.

I reach up, placing both my hands on his face and lick my dry lips. His gaze follows the movement.

"I love you, Kade," I say quietly.

He stops his thumb from brushing against my ear and I can hear the hitch in his breath.

"Say it again."

Still so bossy.

I brush my lips against his. "I love you, Kade *Xavier* Evans."

He laughs, the sound still one of the sexiest on earth.

Pulling me close, he whispers in my ear. "Been stalking my Facebook page?"

"Wikipedia."

With a gentle tug, he pulls me off the bench and takes a bow before the cheering crowd. My face runs hotter by the second. Kade never leaves my side as he guides us to our waiting friends.

Quinn practically springs from her seat, throwing her arms around my neck. Tears glisten in her eyes when she pulls back.

"All I can say is it's about fucking time." She wipes at her eyes and laughs.

"I guess I had to get lost so I could find myself. Good thing he never gave up on me."

Kade presses his lips to my temple, letting them linger for a few moments. "Never. I knew you'd come around eventually. Who can resist this hot piece of ass?"

Oh good Lord. I roll my eyes and melt into his side, grateful for his warmth and love. Gabe walks around the bar and stands next to Quinn, placing a kiss on her head.

"I'm happy for you, man. Sorry to bend the truth to get you here."

Kade shakes Gabe's outstretched hand and does the guy hug/slap-on-the-back thing. "If the outcome is always like this, feel free to bend it as much as you want."

"Work hasn't been the same without you, Adrienne. Any chance you're willing to quit that fancy new job of yours to come slumming back here?" Gabe asks.

Kade twists his head to me and I kiss the corner of his mouth. "I'll tell you later, after my surprise."

The low growl coming from the back of his throat makes

me laugh as fire spreads through my veins. The man I love is standing next to me and I couldn't be happier. Everything is just as it's supposed to be.

Perfect.

Twenty

FOR THE FIRST TIME IN MY LIFE, THINGS FINALLY FEEL IN place. Kade is here, still in love with me as ever before. He was never in my plans, yet he slid into my life so easily. I can't imagine it any other way.

"So what's this surprise?" he asks, running his hand up and down my thigh.

I giggle and pull his hand away. The motion is distracting and I'd rather not crash the car before we get to the house. "No hints." I smirk. "Gotta trust me."

His brow crinkles in confusion, but he doesn't say any more. I should be more nervous about this, but I'm calmer than I've ever been. It's sort of amazing. When you're in love, nothing can go wrong.

Gravel crunches beneath the tires before I pull onto the freshly paved driveway. His eyes widen and I smile. He didn't know about the extra money I put toward the house.

This is going to be fun.

"Did you do this? I don't remember hiring anyone for

it."

I nod, the smile still plastered on my face as the house comes into view. The driveway will be the least of his surprises. "I figured if we're staying here for the summer, I'd rather not spend the time washing our cars."

Eyes gleaming, he turns his head. "What a shame. Just think of the fun that would be. You, me, and a bucket of soapy water?" He blows out a quick breath. "Damn, I'm getting hard just thinking about it."

Parking the car in front of the garage, I slap his chest. "You're always hard. How is that any different?"

He laughs and pulls me over the center console. Once I'm settled on his lap, he grabs my face and runs his tongue along the seam of my lips, which I happily open for him. After all, it's been almost twenty minutes since we last kissed.

"Down tiger," I say, pushing against his shoulders. Desire still running through his eyes, he moves his hands up and down my spine before cupping my ass and pulling me into his rock hard erection. "I still need to show you *our* house."

The smile he gives me could light the night sky. "Finally, you've accepted it." He opens the door and allows me to exit first.

"Well, I have been here for quite a while. It was starting to feel more like my house than yours. Then I realized... it was."

Jerking me flush against him, his lips explore my neck while I run my hands through his hair. "I can't wait to christen every room with you."

Heat rushes to my core, flooding my veins as he nips lightly at my ear. God I've missed this. Luckily, I never have to go without it again. "So would you like the grand tour?"

He runs his hands through my hair again, my heart fluttering and eyes threatening to roll into the back of my head.

"Grand tour, then we have two months' worth of sex to catch up on." A nip at my lips and the roll of his hips means it's going to be a *very* short tour.

"Then we best get moving." Probably should save the master suite for last.

He tries to kiss me again, but I move out of the way, laughing as I pull him away from the car. Any more time spent out here, and we'll end up fucking on the hood of my car.

Hmm…. There could be perks to living out in the country. We definitely wouldn't be able to do something like that in the city.

Dragging him through the door, we pause in the foyer so he can kiss my lips quickly. We move to the den, and another kiss falls upon my lips. Living room. Kiss. His office. Kiss.

I'm seeing a pattern.

Kade doesn't say much, simply comments on my decorating skills. "It feels like a home, not just a house," he says as we walk into the kitchen. He turns in a circle and whistles in approval. "Damn, woman, you did good. Tell me you've gotten better at cooking during the break."

Smoothing a hand over the granite countertop, I shake my head, giving a coy smile. "Nope, sorry. You're still going to have to be Lord Commander of the kitchen."

Thank God we're in the kitchen because the hunger in his eyes is off the charts. I'm finding it hard to keep myself in check.

"Is this surprise upstairs?" He crosses the room, acting like he's ready to leave. "Please tell me it's upstairs because I really want to go up there."

A lump forms in my throat and I lick my dry lips. Kade growls low when I shake my head. He crooks his finger at me and points to the spot in front of him. I want to laugh at his expression as I take a step away, trying to get him to follow. "Don't you want to see the view from the backyard?"

His lips quirk up on one side. "Nope. I want to see the view between your legs."

Oh, good God. My heart beats faster as I chew my thumbnail. Each step I take has him taking two, closing the distance between us as we approach the patio door.

I place a hand on his chest. "Humor me, please? Then you can fuck me for the next three days straight. This time without having to kidnap me."

A blaze flashes in his eyes, making his pupils dilate. He threads his fingers through my hair, pulling my mouth to his. "Make it quick. I need to be inside you. Now."

Somehow I'm able to reach for the door handle behind me, flinging it open and drag him outside. I know the instant he sees it because he's dead still. Not that it's hard to miss.

Kade's eyes dart from mine to the giant wooden playground and back again, a smile playing on his lips with each glance.

I tighten my grip on his hand and shrug. "Well, I figured the kids would need something to do outside while we're here. I know it's a little premature, but I had a vision a couple months back and this is what I saw." I sweep my hand across the yard. "You and me, with lots of kids playing on this set in the summer sun."

Maybe I've jumped the gun. He doesn't say anything, but when he turns to face me again, I can see it.

He loves it.

I open my mouth, but don't have any words. Instead, he cradles my face, eyes glistening with emotion before moving his hands slowly down my body, caressing every curve on the way to my hips. He loves me with his mouth, his tongue stroking lazily against mine. Walking backward, we fall onto one of the cushioned chaise loungers, his body pressing into mine. With the setting sun, this is more than I ever could have imagined.

"Fuck the bedroom. Let's practice making that baby now."

Our clothes strip away and he sinks gloriously inside me, making love to me until the stars come out and the moon casts its silvery glow on the world.

Kade is here, with me.

And I'm home.

Epilogue

Eight Months Later

THE LIMO PULLS AWAY AS KADE'S MOUTH RAVAGES MY body, kissing every ounce of available flesh he can find. And even some spots that aren't. Underneath the massive pile of tulle and silk, his fingers caress my sensitive skin, rubbing the tender spot between my legs, driving me insane.

"Good thing I didn't wear blush today. I'm not going to need it if you keep this up," I pant against his lips.

He smiles, trailing his mouth across my cheek to my ear. "It's not as if people don't know what we're going to be doing later. You can't tell me you've never looked at a bride and said she's going to have sex tonight."

I try to laugh, really I do. Then his fingers slide inside me and nothing else matters as I grind against his hand. Teetering so close to the edge, I'm not sure how much longer I can hold on. I fumble with his pants, finding his straining erection. Wrapping my hand around his thickness, Kade presses into my palm, a strained moan coming from his lips.

"Fuck, I can't wait to strip you out of this dress."

Good thing the divider is up. We don't need to give anyone a show. Although I should have known something was up when Kade told him to cruise around town for the next hour.

Kade's tongue licks inside my mouth, keeping in tempo with his thumb circling my clit. Colors swirl behind my eyelids, sending me spiraling as I grind out the last of my orgasm against his hand.

"I love watching you come. It's my new favorite pastime."

I blink back to life, a satisfied smile playing on my lips. Now it's my turn.

Shifting my dress, I kneel on the bench seat and make quick work of his pants, pulling them and his boxers down to his knees, springing his cock free. The instant my lips wrap around the swollen head, he groans and fists his hands at his side. I know it's killing him to not grab my hair. It's his favorite, and mine too. Being manhandled, shown how to bring him the most pleasure, turns me on even more. However, this was my compromise. Limo sex, but no rough stuff.

Obviously he caved.

After another half hour with the smell of sex lingering in the air, we arrive at the outdoor pavilion where our friends and family have patiently waited for us. Everyone knows. You can see it in their smirks and avoiding stares. Everything is perfect; the ceremony, the venue, our friends and family celebrating with us. The sunshine warms my skin, even with the light breeze. I know it's my parents giving me their hug from above. They're here with us. I can feel it.

Keep it together. Don't cry.

No one cries on their wedding day. Besides, I've cried enough for one lifetime.

Once dinner is done and Kade attempts to smear cake all over my face—unsuccessfully since I distracted him with a kiss before smearing it on him—he leads us to the middle of the floor, ready to have our first dance as husband and wife.

Kade was in charge of the song choices tonight. After all, it is his profession, being the best-selling band on the market right now. Four number one singles, a platinum album, and another in the works. I couldn't be more proud of my rock god if I tried.

Somehow he managed to pull strings and find me a job in the industry after we moved to L.A. Who knew playing scores for major motion pictures would be as fulfilling as my job with the orchestra, who graciously let me come back as a guest during the summer months.

The first few notes of Van Morrison's "Crazy Love" play over the speakers and I can't help but laugh as he twirls me around the floor.

My husband, the comedian.

Wrapping an arm around my waist, he brings our entwined hands to his chest and presses our cheeks together.

It's as if the lyrics were written especially for us as I think back on this past year and our crazy love journey. Yes, I fought him almost every step of the way, but if it wasn't for him pushing me to open and start living my life, we wouldn't be here right now. I wouldn't be staring into the eyes of the man who saved me in more ways than one. A man I love more and more each day.

Our lips brush together as the last few words float around us. "I love you, husband of mine."

He returns the favor, slanting his mouth over mine in as chaste of a kiss as he can muster. "I love you, my wife. And be prepared to stay up all night. The limo was the opening act. Tonight is the main attraction."

The diamond on my finger sparkles under the spotlights, catching my eye when I frame his face with my hands. Here's my future, standing in front of me, pledging his life and love to me for the rest of eternity.

My rock god.

My love.

My Kade.

"I wouldn't have it any other way."

Acknowledgements

What started as me listening to a song one day in my car turned into this beautiful masterpiece. It's no surprise that music is a large part of my life. I put as much music into my every day activities as I can, so to write a book like this was a no-brainer. Music inspires people to do things, either through melodies or lyrics. For me, it was both. John Legend's "All of Me" struck me hard. I listened to the lyrics once and instantly had a story in my head of a girl who had been unable to say the words "I love you" until she finally was able to express herself through song. Many hours were spent reworking this until I felt it was finally the story I wanted to tell. Many people helped me get this book on its feet; I cannot properly express my gratitude enough for each and every one of you.

To my husband, who gives me the support I need to keep writing these stories. His constant encouragement, letting me know how proud he is of me, lifts me up on the days where I question my sanity. Thank you for being my sounding board when I need to vent and telling me that I can do anything as long as I put my mind to it.

Billie – You were the first to read StS chapter by chapter, telling me what made sense and what didn't. Without your constant support and belief in me, I don't think I'd be here today. I love you!

Angela – They're right. You always meet the nicest people in elevators! I'm so glad we met in March and even more so that I can call you my friend. Your support and wisdom has been my rock during this whole thing. And the late night laughs were much needed for both of us. Either you need to move up here by me or I need to move by you because we cannot go this long without seeing each other. You've become one of my closest friends and I'm so glad you're in my life.

Andrea – My twin! Why must you always bring logic into our conversations and make me see what you do? You bring a smile to my face when I want to cry and remind me that the voices in my head are wrong. Every day I'm thankful we were brought together and I can't wait to squeeze you in real life.

Katie – What could I possibly say to you? We met when you read Lessons of the Heart and you quickly became one of my best friends. Your support, your belief in me means so much that I don't know what I'd do without you. I love you more than you know and one of these days I know we'll see each other again.

Tee – Thank you so much for editing my baby for me and making it the best it could be.

Murphy – You deserve a medal for all the hell I put you through this time around. But after all the emails and multiple drafts, you designed the most perfect cover I could have ever asked for. It captured the feel and emotion of this book. You are one of the best!

Minxes (I still want to say Minxens), you are the most amazing bunch of ladies I know. I'm so glad we all found each other and could be a constant source of support and encouragement. Love you all so much!

To all my friends and family, thank you for everything that you do for me each and every day, whether it's with a phone call or just a quick message to say hi. Thank you for making me laugh when I want to cry and always being there when I need you, even if you don't know it at the time. Your love and support mean the world to me.

To my readers, thank you so much for taking a chance on my book. Without you, I wouldn't be able to do this. Each and every one of you brightens my day and reminds me of why I do this. From the bottom of my heart, thank you!

Like the music featured in this book? Follow my Spotify playlist:
http://bit.ly/serenadingtheshadows

About The Author

Jodie Larson is a wife and mother to four beautiful girls, making their home in northern Minnesota along the shore of Lake Superior. When she isn't running around to various activities or working her regular job, you can find her sitting in her favorite spot reading her new favorite book or camped out somewhere quiet trying to write her next manuscript. She's addicted to reading (just ask her kids or husband) and loves talking books even more so with her friends. She's also a lover of all things romance and happily ever afters, whether in movies or in books, as shown in her extensive collection of both.

Other books written by Jodie Larson

Fated to be Yours
Fated to be Mine
Lessons of the Heart

You can find Jodie at:

Facebook: www.facebook.com/jodielarsonauthor
Twitter: www.twitter.com/jlarsonauthor
Instagram: www.instagram.com/jodielarson

Join my reader group to stay up-to-date and get exclusive sneak peeks, giveaways, and more!
http://bit.ly/larsonslovelies

Made in the USA
Lexington, KY
30 March 2017